Jo Riddett was born in Cheshire and now lives in Hampshire. She has written two previous novels, *Children on the Shore*, published in 1986, and *All a Green Willow*, published in 1990.

Also by Jo Riddett

Children on the Shore
All a Green Willow

On the Way to the Wedding

Jo Riddett

First published in 1994
by Hamish Hamilton Ltd

First published in paperback in 1995
by HEADLINE BOOK PUBLISHING

A HEADLINE REVIEW paperback

10 9 8 7 6 5 4 3 2 1

ISBN 0 7472 4724 2

Printed and bound in Great Britain by
Cox & Wyman Ltd, Reading, Berks

HEADLINE BOOK PUBLISHING
A division of Hodder Headline PLC
338 Euston Road
London NW1 3BH

For Jess

1929

August – September

CHAPTER ONE

Maurice Coverdale incurred his mother's wrath when he quit officer training in the merchant navy. Adding insult to injury, he went to work as a farm-hand in the parish of the family home. She cut Maurice from her will and transferred the inheritance together with attendant affections to Bertie, her younger son. Her two daughters looked on in awe, adjusting allegiances, conforming to the matriarchal *fiat* in this as in all else. Mr Coverdale had never managed patriarchy.

Maurice lacked neither temerity nor charm. The one frequently landed him in trouble, the other usually bailed him out. So it was with the farm-hands. His sudden appearance in their ranks aroused suspicion and hostility. He had breached the system: 'What the blazes is he doing here?' He was a Coverdale. Not one of them. Gentry, playing games. Someone ought to see Boss, put him right. But this Boss was not 'one of them' either; brand-new to the place, college-trained, just arrived. Old Grigson would have known better than to hire a Coverdale! The very idea! So someone did see Boss, protested on behalf of the men; but Sutton with his college-trained ways wouldn't budge, said he was suited and they'd signed a contract – a contract! So that was that. And there were some stiff faces about the place for a while.

Not a very long while, though. Quite soon their hostility relented. Quite soon they were calling him Mo, as they used to do when he'd been a nipper playing about the barns on his holidays from his boarding school. Young Mo.

He made them laugh again, as he used to. Well – he always was different from the other Coverdales, young Mo. Specially her. Mrs Coverdale. One in the eye for her, Lady Muck! Slow, sly smiles dawned at this aspect. Shortly, Maurice occupied a prime place at Home Farm, Hollisfont, his oddity turned to advantage, supplying for them something between a mascot and a local hero. At twenty-one he was by far the youngest, but no fool, no fool at all – you had to hand it to him, he was a first-class worker, picked up the knacks fast – well, he'd shown himself handy even as a nipper. And then again, there was no 'side' about him, not like the other Coverdales, didn't come on la-di-da, never had done. Easy to be with, young Mo.

On the other hand, you didn't offer him bed and board. Not in this village. He was out of face, the Coverdale black sheep just now, and you didn't cross swords with Madam Coverdale, President of this, Chairman of that, on visiting terms with Squire. No, you didn't look for trouble in that quarter. Boss let him use the old bothy behind the barn while he found himself lodgings somewhere. Well, it wasn't the Ritz, but it wasn't bad, a bit damp, but Mo didn't seem to bother, quite liked it, so there you are, no point looking for trouble, offering to take him in. Perhaps later, when the trouble blows over. Maybe.

The trouble did not so much blow over as lose some impetus, become unremarkable, part of the local lore. By the end of the year it was simply accepted that the rift was part of the landscape. Maurice Coverdale got on with being a farm-worker and the rest of them up at Outwick House got on with whatever it was they did there, ignoring his existence without apparent difficulty.

In the following year, 1927, Outwick House drew attention. The second girl, Lilian, became engaged, and Moira, the elder, married her young man. The wedding took place at the village church, St Aldhelm's. Bertie was an usher with a rose in his buttonhole. Maurice did not attend. He was not formally debarred, just uninvited. The wedding, a grand affair, was the talk of the neighbourhood for a few days, but not in the presence of young Mo. Not that he seemed in the least concerned. It so happened that he spent that day as top-loader on the haywain in the twelve-acre from which vantage-point could be seen the church, the lane, the *dramatis personae*, the Daimlers, the glamorous guests and craning spectators; but he gave no sign, worked away as usual, the odd snatch of banter like any other time. Not bothered.

It was a good crop, a bumper year, and in the barn in record time, cause for serious celebration at Lower Parvey. Hollisfont had no pub. The men went off to sup their ale at Lower Parvey's and wavered home on bicycles, Maurice leading a chorus under the stars, no ears to be outraged by obscenity, no sensibilities to be dismayed by sprawling limbs and wheels spinning in ditches. A very good binge! That was the way of it with young Mo. He knew how to enjoy himself, did Mo. The village womenfolk, unused to equating enjoyment with inebriation, were not best pleased by these intemperate escapades, and the combination of wifely disapproval and personal sore heads the following morning went some way to redress euphoria. For a day or two thereafter, some of the initial unease would twitch and stir within the chastened revellers: Coverdale was not really 'one of them' – though now, in these hungover aftermaths, it was not his 'gentriness' that set him apart; on the contrary, a common coarseness had been unleashed and their shamefaced resentment was reposed in Coverdale's powers of misrule, summoning up Old Adam. But such hazy half-notions hardly surfaced, were soon subsumed under the daily demands of shared hard work and young Mo's buoyant, carefree banter. Even the censure of the women-folk relented; the escapades were rare enough – haytime, harvest, Christmas – for indulgence to restore harmonious status quo: 'Boys will be boys!' they sighed wryly; and anyway, Coverdale will never stay – he won't stay long! He'll be off one of these days! Never stick it out as a farm-hand.

He was still there two years later, though. Another good hay crop to give the farmer satisfaction every time he passed the ricks. But August was wet. The barley stood limp and blackening with mildew. There came three days without rain but no drying wind either, heavy and humid. Mr Sutton trudged his field boundaries rubbing fowsty grain against the palm of his hand, sniffing, casting it aside, frowning; and at last decided to go ahead and cut, and headed back to the yard.

'We'll go ahead and cut,' he called through the cow-house door to Coverdale. 'Tell Williams to get the horses up. We'll lose the lot if we don't go soon.'

'Right-o!'

'Get your breakfast and go on up with the hook – make a start. Oh – and Mo, tell Dan to go up too, the ditch can wait, we'll be carrying as well today.'

'Right!'

The cheery strains of Coverdale's whistling followed Sutton across the yard. Good decision, that, hiring Coverdale. More good luck than good management perhaps, but good anyway. Though for a minute back there it looked as though he'd put the wrong foot first, made a bad start, upset the whole of Hollisfont. Third day in the place, half their belongings still unpacked where the furniture removers had left them, and he had a rebellion on his hands! Tricky old moment! Local politics, of which of course he knew nothing then. Pretty soon learned! Very tricky, though, for an hour or two; strong challenge to his authority right at the outset. But he'd been right, done the right thing, on two counts: first, you make it clear who's in charge, who's running the show; second, Coverdale turned out to be as good as he'd claimed. Remembering, Sutton grunted a wry laugh to himself. He'd found this youth that evening in the barn, sitting on a bale eating chocolate, suitcase beside him. And he had assumed that he was after the vacancy advertised by the estate office. They'd talked about that, he and the estate management folk during the negotiations for the tenancy, he'd been told that the labour force was under strength. Hollisfont had sent its young men to the trenches to fight the Kaiser like every other parish, and like every other parish, got few back. Under Old Grigson the Home Farm struggled on with the handful of older men, and made a fair job of it too. But at the interview he'd been told that one of those was leaving, had an operation, being retired early; so the post was being advertised. Perfectly natural, then, to assume that this youth with a suitcase was a candidate. And the youth didn't disabuse him. Quick-witted young blighter, Coverdale! Caught the drift, played along, and half an hour later signed up. Cool customer!

'Oh, yes!' he'd told him. 'Plenty of experience! I'm local, worked on this very farm some time back – been away a few years, worked abroad . . .' Could turn his hand to anything on a farm, he'd said. And proved right. Healthy, strong. And a cut above the average – intelligent, prepared to take initiative, use his common. Several cuts above average. That had been apparent there in the barn. What such a type was doing in farmwork might be a mystery but that was his business; he was over twenty-one. 'No,' he'd told him, 'no family!' Travelling light, cheerful. They'd put him up overnight, dossed down among the packing-cases, till he could find himself local lodgings, and he'd fitted in, no trouble, up with the lark and out to the cow-house to the milking . . . And then the balloon had gone up!

You could smile about it now; but not just then! What a to-do! Old Arnie first. Came out of the cow-house like his shirt-tail was on fire: 'You can't hire 'e, Boss! Maurice Coverdale! 'E be a Coverdale – from Outwick House!' Then Williams, then Dan Burtle and a gaggle of them in the yard, clucking and tutting, up in arms – a regular mutiny shaping up. So. He'd let them know who it was who did the hiring and firing on Home Farm.

Tackled Coverdale later: 'You were not quite frank with me, Coverdale,' sternly, not disposed to be made a mug of and getting that clear.

'I told you no lies.' Coverdale had shrugged.

Well . . . no. He hadn't. Slanted the truth, bent it to suit the moment, opportunist, but not planned lies. The actual facts which he then quite happily supplied were simple enough – quit the navy because he hadn't liked it, fallen out with the family and left home, both sides glad to be rid. As to the men here, their objections, Coverdale had said 'Nine days' wonder, Mr Sutton. They'll get over it, they all know me, known me for years. Their trouble is they're still living in the last century, mentally speaking; still pulling their forelocks. Can't blame them – that's village life. But give them five minutes, they'll get round to it, and I can tell you there won't be any more trouble!'

Not short of confidence, either, Coverdale! And he'd been right, there was no more trouble and in a day or two you'd never have known there'd been a fuss. And he'd also summed up the mental attitudes of the older generation in agriculture, which indeed you couldn't blame them for. But with a 1,200-acre farm to modernize, Mr Sutton was very glad to have a Coverdale among the hands.

He let himself into the farm kitchen, breathing the smell

of bacon. 'Yes, serve it out, Marj,' he called to his wife, 'I'll not be a minute, going to telephone the vet – Arnie's got a cow bad!'

Coverdale, in his bothy beyond the barn, fished the sizzling bacon from the frying pan, slapped it between two hunks of bread and turned off the primus stove. The door of the bothy stood open this mild and sticky morning. Seated on his bunk, mug of tea to hand, he chomped his sandwich, watching the hens pecking about beneath the trees in the orchard. Terra firma. About as far from the sea as you can get, this corner of Northamptonshire. Nowhere in England being more than seventy-five miles from the sea, this, appropriately enough, was about as far away as you could get. He took a swig of tea, strong and sweet. Must remember to get another bag of sugar, call in and collect it from Mrs Sutton after work. Or get it from her at supper-time. Good cook, Mrs Sutton, good grub.

The long-established arrangement suited all concerned: he made his own breakfast, had midday snap out on the job, and collected hot supper in a mess-tin from the farm kitchen to eat in peace in his bothy. It was best all round. They liked a bit of privacy, and so did he. They hadn't elbow-room enough anyway, with a couple of toddlers when they first arrived and another on the way. Worked out just right, the bothy. His own idea. Remembered from the magic days of childhood when every chance he'd had he had spent days at the farm, blessed antidote to public school regimentation. And blessed antidote to home, no less regimented.

She had never approved. Not a suitable environment. Farmyards and the company available – they had no place in the plan mapped out, following her sainted father's footsteps up the ladder of success, collecting increasing quantities of gold braid with which to decorate the family esteem. But he'd found ways round her; there were still ways round her occasionally in those days if you were canny. Quoting Juvenal at her had been singularly effective, aged fourteen: '*Oranda est ut sit mens sana in corpore sano.*' It was carved over the entrance door at school. She didn't know Latin. 'Oh, it means: Your prayer must be that you may have a sound mind in a sound body, Mother. They're very keen on that, fresh air and exercise, and the Head says working with animals is first-rate discipline, it's good for your character, he said!' And he'd spent most of those summer hols at Home Farm. Minimum of the boring tea-and-tennis, minimum of her 'gentlemanly pursuits'.

He finished his sandwich, drank the last of his tea and rinsed the mug under the stand-pipe outside the bothy. There were two bits of bacon rind and a few crumbs and he threw them to the hens: 'Here you are, you lot! Say thank you – where's your manners?' He washed his hands, cold water and yellow soap, quite adequate. Bathing was once a week, courtesy of the Suttons, in their bathroom, plenty of hot water. He tested the blade of the hook against his thumb, gave it a couple of honing strokes, pocketed the whet-stone, picked up his jacket and fastened the door against the hens. Hens were excellent beasts in their way but he drew the line at them roosting on his bunk or ravaging the bread-tin. He wheeled his bicycle into the yard and swung himself aboard, the hook stowed in his saddlebag, swathed in sacking. He would have walked, cut across the meadow and past the twenty-acre, presently down to mangolds, if it were not for delivering Sutton's message to Dan. Quicker by bike, seeing he had to go by Pitt Lane; Dan would have gone straight there this morning, ditch-clearing. Dan was the youngest – the least old – of the other hands. Fifty-three. His son would have been working here if he hadn't been killed in France. A lot of others too, they'd have been here if it hadn't been for that war; couple of dozen of them, estate or farm. When it finished, that war, on Armistice Day, at school, they'd all been called to assembly in the hall after tea. Pongo, in full kit, best mortar-board and gown, made the announcement, face as long as a fiddle. You'd have thought we'd lost the war, not won it. All the masters po-faced. Still, some of their chums had been killed, so perhaps it wasn't the moment for smiling. But school was given a half-day hol, and an extra slice of that blotchy fruit cake, Leper's Leg. Back home, that Christmas vac, the vicar preached a sermon about the war and absent friends. Not very festive! Quite odd singing carols in the circumstances, both sisters sniffling into their handkerchiefs like all the grown-up women. Except Mother. Mother never cried. Not she.

'Dan!' He coasted to a stop. 'We're cutting! He says to leave that for now and get up to the barley – all hands to the pump!'

'Cutting?' Dan rolled an eye weatherward.

'Yep! Well, there's more rain about, get in what we can while it holds off – and we're carting too, taking it straight in, see.' He hitched himself aboard the bike and pedalled on. Gather ye rosebuds, Mr Sutton. Quite right! Good motto, that. Perhaps I'll carve it over the bothy door!

Dan was all right. More to him than some of the others, though they were all right too, liked a joke. Except Arnie, of course. Good dairyman, but an old misery, been there since before the Ark. But Dan was all right. The only one who'd offered him lodgings, and his wife agreed, all settled. But Arnie put the brakes on, gave him the wind-up – didn't know I was the other side of the door: 'Don't you go crossing the gentry, Dan! Don't you go upsetting Mrs

Coverdale. She wants 'e out of Hollisfont! I've told Boss – we don't want no trouble!'

A force in the land, Mother. Rather more of a force in the land than Squire! Spencer Seton's more interested in his high life with his curious friends than his 8,000 acres. And very sensibly, he's left all that palaver to his sister to worry about, though she doesn't seem to worry, seems to like it, copes a treat. Miss Honoria is therefore a force in the land; but not like Mother. Not at all like Mother. Quiet, shy little woman, nice and kind. Treats everyone the same, as though everyone is human, even those who've made the dreadful error of not being born gentry!

Well, he'd not gone to Burtles'. Dan got cold feet, thanks to Arnie. But Arnie had done him a favour as it turned out. The bothy was better than any lodgings in the village. He need never go near the village, except to cycle through it on the way to the pub in Lower Parvey. No pub in Hollisfont anyway. No nothing in Hollisfont in fact, a dead-and-alive hole; except for the farm! Best decision he'd ever made. More good luck than good management, perhaps. But everything came right that day! Hadn't planned it – not the farm part; just happened to drop anchor there after slinging my hook from Outwick; wondering if I could cadge a lift if I started walking, long walk back to Hestonborough. Hadn't planned the farm part; that was good luck. Planned the other part, though. Oh, yes! Good management. He sat back in his saddle whistling to himself, pedalling between the hedges he'd helped to lay last year. The barley field hove in sight. Another half-mile.

She had never listened. He'd told her often enough, 'I do not *like* the sea.' But she didn't want to know. It didn't fit the Master Plan. So she didn't listen.

It had been all right at first. The uniform was good fun; very natty. College was all right to begin with too, though the rules and regulations were a bit ominously familiar, much like school.

It was being afloat that was awful. For one thing, the sea-sickness. A lot of matelots got sea-sick of course and it was true that it passed in a few days once you'd adjusted. But it was disgusting while it lasted – have to be mad to put up with that as part of a job for life! But worse was the boredom. Cooped up in throbbing metal twenty-four hours a day, same old faces, same routine, boxed in. Join the navy and see the world? Ho ho! Join the navy and see the bulkheads and miles of rocking water for light relief! The boredom. Oh, the boredom! He had told her.

He swung off the bike, wheeled it into the field and stowed it against the hedge. He surveyed the barley. What a mess! He scooped a handful, sniffed it. Pretty fowsty. He hauled out and unwrapped the hook. In his left hand he took the ash crook which he had personally fashioned for the job, and methodically set to clearing a starting area for the reaper. A wet rabbit scuttled, hunched, from the crop into the hedgerow. 'You forgot to put your mac on, mate!' Coverdale told it.

But it was not only the sea. There was that other matter. On the Upper Deck, in the wardroom, the bull-shit. Officers and gentlemen. Sir! Yes, sir, no, sir. Sir! And no consorting with the lower orders. Discipline. Responsi-bility – to your office, to the Service, and in your case, Coverdale, to your family tradition . . . On board and off. Big hullabaloo when someone let on that he joined the card games below decks. On the carpet, up before the Beak. Severe reprimand from the First Mate. Sir. 'Can't fault your work, Coverdale, but the attitude has to improve. See to it!'

He stood back, honing the blade again. Going to have problems cutting this lot, problems with the reaper. Crop lying every which way and nowhere near dry. Still, he's right, it can't get better, only get worse, so – on we go!

Rather more than a severe reprimand in Port Said, the Captain this time; confined to ship, five days in the stinking sweaty harbour, extra duties. Some smug squealer recognized him, saw him emerging with deck-hands from the red-light alleys and reported him. Hell of a blasting. But they didn't discharge him. No such luck. And he knew why. Not all that high-falutin garbage about the ethics of the Service – 'The Service deals in discipline and reform, Coverdale, not capitulation to insubordinate behaviour.' Rubbish – he'd seen men given the order of the boot for less and no two ways about it. No – it was who he was. Who *she* was, Mother, the daughter of the great-and-famous Courtenay of blessed memory, one-time Senior Captain of the Cunard Line. It was all fixed up, arranged in high places, settled over dining-tables, ratified in the clubs. A cabal held him in place. Also, his indentures; the contractual fee.

But he'd foxed them in the end! Had to bide his time; put up with the measures, which included shore-leave only in the company of other Upper-Deckers.

She wouldn't listen. Father, of course, never came into it. Pathetic old twerp.

Not that she'd been told the more lurid bits. Not by him, anyway. Perhaps some discreet version fit for a lady's ears had been fed to her through the cabal? In which case she hadn't listened to them either. But she had certainly been told by him that he had no intention of staying at sea. She had, eventually, laughed. Actually laughed. A rare event with Mother.

Well. He who laughs last . . .

The distant rumble of wheels and clop of hooves announced the approach of the reaper. He glanced round, assessing his work. OK. Almost ready. Another sound, of a car, was sufficiently unusual for him to straighten up for a look. Oh. The green Ford, heading for the estate office. Mr Know-all Blow; estate manager and pain in the neck. Slowing down, met the reaper. Tight fit in that lane. Make him wait, Williams! The only blot on an otherwise delightful landscape, Mr Blow. Member, along with Father, of the Rotary – or was it the Masons? Had a shot at stopping the use of the bothy, found some law or other, or tried to. Fortunately misfired, some clause or other not clear. Or something. Anyway, misfired. None of his business, the farm, anyhow; that's Sutton's business.

Wouldn't mind a car myself. Matter of cash. Quite a serious matter on an agricultural wage, worse luck. Bike's got limitations. Yes, a Rover. Same as my brother-in-law-to-be is running about in. Lilian's intended, Frank Bellinger by name according to the grape-vine, bush-telegraph. All the qualifications – member of the right clubs, about to be rich, a really nice, rich person next year when he comes into some inherited loot, really nice and rich enough to pass the Outwick House personality test . . .

The reaper rumbled up.

'Hang on – I'll give you a hand! Steady as you go – that's it – further left a bit – all right – you're clear!'

It went badly. Time and again the reaper jammed. Tempers frayed. The men cursed and sweated and the horses stamped and tossed their heads at the crowding thunder-flies. Mid-afternoon the slack sky darkened, brewing rain, more rain. Sutton came. Crossing the tacky stubble, he called to Coverdale, 'You go in to the milking – Arnie's with the vet! Not got the cows in yet – go and take over!'

Skimming down the lane, Coverdale thought, 'Vet only just arrived? Or is this a second call? Doesn't look good for poor old Buttercup either way . . .'

The cows were over their time for milking, tetchy under the swarming flies, lowing and butting about in the narrow lane. Old Peevish, malignant eye rolling at him, had her head down for a mouthful of verge grass, bony haunch unbudging. 'Geddup, y'old bugger, geddon out the way!' He grabbed her tail and gave it a tweak. Over the dawdling backs he hollered, 'Gerrup there! Daisy – Mattie – Bella – goo-on, Bella! Gerrup!' and then swivelled round in surprise. Squire's Bentley, gearing down, progress blocked. It did not carry Squire, nor yet Miss Seton. The passengers were two women he had never seen before and two youngsters craning at the glass partition behind Murston at the wheel. The lead-cow stood unmoving in the stockyard entry. 'Geddon, Daisy! Hup! Hup!' he bellowed. Pitching his bike against the hedge, he thrust through and shoved Daisy into motion. The herd followed swaying into the yard; except Peevish, who had swung athwart, glowering at the Bentley. A child's head leaned from the window now wound down, white-gold fringe over wide solemn eyes. Coverdale shouted, 'Shut the window! Y'll be full of flies!' Murston stared stiffly ahead. Coverdale bounded forward and thwacked Peevish out of the way and the car inched onward, changed gear and passed. Pressed against the hedge, he watched it go. The nearer woman, big-built, sat back in her corner under her veiled hat, but the other leaned across, speaking to the boy at the window, and for a long moment Coverdale looked into an even, oval face with softly defined, parted lips and grey eyes that saw him but withheld expression. The car accelerated away, then slowed again, taking not the road to Hollisfont Hall but the left fork towards the Dower House.

He picked up his bike and wheeled it, biffing Peevish along beside him. He could hear the Bentley winding its unaccustomed way. The Dower House had stood empty for years, ever since Mrs Grantham Seton's death before the war. In the yard the vet's car boot stood open. Arnie was emerging from the bottom byre, bucket in hand.

'Hey, Arnie!' Arnie was always in the know, working round the stead all day, picked up all the know from Mrs Sutton. 'Hey, Arnie, Murston's just driven some people up to the Dower House – what's going on?'

Arnie was glum and preoccupied, his narrow features shut against chat. He grunted, tramping past, 'Squire's folk, from Germany.'

'From Germany? What are they doing going to the Dower House?'

Arnie said, 'How should I know? You want to be getting on with the milking, never mind owt else!' And as he rounded the dairy door called, 'Put Mattie in number four – and there's the watering to finish yet!'

CHAPTER TWO

Grace laid her valise on the bed and looked about her. The room, being in the Georgian part of the house, was pleasantly proportioned. On the top and third storey, it could be said to be an attic, long and low, but this was no garret, and, unlike some roosts of her experience, held an airy lightness, despite the present gloom of the day beyond the three sash windows. She peeled off her gloves and ran her hand over the linen counterpane, prodded the mattress and found it free from lumps. The mahogany bedstead was old-fashioned, hefty in the Victorian way, as was the rest of the furniture which she now surveyed: a chest of drawers topped by a swing-mirror, a pedestal table under a white lace cloth, a red plush armchair and three upright chairs. All the dark wood was gleaming with polish, the lavender wax that faintly scented the air. By the bed was a whatnot and on it, under a parchment shade, an electric lamp. She flicked it on and off, approving. The centre ceiling light would no doubt be fitted with too dim a bulb but that was easy to correct. She sank on to the bed and kicked off her shoes with a sigh of satisfaction. Two days' travelling, even Mayendorff-style, first-class in every sense, was two days' travelling, and they had all been ready to arrive. Both the boys had been very good. Not that she had anticipated otherwise, but Nicholaus had above-average energy for a six-year-old and did not take easily to long periods of sitting still. Max, two years older, was unusually contained for his age. There was never any prospect of Max physically fretting. His abundant energies would be directed in observation and reflection as the train carried them across the Continent, away from home in Berlin, to the boat for Harwich. He had taken her hand, on the dock at Harwich, just for a moment, as they walked behind the porters and his mother and Nicholaus who hopped aboard the trolley and rode on top of the luggage grinning with pleasure under English skies clear pale blue this morning. But even Nicholaus succumbed to the soporific tick-tock of the windscreen-wipers as the chauffeur delivered them the last twenty-five miles from Northampton in warm grey August rain. She glanced at her watch. Tea was being served at half-past. No immediate hurry.

There were patches on the walls where pictures had hung. She saw that the hooks remained, conveniently enough. When her luggage arrived she would hang upon them her own collection, the water-colour of Zermatt, the print of York Minster, the others, loving records of the horticulturist's art, vibrant and rich reproductions of camellias, peonies and roses. The fireplace, on inspection, proved to be in working order. The flue lever plied effectively, and she judged the back-plate to favour up-draughts rather than down. Good. She would have need of coal fires this coming English winter, her first for seventeen years. No tall tiled stoves and heated pipes here, and no double windows penning in their warmth; but a good English coal fire would do very well.

She sat back, unpinning her felt hat and dropping it beside her on the hearth-rug, ran her fingers vigorously through the thick dark bob that was all that remained of her waist-length hair since that vertiginous moment two years ago when she had succumbed to fashion and left her tresses on the hairdresser's floor on Kurfürstendamm in Berlin. The result had met with universal approval – Fräulein Moon looked 'schick'! She'd felt 'schick' too! But then, oddly enough, she had wept that night. It was the first time she had wept since she was a child. In the dark beneath the bedclothes she had been stormed by emotions she couldn't account for. She had alarmed herself, afraid of the uprush of a sort of primitive fear, as though she had lost – well – her 'self'. Quite irrational. She had pulled herself together of course. But she did have a headache in the morning. There was sympathy and aspirins and some gentle teasing: 'Fräulein's head ached from the shock of losing its hair!' and by then she was restored to customary calm and could join in, smile and agree.

She stood up, collecting the hat, and carried it to the white-painted doors of fitted cupboards filling the end wall. Shelves, and plenty of hanging space. She left the hat there and crossed to a window, opening its curtains wider. Below her was the stable-yard, its setts dully gleaming purple-grey in the rain. Some of the loose-box doors were ajar, some closed, all dingy with neglect, the paint weather-stained and peeling. The elegant Georgian clock-tower rose forlornly stripped of its glory, rust streaks attesting the years the fingers had stood dead at thirteen minutes past two. Beyond the block were rose-brown walls of a kitchen garden, here and there the reaching tangle of fruit trees long untrimmed. But beyond that again was farmland, cultivated, ordered, in hand, productive fields rolling and sloping between stout laid hedges, and in one of them a couple of men straining a canvas sheet over a reaping machine, another leading away a horse-team plodding under wraiths of drifting rain, heading back to the farm. That must be the farm they had just passed, the car halted in the lane full of cows herded by the youth with a bicycle. And a bold, inquisitive stare. Curly hair, very dark. Probably darkened by being a bit damp. Probably curlier for that too. Like Nicholaus; only Nicholaus was ash-blond. Nicholaus's hair curled more when it was damp.

A flock of descending pigeons arriving in the stable-yard drew back her attention. She watched them sort themselves and disappear into the shelter of an open loose-box; theirs, evidently, their territory. But not for much longer solely theirs. Mrs Mayendorff's hunters would be arriving. First the restoration of the stables, then the horses. Two were being shipped from Germany, from the country estate, Reissen, the place where Margaret Mayendorff had found such happiness as was available to her within that tortuous alliance she had just quit. The departure to England had little to do with the stated purpose of Mrs Mayendorff being on hand while her boys attended English public school. And less with that other given reason, that the makings of civil war were burgeoning in the Reich, economic chaos fuelling the conflict underlying Mueller's 'Great Coalition'. No, it was to do with the insupportable tensions of a marriage finally past repair and never a success. For Margaret Mayendorff the move had been more of a leaving of her married life, its ugliness and insult, its boredom and loneliness, than a positive move to England. England it was because there was nowhere else to go; and Cousin Honoria had arranged it, offered sanctuary here in the Dower House at Hollisfont. The cousins were alike in some ways, neither favoured with obvious beauty, both with quiet resilience. Honoria was senior by twelve years and now fifty-two. She had never married; neither had her brother. Spencer Seton was known as 'Squire', the owner of the 8,000 acres lying between the trunk road in the east and the market town in the west. He and his sister lived their separate lives under the one roof of Hollisfont Hall. Spencer's colourful friends, sprigs of aristocracy, artists, beau monde, were often in attendance. Miss Honoria had no personal circle. As the years advanced it was she who fulfilled the role of patron around the estate. Her one close and enduring friendship was with her Cousin Margaret, and so it was that in a welter of telegrams and letters these past few weeks, it had been arranged, the sanctuary, the Dower House. All this Grace knew. But the convention prevailed between the governess and her employer that she knew nothing of the intimate realities behind the move. Grace did know, and Mrs Mayendorff knew that she knew, but both valued the professional distance preserved; it enhanced their mutual respect and affection, which were considerable.

Grace had come by her evaluation of professional discretion in the usual manner of lessons learned: the hard way. In her previous post her employer had held her captive to hours of personal indiscretions. At first that was flattering; soon burdensome as Grace found herself ill at ease in the presence of husband and friends she knew too much about, and the unease began to sap her professional performance with the children. That mattered to her. Enough, eventually, to take a decision and extricate herself, quit.

She had never regretted it, though the fact that she had left that family high and dry did trouble her. She had, on that occasion, broken faith with her own tenet of trust. She had defected. The defection was to the Mayendorffs who were holidaying in an adjacent villa at Cap Ferrat. Grace saw them about, the ungainly, quiet English woman, the two little boys who called her '*Mutter*' but were blond and quick and slender like their aquiline father who occasionally accompanied them, though always at a slight distance. When she heard that they were in need of an English governess for those two little boys she applied, presenting herself at the villa.

She had not lied but she had adapted truths. She conveyed that she had experience as a governess which was only true in the sense that as a nanny or nurse over the years in several posts, she had taught her charges to read, taught them English when they were French or Swiss-born, and in the process taught them rudimentary geography and history and botany since learning anything meant also learning something else. She guessed that her style, restrained and self-sufficient, appealed to Frau Mayendorff and consciously applied it during the interview. She got the job.

She knew she could do it, and properly; she would not have applied otherwise. She was jubilant. When she had next to face the unattractive moment of giving in her notice, she surprised herself with her own resolve; come the moment, buoyed along by the success of her own audacity, she outfaced the protests of dismay and indignation. She was, she found, stronger than she had thought herself to be. All her life, one way and another, she had been at the disposal of others. Now, she had disposed herself, and in the process promoted herself, and discovered strength. But she was glad to leave the scene of her defection; she could not deceive herself as to that, justifications notwithstanding.

In the subsequent four years with the Mayendorffs she consolidated her new-found strength and independence. She recognized and was grateful for the fact that Frau Mayendorff's personality made that possible, even easy. Frau Mayendorff valued independence in her staff. She lived within herself, committed to her sons though undemonstrative, unhappy with her husband but bearing her own burdens. The households that she ran for him were staffed with people intuitively chosen for their ability to cope, rise to occasions, oil social wheels where necessary. Guests relished the flawless hospitality, in Berlin and at the country estate, Reissen. The staff relished providing it. The master of those houses would have the rest of his life to ponder just how much stability and order flowed from the wife he disdained as '*dumm*', '*pferdenarrisch*'. His wealthy business friends had been happy to endorse his vulgar taste in the women he made his mistresses, but it had been Margaret who had given that flawless order and respectability necessary to their professional self-esteem. The staff, of course, knew it.

Grace was glad that in the dissolution of that regime she found herself naturally part of the departing wife's household. Not that she would have remained as part of Herr Mayendorff's establishment – she would have left. She was glad that in the natural disposition of things she had no such choice thrust upon her and simply continued to be with Mrs Mayendorff and the boys.

Whether she was glad to be here in England was a matter for speculation. She had, she felt, lost the knack of being in England. Her family tie had consisted of her father, the news of whose death eight years ago had barely touched her. She remembered him as a mild-mannered rather abstracted being whose job as a civil engineer had often absented him from the various homes he rented for his daughter and the woman he had married after Grace's mother had died. Grace, having been seven months old at the time, had no memory of her. She remembered her stepmother, of course, and not without affection though their relationship had never become close. Childhood had been a secure and happy enough time, home, wherever it was, always well run and pleasant. But the liveliest attachments of her youth had been made at the girls' boarding school outside York to which she had been sent when she was twelve, a measure that had cost her parents some financial sacrifices, willingly made for what they saw as a first-class education and a better social experience than they could provide for an only child in their nomadic life. Grace had spent four busy and productive years there, holidaying sometimes with others' families, sometimes with her own.

Her sorrow at leaving Belbrook Grange was amply offset by the excitement of going to Switzerland: the adults – her father and the headmistress – had taken an opportunity on her behalf, and she was to accompany the family of a medical scientist pursuing research in Zurich. Her role was vaguely defined. She was to keep company with the young wife, help with the two infants, live as family. Nobody used the word 'nanny'. The Goughs were of a new breed, emancipated democrats with no use for such divisive concepts. There was no time limit mentioned either – a year or so, or more, they would see how the arrangement worked, and the benefits to Grace were not in question – she would travel, improve her French and German, live in edifying company – it was almost like going to finishing school, was it not, as several of her peers were doing? Grace happily complied. As a healthy sixteen-year-old with no fear of new faces and places, she was simply intrigued and eager to be off. Later, she realized several things: that her father's marriage was collapsing and he had been at his wits' end what to do with his daughter. That her role, defined or not, was indeed that of nanny, and she had been presented with a career willy-nilly. And that she had been very lucky in the circumstances to have been dispatched with those particular people. The Goughs were kind. Meeting as she did with other nursery-maids and nannies, she glimpsed the miseries of working for ill-natured employers. She stayed with the Goughs for six years, four of them war years, the war they called Great because the whole world came to Europe and fought. But not to their corner of Europe. The Great War passed Grace by. At the end of it the Goughs returned to England, but she stayed, recommended to another post. Another amiable family, as it turned out, though very different from the Goughs, this one being French aristocratic stock, not at all emancipated or democratic, but decent employers none the less. Yes, she had always been lucky with employers, unless you counted the last time, and then she had made her own good luck and escaped to the Mayendorffs, broadening her horizons in Germany.

And now, England. In seventeen years of absence she had retained her sense of Englishness while never missing England; one of the blessings, she supposed, of having no deep roots. She had never felt homesick. But recently, in the days of upheaval, the physical process of dismantling life in Germany and travelling and now arriving, she had felt something, something sad and unfamiliar to which she could not put a name. Homesickness for Germany? But it wasn't that. Regret that over the years she had let her school-friend correspondence lapse so that now she knew no one here? No, not that either; those relationships had expired naturally, dwindled painlessly into the past. It was perhaps not unconnected with the faint pang she had felt on the recent birthday that had made her thirty-three? But she had shrugged that off with a comical grimace at the face looking back at her in the bathroom mirror. It could well have been to do with the approaching departure of Max and Nicholaus to preparatory school and her own consequent departure to another post. Reason enough for some sadness; more on this occasion than any before, actually – but it wasn't that. No, it was something else, elusive and baffling: it was when, looking to the future, she saw herself as perfectly well able to cope, well able to look after herself; it was then that she encountered the nameless ache.

A sound – faint, hardly more than a vibration – recalled her to the moment and to a glance at her wrist-watch where she saw that time had moved to half-past four, and the vibration resolved itself into the chiming of a clock out there beyond the faltering rain. From the church? Surely.

Glimpsed from the car just now, that had caught her attention. It had been a fleeting impression only, yew trees and pale rain-blotched stone, but enough for Grace to recognize those pinnacles and the top flight of the tower as fifteenth-century: history lessons – heavens! *twenty* years ago! – had been temporarily enlivened by young Miss Loadsby, who had long eyelashes, stylish clothes and a penchant for church architecture. Before leaving to be married she had culled a swathe of maiden hearts but also implanted in Grace an enduring appreciation of late medieval form. She would take a closer look at this handy example, take that in on an exploratory walk with the boys; and as to exploring, there was some to be done right here as well – the boys had probably made a start, it was that sort of house; there were attics over the Victorian frontage because she'd passed the foot of the small staircase on the way up half an hour ago. Perhaps there were cellars too. She pulled her shoes back on to her feet, ran a comb through her hair. First, a cup of real tea, that elixir of English life that never tasted right elsewhere, and then some preliminary explorations. She quickened her pace down towards the voices and – could it be? – another distant memory revived – yes, it was! – the smell of toasted muffins.

CHAPTER THREE

From the roof of the Dower House on a clear day like today you could see for miles; the village looked like a toy model below. It was, in a way. It was a Model Village, and in a sense a toy, the delight of Grantham Seton, now confined to his grave in the Seton plot beneath the yews of St Aldhelm's, there beyond the end of the single village street. And a very ugly village it was, thought Lewis, scooping up his surveyor's tape and notebook. The street was flanked by uniform red-brick boxes trimmed with brown-painted barge boards behind their privet hedges, uniformly shorn. In an access of paternalistic zeal Grantham Seton had in 1905 rehoused his estate workers, demolished the ancient settlement beyond the river, or most of it. If the surviving dwelling there was anything to go by, the measure had achieved progress of a sort, certainly in hygiene. Aesthetically the step had been a blunder. Perhaps paternalistic pride had had to concede that at some level – at any rate, the new street stood out of sight of Hollisfont Hall. The word was that the work-force had been duly grateful, quitting its traditional patch without regret. Lewis wondered; he doubted whether work-force opinion had been invited. He turned gingerly in the narrow gully and trod towards the back of the building. He was checking chimney-stacks. The house had stood empty for fifteen years. The new residents would be lighting fires to warm the coming winter, and his services had been enlisted; Miss Seton had recalled that there were problems with the library fire which always smoked and with the fire in the nurse's quarters, old Nanny Dodds who, having tended Mrs Grantham Seton to the end, then quietly expired herself at the Cottage Hospital. Lewis manoeuvred between the steep inclines above the Victorian frontage slapped on by some over-confident Seton forebear. He had found no obvious cause for the library's problems. Perhaps a cowl would correct it. He'd think about it, take a look at the stack inside the house later. He already knew why the other fire did not draw properly, he'd seen from the roof of the stable-block opposite; there was a crack in the stucco, quite wide, therefore some shifting in the brickwork behind; could be a patching job, could be reconstruction. It was easier going on the Georgian roof, the leaded gullies broader. He noted the general condition: very good. A couple of loose slates, occasional cricks in the gully joints, but impressive workmanship, impressive quality still substantially sound after two hundred years.

He arrived above the stable-yard, busy with workmen, carpenters, a glazier, a painter, and stood to consider Nanny Dodds's chimney. The governess's chimney, rather. He fished in his pocket for his notebook, in the process found an elderly Mint Imperial and ate it, wishing he could light his pipe. He didn't, since he was on duty and in full view of not only the workers but the various powers-that-be congregated round a hydrant: Mrs Somethingdorff, Mr Blow in full regalia despite the heat of the day, three-piece tweed suit, leggings, tweed hat, estate manager in majesty, and the amiable, dumpy figure of Miss Seton. Lewis would have found her likeable anyway – an admirable person, generous with time and attention, kindly and unassuming, but also astute. The estate and its dependants owed her much; more, he suspected, than was generally understood. But he had additional personal grounds for finding her likeable, since it was she who had set him in his present position as consultant surveyor to Hollisfont. With that under his belt he had the makings of an independent career, was able to stay freelance, saved from what was for him the dreariness of working again in somebody or other's firm. Perhaps it was the war that had shaped his taste for self-sufficiency. Certainly it had taught him the more obvious ground-rules and equipped him with the skills for living solo – he could and did look after himself then and since. Awareness of simple domestic truths had been forced upon him at the Front: if a mug was to be clean, someone actually had to clean it, a shirt repaired, someone had to stitch it, facts that had passed him by as a youthful member of an average, comfortable, provincial household before the war. His one concession to that old regimen was the ministrations of a 'daily', though Mrs Cox came just two mornings a week, cycling the three miles from Hollisfont to his house, Fold Cop, and adequately dealing with basic muck-and-dust removal in the modest abode of a bachelor and a dog of tidy habits, both of whom were usually out all day. Guinness, so called because his dark velvety coat was offset by a coronet of creamy fur atop his benevolent head, rode side-car with the Norton, which was now parked in the shade beyond the stables. Lewis glanced at his watch. Nearly lunch-hour, not long for Guinness to wait for his midday stretch.

Nanny Dodds's chimney would need more than patching. The recent wet spell had obligingly left its mark, staining the stucco in a wide inverted V. The bricks within the crack were fudgy, the mortar dead; yes, reconstruction, and the sooner the better, take advantage of this settled high pressure. Squatting against the stack, he made notes, entered measurements, a rough calculation of materials needed, then flipped the notepad shut, stowed the pencil in his breast-pocket. He stayed for a moment, savouring the sunlight warm upon his face, then heaved himself upright. A clattering rumble drew his attention, a farm wagon swaying into the yard, Williams leading the heavy horse, guiding him, backing him, halting him alongside one of the loose-boxes. Beyond the wagon a door in the wall of the kitchen garden flew open and through it hurtled two young boys, silver-blond, angular children, the smaller one ahead, whooping with pleasure, bounding across the yard towards the horse, clearly their objective. The other, older boy hesitated for a moment, looking back at the garden door through which emerged a woman, her hands cupped and filled with some awkward cargo. She was laughing. The boy laughed too and ran to her, relieved her of whatever it was, or part of it, while she closed the door behind her. The governess. She didn't look like a governess. Not that he'd ever seen one. But she didn't accord with the notion somehow acquired. That bright vignette, the lithe, laughing figure, lent a sudden personal interest to Nanny Dodds's chimney; the governess's chimney. He ran a fresh appraising eye over it, shoved the notebook into his pocket and made his way back to the trap-door above the front attics. He found himself deferring the inspection of the library's inner stack.

They were all still there when he reached the yard. The three from the kitchen garden had been joined by Miss Seton, the boys patting at the horse. Mr Blow was bent above the stand-pipe, pulling at its jammed tap, watched by Mrs Somethingdorff. Deciding that he needed to have a word with Miss Seton, Lewis strolled in that direction.

'Oh,' she was saying, 'is that old fig still fruiting?'

'Do horses eat figs, Aunt Honoria?' The elder boy.

'I rather doubt it, Max! Your mother's the one to ask about that – or Mr Williams!'

Williams had vanished, presumably into the loose-box.

'It's a Brunswick, as I remember.' Miss Seton peered as the governess held the figs for her to see. She took one. 'Ah, yes! We have a Black Ischia at the Hall. Very handsome, but the Brunswick has a better texture.' She smiled, said wistfully, 'That was a superb garden!'

Lewis hung back, hesitated, dawdled past, took himself on into the coach-house until a pause could give him entrée, just as Mrs Somethingdorff called, 'Honoria! Honoria – d'you know anything about the water supply to the yard? Mr Blow says it's separate from the house.'

Miss Seton joined her cousin, followed by the governess and the elder boy. The little one had hopped off after Williams.

Blow unbent himself, puffing and red in the face. 'Won't shift, ma'am. It'll be off at the source, anyway – wherever that is.'

'It must show on the plans,' said Mrs Somethingdorff. 'Surely?'

Lewis was trying to visualize the plans and locate the source when another voice spoke: 'It's in the sluice below the catch-tank.' The party at the tap turned. Lewis craned forward. It was young Coverdale. The only male in the yard without a tie, shirt wide to show a vee of sun-browned torso.

'Oh, yes, of course!' Miss Seton. 'How lucky you're here, Maurice!'

Without surprise Lewis observed that Blow did not share her enthusiasm. Blow shot a dismissive glance in that direction, addressed ma'am: 'I'll send someone to look into it –'

But ma'am was already addressing Coverdale: 'Oh, well done! Where is this catch-tank? And more to the point, is there water in it?'

'Yes, there's water. Tight as a drum.' Coverdale spoke

easily, enjoying himself. 'It's back there about quarter of a mile. I expect the cogs need some attention.'

Blow said heavily, 'Yes, well, thank you, Coverdale,' without looking at him, and to ma'am said, 'I'll send a man along tomorrow.'

But, 'Tomorrow?' she said. 'Is today not possible? If there are to be repairs –'

Coverdale said, 'I can cut along there on my bike now, if you like,' and shrugged.

From his ringside position Lewis felt the full tension of the little drama, watched with interest and amusement. Blow's turn.

Blow raised his voice: 'Coverdale isn't estate, ma'am. He's farm.' Finality applied.

But ma'am was looking at Coverdale who sweetly told her, 'Wouldn't take a jiffy – no trouble!'

Blow flushed. Voice lowered. 'You and Williams are detailed to clear loose-boxes.'

Coverdale tilted his head, innocence personified: 'It's dinner-hour. My free time.' He measured a pause and added, 'Sir.'

In the long ensuing moment nobody moved. From the safety of the coach-house Lewis grinned, almost laughed. With interest he noted that the governess was ducking her face above her figs, also contending with laughter. And then ma'am was saying with delicate but firm neutrality, 'Well, thank you,' endorsing the proposal. 'When you get back perhaps you'll let me know your findings straight away. We may be at lunch, but if you go to the kitchen Mrs Dunkerley will send for me.' And 'Right-o, ma'am,' came the cheery reply. Almost as though he had finished a cabaret turn, Coverdale gave a valedictory wave to his audience and strode away. Well, and indeed he had. It had been a performance. Blow as the fall-man. Quite a performance. Lewis withdrew, not wanting to be caught as spectator. Scraps of old local gossip, the Coverdale débâcle, lay about his mind. Pre-dated his brief contact with Outwick House. What was it that had put young Coverdale so far beyond the pale? Oh, yes – he'd thrown up his naval career and got himself disinherited, no less – though quite why it had been such an issue he couldn't remember, if indeed he'd ever known. Lewis had little appetite for such things, gave them small attention. Knew of course that the boy had spiked Vera Coverdale's guns by going native right on her doorstep. Cheeky young devil, obviously. Quite a performance just now! But, it had to be conceded, attractive, likeable too. Unless you were Mr Blow, of course . . . Chalk and cheese, the two of them. And that was not their first encounter in an arena, either. Jolly entertaining while it lasted. Enough of that, though. He stepped into the bright yard to speak to Miss Seton.

He only just caught up with her, she and her cousin were going in to lunch. Blow, no less red in the face, had stumped off. Lewis could hear his Ford starting up. The governess too, though. She'd disappeared . . . He gave his report. Both women had been stifling fits of giggles as he overtook them, looked charmingly like a couple of guilty schoolgirls caught napping when he made his presence known, but at once recovered, listened with attention, Mrs Somethingdorff – he'd better get her name sorted out – readily supplying permission to examine the inside stack that afternoon. 'Do go wherever you need to, yes. And what happens then – do I ring the estate office? Oh, you'll see to it all? Thank you, yes, the sooner the better – especially Grace's room – start on that, would you? The library can wait.'

Grace. She's called Grace, an English name, an English governess. Then there she was, the two boys running before her. Without preamble the smaller one said, 'You were on the roof, we saw you!' and to his mother, 'Can we go on the roof? *Please!*'

His mother laughed. 'We'll see!'

'Now!' The child beamed, hopping about.

'I said "we'll see", not "yes"!'

'That means "yes" – oh, I want to go now *please*!'

'Not now and not "yes", young man. Now is lunch!'

'Eeoow!' he moaned, but as a last word, not contention.

The one called Max regarded Lewis solemnly. 'Do you get vertigo?' He brought the word out carefully, a new acquisition. 'Grace said people have vertigo on high places some times.'

'Happily, no!' Lewis smiled.

Miss Seton said, 'Mr Gower is used to climbing about on high places – it's part of his job – he's mending our church tower too! Well, supervising it!'

'Oh, can we go up there?' The small one, hopping again. 'Oh, please, when we go to the church, Grace!'

Miss Seton said, 'Oh, Grace – this is Mr Gower, our consultant surveyor. Lewis, Miss Moon, who looks after these two rapscallions!'

'How do you do?' each said.

From this proximity you could see the habit of laughter in her face, a lively face, grey, alert eyes; pleasant voice, which inquired with interest, 'Would that be possible, to see what's going on there? Or would we be in the way?'

'Not at all, perfectly possible!'

'Yeeow!' Hopping and grinning, the younger one said, 'When?'

Lewis thought that Saturday afternoon would be best. The masons finished at midday on Saturdays. 'I'll be there myself then, glad to show you!'

'Thank you! Yes – that will suit us!' said the governess. 'What time will be convenient?'

'Shall we say three o'clock?'

It was agreed. 'And now,' said the governess to her charges, 'inside with you. Hands washed – but Nicholaus, here – take off your jumper, it's covered in hay!'

'Straw,' said Nicholaus, and his mother said, 'Mr Last-word!', everyone laughing.

Lewis took his leave, left the amiable domestic bumblings and set off to release Guinness. What very nice people! Rounding the stable-block, he took off his jacket, loosened his tie; beautiful day. September's a good month – England at its best. He whistled a snatch of 'Scarborough Fair', a tune he'd always liked. One way and another this had been a very satisfactory morning.

CHAPTER FOUR

The board beside the lych-gate bore the name St Aldhelm and set out the nature and hours of services. Across the bottom ran the name of the incumbent: The Reverend Thomas Opie. A wicket-gate some thirty yards east and round the corner in the churchyard wall gave access to the grounds of the Vicarage in which Tom Opie, humming to himself, prepared a corned beef sandwich and brewed a pot of tea, Saturday lunch. In the larder, under a muslin cloth to ward the flies off, were the chop, the peeled potatoes and carrots steeped in water, and the milk pudding – 'Just pop it in a low oven for half an hour to warm through' – his evening meal which today, as every Saturday, it pleased Mrs Cox to leave prepared for him: 'Well, we must look after you, mustn't we!' He had long since abandoned the unequal struggle to convince her that on Saturdays as on other days he was only too happy to cater for himself. The ritual was dear to her for some reason, and after all, it didn't come amiss, some of the puddings were rather good, too. He mixed fresh mustard and liberally dosed the corned beef. He must get another jar of piccalilli next time he was in Hestonborough. He put the remaining chunk of tinned meat on a saucer and took it to the larder to join the chop under the muslin; a pork chop, today. Not mint jelly, then; he'd use up those wrinkly apples, make a bit of sauce.

Returning to the kitchen he poured his tea and settled to his lunch. Mrs Cox, it seemed, did not feel moved to look after her 'other gentleman' to the extent of a ritual weekly supper. Lewis Gower had laughed: 'I don't come up to scratch, evidently, Tom!' 'Ah!' Tom had told him, 'you don't wear your collar back to front! There's something about bachelor clerics that brings out the cherishing instinct in women!' A joke, but not only a joke – it was true, thought Tom; and quite acceptable too on the whole! Also, he thought, chewing his hefty sandwich, I am middle-aged, a bit thin on top, and in general safely within a category to bring out the bustling quality in a certain type of woman. Lewis was still a couple of decades short of that qualification. Mrs Cox's services for Lewis extended only as far as chivvying the dust about in the usual way. The arrangement suited them all well these past few years. Between them the two households gave Mrs Cox 'that bit extra' which she needed as a war widow with two youngsters, living on a pension. She was pleased as Punch this week to have found a bit more extra, courtesy of Honoria Seton, as one of the new 'dailies' up at the Dower House. 'Oh, don't you worry, Mr Opie, it won't interfere with you or Mr Gower, I wouldn't let anything interfere with my two gentlemen for the world!' Pleased as Punch and specially bustly. Mrs Mayendorff had astounded Hollisfont: she didn't want staff living in, she wanted daily help. Hollisfont was not only astounded, Hollisfont was ruffled: 'Whoever heard of such a thing!' Tom, taking a swig of tea, mildly reflected that a splendid tut-tut session had been enjoyed by all. Less acceptable was the upsurge of anti-German sentiment, undiminished by eleven years of Peace. The fact that Mrs Mayendorff was English did not absolve her; she'd married a Hun, had a Boche name, no recommendation to the vassals of Hollisfont who had sent twenty-two of their men to the war and received back five. The rest were listed on the plaque in the south transept, In Memoriam. Including Mrs Cox's Billy. Tom acknowledged that residual tribal animosity was not to be wondered at, unattractive though it was. He noted without surprise that it was nevertheless dispensable when, come the moment, jobs were offered; Mrs Mayendorff was reassessed; her Hun connections were superseded by her kinship to the Setons, English as good roast beef. As to the blond Teutonic children, well, as Mrs Cox explained, they were only kiddies – had no choice where they were born, had they? She hadn't stayed for an answer, swooshing off with her carpet-sweeper. Tom's answer, if he had chosen to give one, might have been: 'No more than your Billy, or Mr Gower or I or any of us poor blighters either side of the firing-line devised by politicians!'

His meal complete, he carried the bread-board he'd used as a plate to the back door, open in the warm afternoon, and scattered the crumbs for the birds. He rinsed his mug under the tap. From the plug-hole came the loathly reek of Jeyes' Fluid, the cleansing force beloved by Mrs Cox. Its stink invariably and instantly recalled army huts, field latrines and military hospitals. Lewis shared his abhorrence on the same grounds, similarly afflicted by this aspect of Mrs Cox's personal crusade against impurity at Fold Cop. He ran more water to dilute the Jeyes' and only succeeded in amplifying the stink. The Lord, he thought, works in mysterious ways: who'd have thought Jeyes' Fluid could be a lubricant to friendship? It had been the subject of their shared laughter, his and Gower's, and the entrée to discovery of common ground beyond the sharing of domestic aid. Turned out they'd been at some of the same camps in England, some of the same places in France; and shared the same opinion of that appalling carnage known as the Great War. Lewis had at last escaped by the dubious advantage of 'a comfortable wound', mutilation short of chronic disablement, just enough to get you out and home. He himself had left less acceptably, though none the less gratefully, a dose of jaundice invaliding him out. He did not account himself much missed. By then, autumn '17, few viewed the Padre with more than tolerant cynicism. He'd done his tithe of burials, committing the mangled remains of youth to the expanding cemeteries, their souls to the Redeemer in whom most of them did not believe; his preaching, such as it was, had been to the converted. As ever, it seemed. He could not claim with certainty to have achieved a single convert in his thirty years' ministry. Though you never knew, of course. Possibly that alcoholic in Walsall, before the war? Good days in Walsall, converts or not, rough and busy times they'd been, plenty of action in those crammed and grimy streets below the smoke-stacks, plenty to support the sense of high purpose, the right work in the right place, among the victims of poverty burdened with troubles, bad housing, debt, ill-health, guilty or defiant with alcohol, VD, petty crime, abortions, sex for money, life of the real and earnest variety with its own sturdy virtues of resilience, generosity, tolerance and humour. His return there presented a cheering objective as he straggled through the wastelands of the war. But when he was eventually discharged from hospital and handed in his uniform, he was posted not to his beloved Walsall, but to some Cloud Cuckoo Squirearchy. You're not supposed to argue, but he did, a bit. He got his knuckles rapped, of course: Pride, Spiritual Pride, Mr Opie. The squirearchy, which was called Hollisfont, he was sternly reminded, was furnished with souls in need just as was Walsall; the Lord's work lay everywhere, did it not? He'd had a shot at constructive humility; but he was decidedly grumpy as he headed for St Aldhelm's, and it took a while to achieve new perspective. They'd been right, of course, about spiritual pride. And right, of course, about the souls. The bodies were better nourished and clad and there were fewer of them per square yard here in

Hollisfont; but per capita – if you could endow souls with capitas – the needs were much the same, much the same.

He shook out the tea-towel and draped it where Mrs Cox had left it, neatly pendant from the draining-board. Time to make himself presentable for the afternoon's appointment. His plimsolled feet made no sound across the flagged kitchen, the stone passageway into the hall. He paused on his way to the stairs. He frowned in concentration. No good! He'd have to look it up again. He went into his study and flipped open the diary. Bellinger . . . Bellinger. Coverdale/Bellinger 2.30. Got that? Bellinger. He flipped the diary shut. No need to remind himself of Coverdale – Coverdale he knew all right! Young Lilian of that line; bride-to-be come next May. He turned away and then turned back, struck by something – he found the page again. Yes, that was an error, it should be Bellinger/Coverdale – groom first, bride second. A small grunt of a laugh escaped him. He shut the book again, not troubling to correct the error. Its irony amused him. As he jogged up the stairs, peeling off his flannel shirt, he could not but reflect that whatever the components of Mr Bellinger's personality might be, one would have to be a ready compliance to stand second in Coverdalian concerns. He was quite interested to meet Mr Bellinger, curious to see this latest recruit to the Coverdale ranks; be a different sort of lad from Moira's. Vernon was an earnest, sober sort of chap, quiet and formal like Moira herself. Lilian's temperament would look for something . . . livelier; but the candidate would have had to pass muster with Mama, nothing too unconventional in his behaviour.

He hummed to himself, finding a clean shirt, his bib and collar, socks; he often hummed; liked music; hadn't a bad singing voice, actually. Clipping his clerical back-stud into place, he mused upon St Aldhelm, who had stood on the bridge in his parish of a Sunday morning loudly singing his native Saxon songs in an attempt to lure defecting peasants into church; desperate measure! He'd thought of trying it himself on the bridge at Hollisfont – snatches from Gilbert and Sullivan, perhaps; well, not entirely seriously, but there were moments when any methods to increase his meagre congregation seemed worth considering. Dum dum dum, trala tra lalaa . . . Now then, specs. Where did I leave them this time? Had them when I was reading in bed last night. Have I had them today? Don't need them yet for any but small print but it's possible there'll be some small print on the afternoon's agenda. She said something about hymn-books. Hymn-books, kneelers – 'tatty' she called them! Tatty. Well, I suppose they are, some of them. Hymn-books, kneelers and the red carpet to be checked for moths. The impressive mills were in motion. Been just the same with Moira's wedding. Eight months away, but we're checking everything! Ah. Specs! Where's the case? Oh, good, under the books here. Might just need them if she wants to choose hymns together with – what's his name? Bellinger! Clean fingernails? Clean handkerchief. Shoes all right? Give them a bit of a buff downstairs.

Back in the kitchen he decided they needed more than a bit of a buff and took them off again, gave them a bit of Cherry Blossom as well as a bit of a buff. He should really have pressed his trousers; the bicycle clips had left their mark round the turn-ups. Oh, well, too late to bother now. He screwed the lid back on to the boot-polish, dropped it with the brushes into the drawer by the sink and wiped his hands briefly on the tea-towel. His bicycle clips had been a feature of his last, indeed terminal, visit to Outwick House three years ago. Summoned thence, and arrived, in the impressive presence, in her study, he was made aware by an eloquent glance that he had omitted to remove them, his bicycle clips. Mrs Coverdale had never concealed her preference for his predecessor, the Reverend Giles Phillotson, who had indeed been a very nice old man, but more to the point for Mrs Coverdale, was a product of the Right Background, a scholar and a gentleman. In the event, the bicycle clips were the least of their problems that day when the purport of the summons turned out to be her requirement that he should have her errant son turned out of the village. Using what she referred to as 'your moral authority', he was to go to the farmer and make plain that the 'absurd and intolerable situation be terminated immediately' by Mr Sutton dismissing the reprobate. Tom sighed, remembering. It had not been an easy interview. His attempts to define his role as conciliator in life's conflicts were cut short. Not easy. His own rising temper was, he hoped, better concealed than hers. 'I have, Mrs Coverdale, no authority, even if I thought it appropriate, to attempt to instruct or persuade Mr Sutton towards one course or another –' And she had pulled the bell-cord. 'I see,' she had said. 'You will excuse me, I have much to do.' And to the maid who appeared: 'Mr Opie is leaving.' He had not been invited to Outwick House again. Not an intolerable privation for either of them; he sighed again. He had cycled down to see the boy, thought that an appropriate pastoral call. Another barren exchange, really, the boy grinning, cagey, truculent. 'Me? Talk to her? Not on your life!' Quite a likeable boy. Young for his twenty-one years; handsome, and aware of it; no fool, but foolish with cockiness pro tem; stubborn. Like his mother, there. But quite unlike her, hotheaded, was Tom's guess. He saw him as a youth at the mercy of impulse but imagining himself to be a free spirit, and Jack the Giant Killer. Tom hoped his awakening would not be too rude, if it ever came. Since then, they always waved to each other in passing. He never came to church. His mother did from time to time; and inclined her head, cool and correct, gloved handshake on quitting the church porch after service. Such interchange as was unavoidable in the planning of weddings was conducted through the brides, Moira a couple of years back, now Lilian.

Restoring the tea-towel to its appointed place, he heard the Norton's engine gearing down, always a welcome sound, but today a couple of hours earlier than expected. He hurried to the front door. Lewis was fishing two bottles of beer from the side-car: 'I've brought our tea!' Then, taking in Tom's appearance: 'What's this? Full fig!'

'On duty – Coverdale wedding!' Tom hopped down the steps. 'You're early, aren't you?'

'I've got a duty too – people from the Dower House, the kids want to see the tower!'

'Do they, do they?' Tom was pleased. He was personally fond of St Aldhelm's; over the years he had unearthed much of its history and was always pleased when interest was shown.

Lewis felt obliged to explain: 'I think it's climbing things that's the attraction!'

'Ah!' said Tom. 'Well – a very proper predilection in the young!' He went on, 'What time do you expect to be finished, then? I should be through with my business by three.'

'Mine starts at three – I've come now to have a look over the week's progress before they arrive, then, well, if all they want is the tower, I'll be with you by half-past.'

'If they want to see more, don't hurry,' said Tom. 'Hello, old fella!' He greeted Guinness, leaned to pat the dog who sleepily thumped his tail, curled in the side-car. 'Take him into the study if you want!'

'Oh, he's all right here, he's in the shade. But I'll put these in the larder.'

'Carry on – I'm off to lug the carpet out.'

'Carpet?'

'The ceremonial red, for the bride.'

'Good Lord!' Lewis laughed. 'It's only September!'

Tom smiled: ''Twas ever thus!' he said.

From the top step Lewis called, 'I've brought the binoculars – see if those kestrels are still about.'

'Excellent!' Tom called back.

As he let himself into the vestry he reflected that it would have been better sense to have lugged the carpet out before lunch, in his civvies rather than now in his best bib-and-tucker. Oh, well. It stood rolled and wrapped in sacking up-ended against the wall beyond the cupboard. It was a heavy old brute! Well, it was twenty yards from the lych-gate to the porch and this was no ordinary carpet, this was prime-quality Victorian carpet, bespoken for a Seton marriage, 1860s. Miss Seton's parents. And Spencer Seton's too, of course. No marriage for him, none for Miss Seton. No more Setons. The end of the line. He lugged and heaved the thing through the door into the chancel and bumped it down the steps into the nave where it was to be unrolled for inspection. 'Well that's the obvious place!' she had told him. He untied the sacking in readiness and shoved the roll against the base of the pulpit, dusting off his hands.

It was still, very still in the church, gilded dust motes hanging in the fingers of sunlight reaching from the Perpendicular windows mercifully free from devout Victorian improvement, clear simple glass and simple clear light. Behind him the east window, reglazed by Grantham Seton and crammed with saints and lilies, Our Lord well haloed and complete with Lamb, grudgingly admitted a curious gloom, not radiant at all. Alas for Victorian zeal, untempered with discretion! Hands lightly locked behind his back, Tom strolled about his favourite building. The scent of chrysanthemums met him as he passed the lectern, Mrs Hobbs's turn on the roster this week, the blooms embowered in beech leaves in the gleaming brass bowl. Those handsome incurves, creamy white and bronze, were from the Hall's hot-houses; the Hobbses' garden jostled with cabbages and beans, and contributed lavishly to the Harvest Festival, but did not furnish flowers, apart from the rambler rose in the front garden. Pink. Very pretty. Miss Seton, with her usual quiet, self-effacing competence, made sure that for whatever reason, St Aldhelm's was never without its flowers. He paused before the plaque commemorating his predecessor: The Reverend Giles Phillotson, Vicar of this parish 1866–1920. Quite remarkable. Fifty-four years. A longer span by far than any other recorded on the Roll of Vicars and Rectors. The first incumbent, Baldwin de Clyfforde, had served two years before something or other carried him off – another benefice, or death. The Reverend Giles had by all accounts been a robust and vigorous man right up until the influenza which took him off in a matter of days, aged eighty. Tom wished he had known him. He knew his widow, Dorothy, who had shown much kindness to the successor, gently insisting that he should keep the furniture, aware that an ex-army bachelor cleric would be hard put to it to provide for that substantial Vicarage. She still lived in the snug little house to which she had retired in Hestonborough. He enjoyed his occasional visits; she was frail now, not surprisingly, at ninety, but gently cheerful as ever. He strolled on. One day his own name would be added to the Roll: Thomas Opie, 1920– ? Well, whenever that should be, he hoped that as with his predecessor, it would be the Ultimate Posting, rather than another parish, that would decide it. Yet how he had sulked at the prospect of Hollisfont! A lesson in trust. Which is, he mused, still and always the most difficult of lessons; never fully learned, for an average mortal, like me.

He glanced at his watch. Twenty-five past. Another five minutes – they would arrive on time if Lilian had anything to do with it, and she would. *What* was his name again? Oh, dear. Ah! Bellinger. Think of bells. Which should not be difficult: the repairs to the tower are at last in hand because of bells, wedding bells: Lilian's wedding was to be celebrated by the full peal which had been rung on Moira's wedding day but not since, as a crack had soon afterwards been detected in the tower's north wall and five of the six bells 'laid up' until it should be repaired. The attendant official procedures, true to diocesan form, dawdled and trailed on, papers and documents and signatures for this, for that and for the other, weeks into months, months into years; until Mrs Coverdale entered the arena. Ah, then, the system met its match! By the end of the week the scaffolding was up. He smiled, amused, also contented, that the bells should ring out again, whatever the means. Bellinger. Yes, he'd got it now. A beautiful ceremony, the Solemnization of Matrimony. Beautiful, melodious prose, for all the great ceremonies, the Order of Baptism, the Order of Confirmation, the Solemnization of Matrimony, the Order of the Burial of the Dead. Of which he had personally partaken of two, would one day, albeit passively, partake of another, and once upon a time had been in prospect of partaking in the third. He had been in love, he supposed. Elated, obsessed, physically in chronic arousal for a few months – a serviceable definition of the condition? An experience he was grateful to have had, inasmuch as it enhanced his understanding of human exigencies. He had, though, no regrets that the relationship had not withstood the test of separation, his absence at theological college. It had fizzled out; she had married someone else eventually. And he, he was that curious commodity, a 'confirmed bachelor', and most content. He knew he was a disappointment to the match-makers of the world, of whom there were a few in every parish, and who subscribed to the notion that 'a vicarage needs a woman – Vicar needs a wife, needs a woman's helping hand . . .' With all due recognition of the value of female virtues in any situation, he could not agree in this particular. Company? Never a problem; he enjoyed his own, and folk were very hospitable too. He did not feel starved of companionship. Might yet get a dog. It would have to be as charming as Guinness . . . Yes, marriage was right for many, and just as well; but not for him. He was fulfilled sufficiently in performing marriages for others. The Reverend Giles had united Grantham Seton and his bride in 1869, here before that altar. How many others down the years, in this lovely place, other priests, the same beautiful form of service . . . Half-past: the old clock lumbered into action: B-O-N-G! And here they were, the hefty oak door creaking open to admit clientele, if that was quite the word. Miss Coverdale appeared.

On the roof of the tower Nicholaus thrust himself out between the castellations, Grace's restraining hand grasping his arm. Max stood slightly back, assessing the possible onset of vertigo. 'And that,' said Lewis, 'is the Hall, of course,' pointing to roofs beyond the tree-tops to the west. The river cut slow dark curves through farmland, embraced the broad grounds of the Hall and passed from view. 'And that, over there,' he told the boys, turning and pointing away north and west, 'is where Hector lives, the Home Farm.' Hector was the heavy horse who could not eat figs because they might give him colic, but had eaten carrots – two, one for each boy, supplied by Mrs Dunkerley.

'Can we go and see him?' Nicholaus jiggled and Grace

hauled him in. 'Careful!' she said. 'Yes, we'll go for a walk that way –'

'When? Can we go now?'

Grace slid her arm round his shoulder, drawing him to her. 'One thing at a time,' she told him mildly. 'We're seeing the church now.'

'Eeow . . .'

Max was examining the flag-pole. 'Is there a flag?' he asked of Lewis.

'Yes – well, three, actually! The Union Jack, the flag of St George and the Seton personal standard.'

Max said, '*What* was the first one?'

'The Union Jack – the British flag!'

'Why is it called that?'

'Because the three different flags – erm – of England and Scotland and Ireland which are all crosses – different crosses – are – they're put together, to show that we all belong together under one king, in Great Britain, a Union, you see . . .' Lewis frowned, grappling with his explanation, and appealing to Grace said, 'But I'm blessed if I know what's happened to Wales – do you?'

She laughed. 'No! Perhaps it just didn't fit in – theirs is a dragon, isn't it?'

Max said, 'But why is it called "Jack"?'

Lewis raised eyebrows to Grace and shrugged helplessly. 'I don't know! Why *is* it called Jack?'

'I don't know either.' She smiled, and told Max, 'We'll look it up when we get home.'

'Golly!' murmured Lewis. 'There's more to it than you'd imagine, being with children! You obviously have to know a lot!'

Grace laughed again. 'No – you just have to find out a lot!'

'Where are the flags?' said Max.

'I expect they're down in the vestry,' said Lewis, and added triumphantly, 'The vestry is the little room at the back of a church where the Vicar keeps his special robes!'

'I know,' said Max politely.

Grace grinned at Lewis as he ruefully smiled at her and said, 'Oh, well . . .'

Nicholaus, leaning out again and contemplating the scaffolding beneath, called, 'We can get down that way!'

'I think not!' Grace retrieved him. 'We'll go back the way we came, thank you!'

They stood for a moment taking a final look at the panorama. 'It's beautiful country,' said Grace. 'Wonderful view up here.'

Her smile was delightful. Lewis smiled back.

Only the river moved. But then from behind the Home Farm's outbuildings a figure emerged and, mounting a bicycle, set off along the riverside lane. 'It's that man,' Nicholaus told them. 'He found the water for the horses.'

Lewis agreed: 'Yes. Young Coverdale. He lives at the farm.'

'He came with Hector.'

'That's right.'

The cyclist crossed the bridge, taking the Hestonborough road.

'Where's he going?' asked Nicholaus.

Lewis laughed. 'I don't know! To Hestonborough, I expect.'

'Oh.'

But the cyclist left the road, took a trackway to the right, slowing down and swinging off on to one foot, one pedal, coasting to a stop.

'Is that Hes – Hes –?'

'Hestonborough. No, that's Poundell. Hestonborough is our local town – about seven miles away – you might have come through it on your way to Hollisfont.' He turned to Grace and told her, 'The village used to be there – at Poundell. All old, old cottages, wattle and daub and thatch, pulled down thirty-odd years back when the new village was built.' He nodded towards the single red-brick street.

Grace raised her eyebrows: 'What a pity!' she said with feeling.

'Isn't it!' Lewis emphatically agreed. 'I'm sure they could have been restored, modernized – and for half the price too!' He shrugged. 'Progress, I suppose. Progress in the terms of the philanthropic spirit of the times.'

The figure and the bicycle had disappeared behind greenery, low scrub bordering a copse. Lewis said, 'Well. Down we go?' Grace nodded. He said, 'I'll go first,' stooping through the little door on to the spiral of stone stairs, 'then if you slip you can fall on me!'

As they descended he said over his shoulder, 'There's one cottage left – an old gipsy family – quite an interesting story. The old man claimed ancient rights – quite a wrangle, apparently – lawyers and court proceedings and everything, but the old man won, and his son's still there, an old man himself now, must be about eighty, but the rights hold good – until he dies.'

'What then?' said Grace.

'It'll be pulled down, probably.' He was at ground level and stood to hold the door for them. To his surprise he heard voices behind him in the body of the church. The wedding conference still going on! A smart Rover car had been parked outside when he and the tower party had assembled but there had been no one inside and he took it that the conference had transferred to the Vicarage. They must have been in the vestry. They were here now. And a strip of plum-red carpet lay the length of the nave, Lilian Coverdale pacing it and saying, 'Well, it's all right – but this awful smell of camphor! We'll have to do something about that!' Then, catching sight of Lewis, she cried, 'Oh, good! Hello, Lewis! I wanted to see you – how are the repairs? Going well?'

Grace felt herself assessed, encompassed in the broad smile of greeting. The young woman strode towards them. 'You must be our new neighbours! Mother didn't see you when she left her card though she did meet Mrs Mayendorff! How d'you do!' She extended her hand. 'I'm Lilian Coverdale – Outwick House – you know?'

'How do you do?' said Grace, her hand firmly grasped. Lewis Gower was saying, 'This is Miss Moon – and this is Nicholaus, and Max –' but Grace was struggling with a concept: Coverdale? That farm-boy and this – surely not! But there was indeed a strong likeness: hair, shape of face, stance . . .

'Come and tell me what you think!' The young woman was striding off again, elegant blue-shod feet along the carpet. 'I can smell camphor, can't you? Awful!' She waved a hand at the two men hovering near the pulpit. 'They claim they can't smell a thing!'

'Phoo!' said Nicholaus, following her.

'There! There you are, you see!' Miss Coverdale was pleased. 'Which one are you? Nicholaus. Nicholaus can smell it! Trouble is with you men that you smoke too much – can't smell anything – ruined your sense of smell! Isn't that right?' She summoned Grace.

Grace smiled and came up with diplomacy. 'It could be that!' But Miss Coverdale was already speaking again, addressing the boys: 'So you've been up the tower? Did you like it up there? Years since I went up!' And encompassing Grace again, 'Wonderful views! Lovely country, isn't it? D'you think you're going to like it here? Come and meet my fiancé! He was in Germany last year – motoring holiday, weren't you, Frank? This is Miss Moon – Frank Bellinger, my fiancé!' And then, 'You know Mr Opie, of course! Oh! Haven't you? Our Vicar, Mr Opie!'

Grace shook two more hands, 'How d'you do – how d'you do,' the one belonging to a personable young man in open-necked shirt, cravat and hacking jacket, the other to a man older though not old, genial mobile face with shrewd, humorous eyes above the sobriety of clerical dress.

'And what part of Germany do you hail from?' Mr Bellinger inquired cheerily.

'Berlin,' Grace told him. 'Berlin and a place called Reissen, in the country, Saxony as was.'

'Mm, yes, didn't get up that way – went in through Strasbourg, took a look at the Blue Danube, Freiburg, Ulm, down to Munich, all round there, jolly nice. Thought I'd take Lilian, honeymoon trip – on into Austria. Like to take a quiz at Vienna – on the way to Italy, y'know – Grand Tour. Might skip Germany, though, getting a bit so-so – Jews and Communists – exchange rate out of hand, mark not worth the paper it's printed on!' He put it to the men of the party.

Lewis fielded: 'Mm, they're having a difficult time.' And opened a different subject. 'That the car you toured in? I'm thinking of a Rover myself, they seem good cars?'

'Oh, first-rate, first-rate! Come and have a look, have a look-see! Leave the carpet to the ladies, eh!' The confidence of the tone was modified by the glance at his fiancée, a request for clearance which was rewarded with an indulgent laugh. 'Oh, MEN!' she put it to Grace. 'Have to play with their cars, don't they? Boys will be boys! Shall we let them go?'

Grace, putting herself to bed that night, recalled that she had not been given time for an answer: the question having been rhetorical, Miss Coverdale supplied her own answer. 'Off you go, then!' she had said. 'Only don't be long – this carpet has to be rolled up again!' The Reverend Opie, designated neither man nor boy, had been left with the women and children. Which he didn't seem to mind at all. He was very nice. Knew a lot about the history of St Aldhelm's, and obviously enjoyed showing the boys how the organ worked and why it wheezed.

Grace wound the alarm-clock, plumped the pillow and got into bed, settling her feet on the hot-water bottle and ruminating on her day. Central to her ruminations, she encountered the enigma for which she had never found a name. Not for the first time, she thought it odd that no satisfactory name, no proper word, had ever been devised to express the enigma that was after all at the core of human society, the affiliation, in pairs, of opposite genders. It was called 'falling in love'. Vague, imprecise. It didn't explain anything. 'Sex' was a word too gross for her taste and anyway inadequate, signifying as it did that primitive, functional business common to any old animal – merely anatomical. 'Sex' was that ugly coupling, mindless, which she had witnessed with distaste – the chimpanzees at Berlin Zoo. That had nothing to do with human affiliations, the higher faculties selecting a partner for life. But there was no word for that. 'Marriage' was the possible end-result of the selection but not the initial process. Miss Coverdale and Mr Bellinger, the contract symbolized by the handsome diamond on Miss Coverdale's ring-finger, had made their selection. But on what basis? They were, presumably, 'in love'. There had been little evidence of the phenomenon 'being in love' as manifested in books. Books – though they did not explain the enigma – did describe the symptoms: tenderness, agitation, mutual awareness and concern, for instance. Come to think of it – how extraordinary! Now that she thought about it, the two had been more like a pair long married than a pair tender, agitated, mutually aware and concerned. Which brought her back to the enigma! What *was* it that brought people together – but then seemed to get lost afterwards? For though Grace had never previously met an engaged couple, she had lived her life with the married variety.

Personally, Grace had little experience to draw upon. She had been kissed, when she was seventeen. Behind the bathing huts at Cannes. A student on holiday. Pierre. He'd gone back to Paris two days later, back to university. He was good-looking; it was quite nice, the kiss; but rather worrying, lots of people about and she should not have been behind the bathing huts, she should have been on the sands with the little Lascelleses and their buckets and spades. But it had been quite nice. Other experiences had not been nice at all – the inebriated gropings of Herr Mayendorff's house-guests from time to time – pure chimpanzee! Horrible. Especially the one who'd come fumbling into her room at one o'clock in the morning. Reeked of brandy. Thoroughly drunk, and just as well – too tipsy to resist when she bundled him out. Ugh!

She reached out from beneath the bedclothes and switched off the lamp. It had been a good day, one way and another. Lovely at breakfast when Mrs Mayendorff had told the boys that they could indeed have ponies. And then more exploring because it was Saturday. In any case, lessons hadn't started yet, it was still holiday time. Lessons again on Monday. Mrs Mayendorff did not intend the boys to go to boarding school yet – for one thing she had not had time to find one, personally visit and assess possibilities; and for another, she thought it was as well for them to settle in, get used to England and the English, adjust. Through Miss Seton a tutor might be found to initiate them in the maths and science they'd meet in their new school, which Grace had suggested would be wise as she was out of touch with modern developments in those subjects. She'd mug them up somehow if she had to, but apart from anything else it occurred to her that it would be useful for the boys to have another teacher, and a man, as part of preparation for the wider world, and Mrs Mayendorff thought that made sense. Meantime, holidays, and further explorations today. They had walked across the park this morning and found some conkers. Beautiful parkland. English, and English light, quite different from other light, unique. This morning she had felt that she had arrived, childhood memory matching the moment. And this afternoon, standing again in an English church, spare, uncluttered, delicate but strong in its simple lines. Classical, not Baroque. Grace had not been moved to take her pencil and drawing-pad into those curvaceous, complex, exuberant Continental churches, alien to her taste. Perhaps she'd try her hand again; the pencils and pads were still there somewhere at the bottom of a trunk. Perhaps she would. Mr Opie had given ready permission when she asked if she might come again to browse on her own: 'Yes – please do! It's always open.' So perhaps she'd have a go at drawing again, see if she still had the knack after so many years . . . She shifted the hot-water bottle with her feet, reached down and hauled it up, turning on her side and settling it against her tummy ready for sleep. Guinness! What a wonderful name for that dog! And what a nice man Mr Gower was; very kind. Very easy and friendly with the boys, and sensible, quite firm in a calm sort of way when Nicholaus got a bit dotty and excited with the dog. The boys took to Mr Gower. Very pleased with the offer to show them some caves, 'Only small ones, you know, but big enough for you two to stand up in!' Somewhere along the river, but too far to go today, probably next weekend. Eyes closed, she drowsed. Yes, a good day. But with the last of her consciousness a question recurred: 'That farm-boy and that chic young woman . . .?'

1929

November

CHAPTER FIVE

Mrs Coverdale switched on the ormolu desk-lamp beside her and adjusted its silk shade, directing light on to her list. She glanced at the clock on the mantelpiece, noted that it was quarter-past four and that the fire needed attention. Betty was late again about her duties.

She turned back to her list. It was headed 'Christmas card order. November 1st 1929'. To her left were other documents enclosed in labelled folders: Women's Institute, Parish Council, League of Pity, Earl Haig Memorial Association, English Embroidery Guild, and Benevolent Society for Poor Relief. To her right lay her diaries, one personal and domestic, the other recording her public engagements, and the bulky folder marked WEDDING. Facing her in a dozen silver frames, for the desk was on the grand scale, were photographic portraits attesting to years of family life: of her late father in full uniform as Captain in the Cunard Line; of her mother coiffured and gowned for a County ball; of herself and Henry as guests of honour at the opening of the King George V Veterans' Wing, Hestonborough General Hospital, 1922; of their elder daughter and her groom outside St Aldhelm's on the occasion of their wedding; of the granddaughter from that union disposed on a fur rug: of Lilian, the studio portrait on her recent twenty-first birthday; of their youngest, Bertie, at the Open Day upon which he received the Science Award, the youngest recipient ever in that illustrious school; and others of her children in early years, Moira, Lilian and Bertie. There were none of Maurice. Three and a half years ago on

14 May they had been stripped from their silver frames and burnt.

She took up her pen, totted up the Christmas card list again: 187. She finally wrote '200', counting the additional dozen or so for Henry's use. From the top right-hand drawer she took her address book and the clutch of business cards paper-clipped together. She consigned Petterson Press to the waste-paper basket. Last year the order had arrived three days late. She selected Castledean Printing and copied the address under C in her book, turned to P and crossed out Petterson Press. Their laxity had cost them a substantial account, amplified this coming year by wedding invitations and place-cards. She flipped open the folder marked WEDDING and drew out Castledean's sample design. Excellent-quality board, discreet format. Fairly expensive, but then cheap's cheap, as the saying went. She returned the sample to its place and closed the folder. Aligning her list, she perused it. Two for Hollisfont Hall. Honoria Seton had her own separate suite of rooms and her personal letter-box. Next on the list, new this year, Mrs Mayendorff. Pleasant woman, as one would expect, of course; though her dress sense left something to be desired. But then she was primarily interested in her horses; rode with the Pytchley, had two hunters shipped across from Germany, very good bloodstock according to Henry. Her eye moved on. Bracketed with 'Dower House', Grace Moon. Her gaze lingered critically. Lilian was insistent. A good thing when Lilian became Mrs Bellinger and achieved proper perspectives. She was becoming headstrong. Rather tiresome. Moira had always been co-operative. Sign of the times, these post-war years; standards eroding. The Moon girl business was becoming irritating. Possibly above average for what one would expect in a governess, but a governess all the same. As to this latest wild idea that she should be maid-of-honour at the wedding . . .! However, there were six months, time for this present infatuation to cool. She passed down the list, leaving Grace Moon undeleted, yielding a principle though with some reluctance; but the card would bear Lilian's signature, not her own.

'Come in!' she called in response to the tap at the door.

'Your tea, ma'am.' Betty bore in the tray.

'The fire,' said Mrs Coverdale, 'needs attention. Do you know what the time is?' Mrs Coverdale's voice was one of the striking features in a striking persona. It was low and musical, the delivery regulated, in accord with an immaculate elegance and a compelling presence. She regarded Betty.

'Yes, ma'am.'

'Then it is difficult to understand why you are again late. There is no room for laxity in an ordered household. Perhaps you are not suited to service. Please tell Mrs Dyer that I would like a word with her on the matter. I'll see her here at half-past five. Put the tray down now. And attend to the fire.' She resumed her work, attuned to the mending of the fire and the departure of the girl, the soft 'clunk' of the door.

She laid down her pen and moved from the desk to the tea-tray, set upon the exquisite little table, prime among her possessions. American eighteenth-century, a collector's piece in glowing walnut, one present among many from her father on the occasion of her marriage. It would go to Moira in the fullness of time. One of the items transferred thence in the rewriting of her will, three and a half years ago. She poured herself a cup of tea. She carried it back to the desk, where she consulted the memo sheet attached to the WEDDING file. It confirmed that it was a full two weeks since Henry was supposed to have made inquiries about the organist. She stirred her tea, distributing the lemon. Another reminder, another prompting, then. To-night, at dinner. How many times in the course of her duties she found herself obliged to do the thinking for others as well!

Towards the end of the Turbot Dugléré Mrs Coverdale said to her husband, 'I hope you have spoken to Canon Topping.'

Mr Coverdale retrieved his attention from wherever it had been, considered the remark and supplied his response: 'No.' He lifted another sliver of turbot and forked it into his mouth. Having eaten it, he said, 'I've not been in Peterborough this week.' His voice was, like his younger daughter's, plangent, but in his case unexpressive, except perhaps in conveying lack of interest. Hair now silver about his temples lent an air of distinction to features handsome but without authority. His glance, when released, revealed sceptical brown eyes. Usually, as now, the glance was withheld, directed to his own affairs behind lowered lids. He continued to eat. So did Lilian and Bertie, each peacefully preoccupied with Mrs Dyer's cooking.

'I should be glad of an answer from Topping soon, Henry,' his wife told him. 'There is no cause to wait upon going to Peterborough. You may write, or use the telephone.'

He finished his turbot, laid together his knife and fork and blotted his lips with the napkin. 'In this instance, vis à vis is preferable in my opinion.' He returned the napkin to his lap.

'The preferable method is that which achieves results soonest,' said his wife. 'If the organist is not available I shall have to look elsewhere. I need to have the matter settled.'

Lilian looked up. 'Why not go straight to the chap himself? Why bother with old Topping?'

'There are proper channels for such things.' Mrs Coverdale turned to her daughter. 'Lilian,' she said, 'rather too many vulgarisms are finding their way into your speech of late.'

'What? Oh, *mother*!' Lilian laughed. '*Everyone* uses terms like that nowadays!'

'That,' said Mrs Coverdale, 'would be no recommendation even if it were true, which it is not.' She turned to her son. 'Mrs Dyer tells me that you have not yet put out your evening suit, Bertie. It was to have been aired today – put it out for the maid please, after dinner.'

'Oh, he won't be needing it!' Lilian declared. 'We've got a partner for Grace – we've got old Lewis – oops! Sorry! We've got *Lewis*.'

Mrs Coverdale did not immediately respond. She chose instead to press the bell for the removal of the fish course. In the ensuing minutes' business she had time to collect herself, repress annoyance in favour of composure. Taking up her cutlery to broach the Veal Orloff, she carefully inquired, 'Why was that thought necessary?'

'Mm? Oh – Lewis? Well, it's nicer for Grace – much better partner than Bertie! And anyway Bertie didn't want to come!'

Bertie addressed himself to his food, secure in the knowledge that his comments would not be invited on this occasion any more than on others.

'I was not aware of any reluctance,' said Mrs Coverdale. 'Bertie knows his duties.'

'Well, it's nicer for Grace anyway. Lewis is her sort of age.' Lilian's tone veered towards defiance. 'She doesn't want to be stuck with a boy all evening!'

Quietly, Mrs Coverdale inquired, 'Indeed? She has said as much, has she?'

Now flushed, Lilian retorted, 'Of course not! She wouldn't dream of it! She doesn't even know yet! It's just obvious!' She sawed a piece of veal. 'And Frank thinks so too – it was Frank who asked him!'

There was really nowhere for the exchange to go. The seasoned tactician in Mrs Coverdale recognized the check and held fire. Not that she was in doubt as to her ultimate mastery in the field, long-term. But this skirmish with her daughter outmanoeuvred her, presenting a *fait accompli* involving participants beyond immediate range in the persons of Frank Bellinger and Lewis Gower. She chose simply to incline her head in fastidious withdrawal. To mark the stratagem she changed the subject. 'Marsh has made an excellent job of the lower path, Henry. You must see it in the morning. The York stone looks very well.'

Similar trivia occupied conversational space for the rest of the meal. They did not dispel the vexation lodged beneath Mrs Coverdale's composure. Lilian's indiscretions! The one now compounded with another. First inviting the Moon girl to Frank's birthday dinner-dance and now recruiting Lewis Gower to make up numbers. The provision of Bertie as a necessary partner had at least limited the solecism. Lewis Gower was quite another matter, promoting an impression that Outwick House was disposed to recognize and even endorse that connection. Mrs Coverdale was not disposed to recognize or endorse that connection. It was absurd. Lewis Gower belonged by adoption to her circle, arriving there two years ago as a friend of Moira's intended, Vernon. Lewis, a member of the same golf club and the same tennis club as all that group, was mooted as a possible best man at Moira's wedding and would have been but for the return from overseas of Vernon's elder brother. At the time of Moira's wedding Lewis Gower was paying suit to her best friend, Charlotte, who as chief bridesmaid was intended to catch the bridal bouquet and did, to general applause and in anticipation of Charlotte Inglesby soon becoming Charlotte Gower. Mrs Coverdale shared the general regret when that suitable match did not ensue. The why and the wherefore were never satisfactorily explained. Moira asserted that Lewis lost Charlotte through indecision as to a marriage date, which may have been the case, though Mrs Coverdale saw his hesitancy as soundly based since he was at the time negotiating promotion in his career and yet unsure of the outcome. Whatever the reasons, that desirable union had not come to pass, which was a matter for regret, although Charlotte had since made another. Lewis, who then disappeared from the circle, had not. He reappeared in Hollisfont with his appointment to the estate, still bachelor and unattached. It was keenly irritating to Mrs Coverdale that it should be Lilian who was publicly giving credence and support to this present absurdity, his association with the Moon girl. Consuming her Poires au Vin Rouge, she pondered again the perplexing inmates of the Dower House. Miss Moon clearly had no sense of what was appropriate, but did not Mrs Mayendorff? Miss Moon, for all her appearance of *savoir-faire*, obviously lacked natural discretion. But Mrs Mayendorff? Mrs Coverdale must reluctantly acknowledge a degree of *laissez-faire* surprising in a cousin of the Setons. She employed no resident staff, simply women from the village on a daily basis: Mrs Cox, for instance, a charwoman with no training in service. At tea in the drawing-room it had been Mrs Cox, clad in the flowered overall in which presumably she performed cleaning duties, who brought in the tray; and on the tray, a crude pottery jug alongside decent china. But then Mrs Mayendorff herself had presided in jodphurs for which she made scant, casual apology, as though it hardly mattered. The governess had brought the children in, which was perfectly acceptable, of course, but had then herself stayed, her manner, and the presence on the tray of five tea-cups, seeming to suggest that this was not abnormal. It was perhaps on this occasion that Mrs Coverdale had conceived the antipathy amounting almost to dislike towards Miss Moon. Neither then nor since had she seen her antipathy as personal. She saw it as the natural and appropriate response to irregularity in social affairs. She had heard of the woman's existence from Lilian, had paid little attention to Lilian's accounts of her over the weeks, had not understood that a friendship was emerging there, had assumed Lilian's eulogies were just more examples of the exaggerated language of the 'bright young things' with whom Lilian liked to identify. It was when she met Miss Moon at tea that she recognized the measure of the governess and the likely nature of Lilian's involvement, not as one *de haut en bas*, but as one equal. This was no pale little nonentity. Miss Moon was well turned out, even stylish, carried herself with ease, much at home in the drawing-room, and was not Lilian's junior, nor contemporary, but ten years older – over thirty, anyway, a guess supported by scraps of history gleaned during tea. Miss Moon would go, of course, when the boys went to their preparatory school. But that, for some reason, was being postponed for a year. One did not press for explanations, any more than one sought to know more of Herr Mayendorff than one was told, which was that he remained in Berlin for business reasons – he was an industrialist of international standing. Obviously a man of ability. One would be interested to meet him in due course. And one could barely help wondering how such a man viewed the degree of informality permitted by his wife. Her manner with employees was . . . almost familiar. Seeking categories to accommodate the impressions of that afternoon, Mrs Coverdale designated her hostess 'eccentric'. She was not so easily able to sum up the governess. The governess remained something . . . discordant, and presently highly irritating in the scheme of things.

Mrs Coverdale directed coffee to be served in the drawing-room, but her own to be taken to her study. 'I have a report to check.' On leaving the room she said to her husband, 'Canon Topping, Henry.'

Solitary in her sanctum, pen in hand, checking the League of Pity draft report, she found ease from vexation. But she was more than merely vexed – Lilian's tiresome gaucheries would be handled and curtailed; words and methods would be found – these skirmishes touched a deeper nerve. Stirred memory. Neither the adjustment of a will nor the ritual destruction of once-cherished portraits had exorcized that episode. That skirmish had broken bounds, running to rout. But victory?

Attention strayed, fingers slackening on the poised pen.

Her gaze rose, finding its talisman, set in silver, the image of James Maurice Courtenay, mariner extraordinary, supreme gentleman and revered Papa.

Thirty-five years ago, beside him at her mother's open grave, Vera's black veil concealed no tears. Her heart beat for the man beside her, bequeathed by Mama's departure. Hers, all hers, now. As his only child her role was not in question. For he would not remarry, Vera knew. He had married late and without conviction, and no male heir, no son, had justified the union. He would not remarry. He was beyond middle years, and his true espousal remained his first one, to the sea.

Their life together, Captain (Rtd) and Miss Courtenay, sufficed him, and fulfilled her. Her marriage, when it came, was by his wish. Perhaps it was no more than a whim, an invalid's querulous fancy, one afternoon, for an heir, regeneration through a new generation. Wish or whim, it was, as ever, enough. His daughter, ardent in constancy, would see to it.

Henry Coverdale served the purpose. Vera Courtenay was handsome, well connected and rich. Among other possible candidates, Henry Coverdale, equally well endowed, was immediately available. A daughter was born to this suitable union in the first year. But Vera required a son. Her father waned, propped among cushions. Five fruitless years passed. Perhaps it was will-power that prevailed. In time, in life, she laid in her father's wasting arms the lusty, bawling boy that she had borne him. Where Mama had failed, Vera victrix.

Baptized Maurice Courtenay Coverdale, the heir inherited. Through a codicil, monies were allotted for his training in the merchant navy. That was axiomatic – given normal health, the boy's path lay in Captain Courtenay's footsteps. Further personal monies, a small trust, were endowed for his majority. On his twenty-first birthday, in the final year of officer training, he would receive the *bonne-bouche*, reward for achievement, and supplement to the needs of an officer and gentleman launching his career. The frail signature endorsed the future years.

Captain Courtenay survived two of those. This time the tears flowed profuse and silent behind her veil, and that bereavement never left her, nor her constancy. Serving him, she raised the boy, shaping him, polishing his speech, curbing obstinacy, correcting posture, supervising mind and manner, creating the gentleman who would rise to carry gold braid with dignity and pride. Two other children came in quick succession, another girl, another boy; but they were irrelevancies, the product of the least agreeable aspect of marriage, from which she then withdrew, taking a separate room. She saw no reason to put up with it further.

Henry Coverdale accepted this *fiat* as all others. Conformity was in his nature. Undemanding anywhere, he was most comfortable in a boardroom or a club where his modest intelligence and superior wealth guaranteed him minimal exertion. With his family, had he troubled to think about it, he was basically bored. He did not at any time constitute an obstacle to his wife's objectives.

Nobody did. Until three and a half years ago. The boy had grown to six-foot youth, handsome in his uniform and flattered by its glamour, well pleased, to begin with. He progressed through the system, ascended via examinations according to expectation. His mother watched, obsessed and satisfied. But when in time he voiced doubts, she dismissed them. Intimations of discontent, discord on home-leaves, she dispatched. Mere juvenilia. As they intensified, she raised her barriers of resistance, and even her voice, enough to surmount his. Always, she prevailed. Naturally. Not to prevail in this perfected plan was so unimaginable to her that when at length he faced her, shouting, no less, 'I loathe the sea! And I won't stay!' she laughed. She stared at him for a moment, and she laughed. And left the room. And back he went to sea. Naturally: the wheel had turned, his indentures held him in place, his commission was assured, the objective was achieved – and maturity would salve juvenile disaffections.

The party she arranged for his coming of age was necessarily postponed a few days – his birthday passed while he was in dock, though not on leave, in Southampton. Outwick House was garlanded, its larder replete with festive fare, the superb cake in place upon the sideboard, ready for the guests who would arrive the following day. Many guests, people of consequence to join the family in celebration of twin joys, her son's majority and assured commission.

Tomorrow they would gather. Tonight he would arrive. Serene, she waited.

When he came he was not in uniform. He did not greet her. He unfolded and held before her a document. It was his discharge from the Service. And then – he laughed. And dropped it in her lap.

When he spoke, he administered the *coup de grâce*: 'My little *bonne-bouche* was just sufficient – to buy me out! . . .'

The embers shifted softly in the grate. Her gaze wavered and lowered away from Captain Courtenay. She grasped the pen, marshalled herself, resumed the work, correcting and amending. And salvaging herself from descent into the squalid sequel to that *coup de grâce*. Day by day afresh she turned from that flagrant devilry. . .

He had gone, left Outwick House, her screaming answer to the *coup de grâce*, 'Get out! Get out! Out, out, out –!' And he had gone. Picked up his luggage, softly closed the door between them. Two days later she heard; the news crept back. He was living in the village. Living in a hut at the Home Farm. Employed, the hour he quit her, by the farmer, the incumbent there so new to the district as to be ignorant of local lore. He had enrolled a Coverdale as a labourer.

Any doubt as to the full malignity of Maurice Courtenay Coverdale's intent was daily nullified. He stayed on, and on. Living out vindictive provocation.

But she would not provoke. She was inviolate. She had disowned him. He no longer existed.

She completed her review of the draft report.

At ten past ten she clipped it in its file. She took her diary and entered the day's events. She made a note of the AGM of the BSPR next week and left her desk, turning out the light, and carrying away to her night's rest the certainty of her own rectitude.

CHAPTER SIX

Lewis ran some more water, topping up the heat, and lay back again, enjoying his bath. He was in good spirits. The Rover had been a snip at the price, even with its high mileage – Frank, who had moved on to an Alvis, had kept it in spanking condition, a keen motorist with mechanical nous. Parting with the dear old Norton had been quite a wrench, come the moment, but there were no regrets. A car was better. Better for Guinness too now he was no longer a mere youth, and with winter arriving. A splendid acquisition. He slid down the bath, creating a wave, and back again, watching it furl round itself. Altogether better. A new dimension. Tonight he would collect Grace. And take her home. He reached for the nail-brush. The world is your oyster! Well . . . Hestonborough and district, anyway! The ragged scar on his right arm, bleached like bone, wore its bathtime border of flaring red, plumped up by heat, its central seam defined by the swerving line of greyish dots, stitch-marks, twenty-eight. Very neat, considering. There was another across his back which he never saw. 'It's the arm that you will have to work on – back won't give you trouble once the ribs settle down.' The army surgeon at Base Hospital after Béthune: 1916. Young man, old as Methuselah, ashen with fatigue, somehow still caring, up to his neck in other men's blood and guts. 'Play any sports, do you?' 'Tennis and golf.' 'Mm. Not tennis for quite a while, but a bit of gentle golf, easy stages. Do the muscles good once the physios have finished with you. 'Fraid the thumb won't be quite A1 again – but you should get most of the articulation back.' 'Thank you. Thank you very much.' 'My pleasure!' Weary smile with red-rimmed eyes.

Bathtime was usually recollection time, with gratitude for Dr Penn who had mended him; patiently scooped together the bloody shards and rescued his right arm. He'd been right too about the golf, and eventually the tennis – 'quite a while' was right, almost ten years, but he could and did play again, competently enough to rejoin the tennis club without being a liability on the courts; he'd practised with the aid of forbearing acquaintances on the municipal courts till then – rather tatty shale; really appreciated the club's top-quality grass again. He'd always been keen on sports – not the hurly-burly of team stuff, footer or rugger. One-to-one or two-to-two sports, subtler, more intense, more interesting. Not many of the old pre-war lot there. Not many left; too many lying across the Channel in cemeteries or unmarked graves. Vernon had survived unscathed, that is without actual wounds, though he'd almost snuffed it – exposure, fourteen hours in the water after HMS *Arethusa* went down. But he hadn't snuffed it, he'd survived to piece together old friendships with others who'd scraped by, to return to Hestonborough, and to get himself a wife. And indeed a child, now. Girl? Yes, girl. Never very hot on correspondence either of them, news came sporadically and by bush-telegraph since he'd left the district, gone down south. In marrying Moira, Vernon had married his mixed-doubles partner; there'd been tennis racquets in icing on the wedding cake – big as the Eiffel Tower. And Charlotte had been thrown the bridal bouquet. She'd caught it too – good eye, good co-ordination! Excellent tennis player, his own mixed-doubles partner and at that time destined to become his partner for life. Oddly, and dreadfully, enough, it had been at that moment when she caught the bouquet and the cheer went up that he knew:

he knew that he did not want marriage. What a mess! He was not exactly ashamed of himself, but not proud either. He had prevaricated, mucked about, fudged along. She knew, of course. He could see it in her eyes, but he was craven, didn't face up to it; should have done. Not entirely dishonourable. He had, as it were, 'tried', played for time, hoping that it would either come right or that she would turn up one day cheerfully taking the moment on herself, quite happy to quit. Neither solution had come to the rescue. It just got very undignified and then she was crying, poor girl, and it was a sad and horrid parting. But it had been the right thing. For him and for her. She was married to Mr Right within a year. Charlotte was ready for marriage. He was pleased for her, very; and relieved. It somehow exonerated him, though he'd given the tennis club a wide berth since the parting – had he imagined the reproach in glances or was that his own seedy guilt? He'd given Hollisfont a wide berth too, but that was from anger. Vera Coverdale had delusions of grandeur – *folie de grandeur*! He grinned, swashing his scrubbed nails in the water and returning the brush to the soap-dish. Very apt! She loved to deal in French phrases. Told him his behaviour towards Charlotte was '*pas comme il faut*, Lewis'. The nerve of the woman! The arrogance! She was basically potty, of course. Lived in some fantasy, Queen of the May. That business with the boy – ludicrous! He heaved himself upright, pulled out the plug and towelled himself down. Frank seemed to have the measure of her – or some instinct to keep his head down! But then he probably did not get any stick from her; thoroughly Approved; have to be to get as far as engagement to Lilian; The Right Type. He took up the smaller towel and set about his hair, peering in the steamy mirror. Lilian, he observed to himself, had more than a touch of her mother in her. Difference in style, but more than a touch bossy, a tendency to take people over. Like with Grace. Though actually it wasn't quite like that. Grace could take care of herself. And Lilian was involved in some sort of hero-worship – well, heroine-worship, more like a crush-struck schoolgirl. Managerial, yes, but admiring, a bit in awe. Well, there was much to admire in Grace! More to her than met the eye. And what met the eye was jolly admirable! He chucked the towel aside and took up the toothbrush, examining himself in the mirror and testing his recently shaved chin for any missed bits. Yes, there was much to admire in Grace! Tonight promised well – pleasant setting, flawless Coverdale competence, but minus madam, thank God! He'd have thought twice about going if she'd been part of the arrangement – even for Grace! Or would he? He ran his tongue over his brushed teeth. No. For Grace, he'd have gone anyway. He shrugged into his dressing-gown. A sandwich and a cup of coffee before dressing. Penguin suit. Fortunately it still fitted him. Years since he'd worn evening dress. Years, too, since he'd felt so . . . happy!

Lilian, fox-trotting in Frank's arms, said gleefully, 'Look, Frank! Look – they're going to dance again!'

Across the thronged dance-floor of the Royal Oak's private ballroom, Grace and Lewis were leaving their table. Frank looked. 'Well, old girl! That's what they're here for!'

'Tch! Frank! You know what I mean!'

Frank laughed, 'Steady, old thing! Champagne's gone to your head, eh?'

Lilian lightly biffed her fiancé's shoulder. 'No, it *hasn't*!' she cried. 'It's obvious – they're really hitting it off – I mean, well, you know?'

'What?'

'Oh, *Frank*! I mean – he's really *keen*!'

Frank, to whose head a considerable quantity of champagne had risen, pulled his fiancée close and ran his hand round her backside, nuzzling her neck. 'Like this you mean?' he heavily breathed.

'*Frank!*' she protested, and pushed him off. 'Don't do that!'

'Sorry, darling.' They fox-trotted on.

Whoever invented ballroom dancing, thought Lewis, was to be congratulated. Licensed embracing. She smelled wonderful, female hair, some scent, face-powder, woman. He wondered whether his own smell left a little to be desired; he was sweating under the penguin gear. Could hardly take your jacket off and cool down. Still, it was clean sweat. Stop thinking about it. Under his hand her body moved in its silken dress, deep blue, swishy round the knees. Silken knees, too. She danced very well. 'Where did you learn to dance?' he asked, smiling down at her.

'At school!' She laughed. 'Miss Dewsbury plonking on the piano. All girls, of course.'

'Very effective, all the same – you dance very well, if I may say so!'

'You may – thanks! So do you.'

'Do I? Oh – thanks! It's ages since I went to a dance.' Letting her know. Letting her know it was ages since he'd held a girl in his arms, had a partner.

'Me too.'

He wondered how to find out about previous partners in *her* life.

She said, 'Most of ours were waltzes – at school. Actually, come to think about it, it's a wonder it wasn't minuets!'

The music came to an end, da-di-di-di DUM dum, immediately followed by an announcement from the MC stepping before the band: 'And keep your places, ladies and gentlemen! By special request – the CHARLESTON!' There was a surge of applause, but Grace shook her head laughing: 'Not me, I'm afraid!'

'Nor me!' He took her elbow, steering back to their table as the band struck up and a score of couples laid about the Charleston.

They had the table to themselves. Lewis leaned across Grace and took up one of the bottles of champagne left after the meal had been cleared away, held it up in question.

'Mm, please!' she said. They raised their refilled glasses. 'Cheers!'

The racket from the Charleston was at full pitch and Lewis shifted his chair closer to hear what she was saying: '. . . vineyards somewhere – I thought possibly that south slope under Chilley Hill.'

'Vineyards?'

'The Romans.' She inclined her head towards him, competing with the din. 'Yes, we were looking up about the Iron Age camp . . . you know? In that book of Tom's, and there's a bit about the Romans –'

'Romans, in Hollisfont?'

'That's right, and Miss Seton says she's got another book – well, a monograph written by the old vicar – Phillotson. He wrote a monograph about Beaker People living in those caves, used to be bigger or something, anyway, Beaker People lived there!'

'Good Lord!' He thought for a moment. 'D'you suppose we could find something if we scratched about?' His interest in history, hitherto negligible except inasmuch as it treated of the science of structure, had markedly increased in the company of Grace. Their time together these past two months since they met had been spent in search of local history, the basis of a scheme of British history she was teaching to the boys – who were always of the party, of course. Until tonight . . .

'Shall we look?' he said. 'Next weekend? Take trowels – it's trowels they use to scratch with, isn't it?'

She said, 'We can try! I'm not sure how you go about it, though I know you have to be very organized . . . very careful. But I expect whatever there was has been excavated already, by the Rev. Giles! I'll ask Miss Seton. She'll know, or Tom.'

It was very pleasing to Lewis that the three people he liked best liked each other so well. Over the weeks, friendship had flourished from their common interest in local history. It started with Grace's visits to St Aldhelm's, as Mrs Cox had been at pains to relate: 'She's there a lot, doing her drawings, sketching and such!' With, predictably, the Cox innuendoes, eyes disingenuous, flipping her feather duster. 'He always goes over, does Mr Opie – when she's there, you know?' The idiotic Mrs Coxes of this world! No chance missed, no opportunity to wield a wooden spoon relinquished. Mrs Cox was perfectly aware that Lewis was susceptible in that quarter. Knew, to call a spade a spade, that he was – well – falling in love . . .

'But we can try! Next weekend? I'll find a trowel or two!'

Grace nodded. 'I know Cossack and Dandy are with the blacksmith on Saturday morning but the boys could be free by the afternoon, I'll check up with them.'

Lewis was wondering whether the time had yet come for expeditions without the boys to be possible. Fortified with champagne, he saw the expedition to the caves in which adults could not stand up as a very attractive proposition without the little Mayendorffs.

'Golly!' said Grace, laughing, as Lilian and Frank jazzed past, Lilian flailing to some purpose, Frank just flailing. 'The *energy*!' She waved back as Lilian beamed and flapped a hand at her. Lewis had only a sketchy idea of the details of that curious friendship – curious because the two were so unlike. His version of why Lilian admired Grace answered well enough: Grace was attractive in herself, easy to like; she dressed well, which would have importance for Lilian, life lived abroad set her apart from the average provincial English female . . . lent her a kind of glamour, 'Continental'; and of course she was new upon the scene, novelty would play its part, and Lilian's temperament would prompt her to lay first claim to acquaintance. But quite what satisfactions lay in that for Grace, he couldn't see. For him, a little of Lilian went a longish way. But then they were the same gender, women found things to talk about together. And how much they saw of each other was an unknown quantity – Lilian had given Grace a tour of the arboretum and another of the Hall's hot-houses, he didn't know of anything else. Grace said little. Had she met Mama, for instance? How would that go down? Although he had spent many weekend hours now in Grace's presence, the boys were also present, and conversation directed accordingly. As though in some response to these very ruminations, Grace, regarding him above her champagne glass, said diffidently, and leaning close for audibility, 'Lewis, can you tell me something . . .?' She was hesitant, as though about to venture an indiscretion. 'Well, you know that farm-boy? Coverdale? Well . . . *is* there any connection with Lilian's family?'

In that one request one certain assumption of his had been refuted: the intimacy of the curious friendship had not extended to include that item of personal history. He was very surprised. 'Yes!' he said, his surprise evident. 'Oh, yes – he's her brother!'

'Her *brother*?' Her surprise was the greater.

She must in her private puzzlement have got as far as designating the farm-boy some distant lesser sprig, but her astonishment was total. 'Yes!' he told her. 'Maurice. The family black sheep!'

She now appeared more discomposed by the fact that she had asked than by the answer. She said, 'Oh,' rather briskly, as one retreating from intrusion.

He was intrigued, somewhat amused, endeared by her discomposure, a new and altogether charming aspect of her. He said, 'Oh, it's all right, it's no secret! I'm surprised you didn't know – Hollisfont's little drama!' He was surprised to find that Lilian evidently endorsed her mother's lunatic embargo to the full. Such a notion, inasmuch as he'd spared any thought to the matter, had not occurred to him. It did not enhance his view of Lilian, either. He was unsure how to proceed, aware that Grace too must be assessing Lilian's candour, or lack of it. He smiled reassuringly, took a conciliatory line. 'It's old history – ages ago – all a bit silly, but you know . . . family feuds . . . people get stuck with attitudes. I don't suppose there's much animosity left now – just habit, really.'

The Charleston and its din had come to an end and couples were heading back to their tables. He said, 'I'll tell you the tale later if you like?' To which she answered, composure returning, 'Well, if it is really no secret – then yes, I'd like to know!'

'Phew!' said Lilian, arriving and subsiding on to her chair. 'I need champagne! Isn't it *hot* in here! Grace, you always manage to look so cool and collected!'

Grace smiled. 'I've not just been doing the Charleston!' she said.

'It was a likeness rather than the name. Well, the two put together. But many families in a district can have the same name – from way back. It was a likeness, I thought, when I first met Lilian . . .' she tailed off. The Rover's engine hummed behind the arcing headlights catching the glint of frost on leafless hedgerows. Beside him she sat nestled in her *Peltzmantel*, high collar up round her ears. She broke her own silence. 'It's not a very attractive story – from anyone's point of view. I mean, neither emerges with honours.' She gave a perfunctory laugh.

'I'm a bit sorry for him,' he said, 'if anyone!'

'Are you? Why?'

'Well, he was only a kid – still is.'

'Hmm.' She had another question which by implication might affect her judgement on that score. 'Why did it matter so much to Mrs Coverdale?'

He changed down to second gear, taking a corner. Instead of immediate response he asked, 'Have you met her?'

'Yes, once – she came to tea.'

'How did she strike you?'

'Umm,' Grace considered. 'Very . . . formal.' She shrugged inside her coat. 'She must have had some pretty strong reason – to turn him out!'

Lewis said, with a shrug in his voice, 'Well, I don't know that much about it. But she doesn't like to be crossed – that's common knowledge!'

They reached the bridge into Hollisfont. He was thinking, Oh? So you haven't seen her more than once – haven't been admitted to the presence at Outwick? Well, well! They travelled the single street, took the left turn for the Dower House. Frank's car was not yet outside Outwick House. He must have taken Lilian the long way round . . . should have thought of that myself . . .! His inner attention was turning on the imminent parting. Its potential for an embrace more crucial than in dancing. But she was still absorbed with the Coverdale saga. 'Mmm,' she said, 'I see. And she expected him to . . . go. Didn't expect him to . . . do what he did.'

'That's right!' said Lewis cheerfully, intent upon closing the subject. 'Well, she'll get her wish fairly soon, because the bothy – that's the place he lives – is due to be pulled down in the spring!'

The car nosed slowly over the gravel under the flanking beech trees of the Dower House drive. Light from the hall spilled on to the forecourt, all the other windows dark. He pulled to a halt and switched off the engine.

'Why is the bothy being pulled down?'

He was sorry he'd mentioned it. 'Well, it's not deemed fit for habitation – it contravenes a by-law and the estate office has decreed it has to go.'

'Mr Blow,' she said.

'Yes, Mr Blow.' He turned off the headlights.

'He does seem to have a talent for upsetting people.'

'Blow?'

'No – the boy.'

'Oh. Mm.' He turned to her.

'Well!' she said, her hand on the door-handle. She half turned, smiling, the curve of her cheek faintly lit from the hallway light, enchanting. 'Thank you very much, Lewis. That was a lovely evening – and thank you for running me about . . .!'

'Grace!' he said, and drew her in one movement into his arms, his mouth finding hers. She made no resistance. He kissed her. The kiss she returned was a girl's kiss, no less, no more. But she made no resistance. He kissed her again, warm and encouraging, moved by her inexperience, pleased and proprietorial. She was sweet, so sweet . . .

She was pleased, and shy. 'I – I'd better go now!' She smiled.

He did not immediately relinquish her and she said, 'I must go in now, Lewis – thank you for a lovely evening!' and drew from him, opening her door.

'When can I see you again?' He was reluctant to release her.

The door open, she said, 'Next weekend – the caves? I'll find out what the boys are doing –'

'Without the boys,' he said. 'Another evening. You can come out in the evenings?'

'Well, I –' dubiously.

'Yes, you can!' he urged. 'Look, I'll telephone you – tomorrow? Any evening, whatever suits you, you decide, and tell me tomorrow!'

She laughed softly. 'All right. I expect I –'

'Yes! Of course you can!' He grinned, happy.

'Goodnight, then!'

'Goodnight, Grace!'

'And – thank you!'

'Thank *you*!'

CHAPTER SEVEN

Habit got Grace out of bed to start the day before she remembered that she had the morning off. Mrs Mayendorff had told her, 'Lie in! Come round slowly – after all, it's Sunday!' Half-way across the room and half in her dressing-gown in the dark, the chill already penetrating her winter nightie, she remembered. She twitched aside the curtain and peered briefly into the stable-yard, grey and frosted in the half-dawn, deserted and still as night. She scuttled back to bed, dropping her dressing-gown beside the blue silk dress and the fur coat, neither of which she had hung in its proper place, just left them strewn at one o'clock this morning. She curled back under the bedclothes, claiming the warmth. In her encounter with the vertical position she had time to notice that all was not quite normal; she appeared to have a hangover. *Ein Kater.* That faint incipient headache, a languor located round the knees and the potential for queasiness that she had met once before, New Year's morning, 1926 at Reissen. The aftermath of red wine and brandy and Kümmel, in unaccustomed quantities, and not surprising. But this was, rather. Champagne only. Not much, at that. And supported by a handsome meal. Perhaps she had had more than she realized? She and Lewis had finished off that bottle, of course, but even so . . . Half-heartedly she considered getting up after all and getting herself some coffee and toast; but inertia won, aided by present warmth. She drowsed, not quite comfy, a little morose, neither body nor spirit at ease. Had she been a bit tiddly? Drunk? How had she behaved? And how, much more to the point, had she appeared to others? To Lewis? The hot-water bottle was assertively tepid and she pushed it from her. No – she couldn't have been drunk: she could remember everything perfectly clearly, unlike at Reissen. Tiddly, though. Not fully herself. Fully herself, she would not have asked about the farm-boy. Never ask, never invite gossip. A golden rule. Fully herself, would she have allowed the kiss?

She was thirsty. Up here there was water available at the bathroom tap. It was not an appealing remedy. But neither was getting dressed and going downstairs and communicating with the world, not quite yet. Go back to sleep awhile.

She dozed in a taut sort of way, her mind refusing to co-operate. The kiss? Yes. She would have allowed it. She had known when she was choosing her outfit, selecting the earrings, setting her hair, that she was anticipating . . . what, exactly? An advance from Lewis on this first occasion of their being alone. No children present. She turned on to her back, eyes half-open. Grey light had crept into the room, pale rectangles behind the curtains, shadowy form, furniture, planes and shapes emerging. First occasion. It was. The beach behind the bathing huts in Cannes could not signify, not signify at all. It was, last night, the first occasion on which she had been alone, of her choice, in a role non-professional, with a man. Socially. In circumstances where she was not, simply, the governess. And yes, she had expected, and required, the kiss. And achieved it. Them. More than one. The close smell of male; the warmth of his face against hers in the dim, cold car; the brush of tweed overcoat collar bunched against her cheek as he came near. And he liked it – liked her; wanted to see her again, and soon. And kiss her again.

She shifted on her pillow, drew the eiderdown up, breathing the warmth of her own breath. She had agreed. He was going to telephone her. And what was she going to say? She blinked. Presumably, 'Yes'. She had already said 'Yes' by implication. But what, by implication, had she implied? Was she implying that she was . . . available, available for that enigmatic process . . . with Lewis Gower?

She knew that she liked Lewis Gower. Oh, yes, she certainly liked him. And yes, she had required a kiss. What else, if anything, she required, she did not now know. Not this morning. Last night, choosing her earrings, dabbing scent along her arms and round her neck, she had not only anticipated an advance from Lewis. Fancy had run on, neither bidden nor checked. The unknown future, the post she must next year seek, another family, another roost, other walls to hang unpacked pictures on, another home through which to pass . . . then another, and another . . . and for the first time restiveness in place of quiescence; and the nameless ache attaching to her well-honed independence . . . and the unbidden tentative probe, testing the title: Mrs. Mrs . . . Gower?

But this morning? Where was that concept, that invitation to herself? Where had it been when she was dancing? How do people know, know what they want? She liked him, oh yes, certainly, but . . . was this how it started, falling in love? And where did it take you, after the dance-floor, beyond the goodnight kiss at the door? Into another world – that other world . . . the universal zoological, coupling world. She shifted, turning on her side, drawing up her feet. They were cold. She needed . . . coffee. She sat herself up, ran an unmoist tongue across dry lips; recently kissed. Have a bath. Get up, have a nice hot bath, get dressed and get some coffee, get going. Get . . . out of bed.

Nice hot bath. She soaped herself copiously, vigorously applied the loofah. Better already, better still after coffee. Daylight. The pigeons clattering beyond the window, someone in the stable-yard by now, probably Mrs Mayendorff, she liked to attend to her horses herself; the boys would be with her this morning, loved helping with the horses. She rinsed off the soap, climbed from the bath and towelled herself dry. No central heating but the bathroom not cold, always plenty of really hot water, steamed the place up. Brassière, vest, knickers, she'd brought her undies in here to be in the warmth, suspender-belt, stockings, lisle this morning, not silk. Slippers, dressing-gown. Back to the bedroom. Thick skirt and woollies. There now! Much better! Feeling much better. Not much hangover left! Open the bedclothes up to air. Light the fire, warm the room up – come back up here after coffee, morning off, and browse through the photograph album lent by Miss Seton, local history in the making . . . The kindling caught and she stood back, returning the matches to the mantelpiece and setting the fireguard in place. Good little fireplace, no problems since the chimney had been repaired. She wiped her hands on the cloth she kept there for the purpose and tidied the room. Blue dress on its hanger in the wardrobe, *Peltzmantel* on the broad padded hanger, also in the wardrobe. Tissue-paper in and round the dancing shoes, into the bottom right-hand shelf. Now, slippers off, brogues on. Bit heavy? Well, it's cold. Cold feet. Brogues today. Stooping to tie the laces, she thought: Coffee. Handkerchief, and I'm ready. One in the *Peltz* pocket from last night still clean, that'll do. The *Peltzmantel*: 'Oh, they're commonplace in Germany – fur, or fur-lined – hard winters.' A summary glance from Lilian, inclusive of astonishment that had drawn from her that response, almost apologetic! An abrupt reminder of aspects of English life, long lost; peculiarly English structures and boundaries; and for a moment she was the governess again, not just a woman with her friend. A personal friend; another 'first'. Friendships with women, of course she had had those all along the way, but since schooldays until now, none that were not within her professional role – acquaintance, nice friendships with other employees – housekeepers, cooks, nannies, other governesses. But here in Hollisfont a personal friend, beyond that enclave in which she was a governess first, a person secondarily. Except for that tiny, fleeting glance; which had delivered a tiny, fleeting jolt. She buffed the fur with the back of her hand, enjoying its texture. It was actually a rather expensive purchase, she'd dipped well into the small legacy from her father to make it. And for the blue dress. And for other things – well, she loved clothes, good clothes, and providing she kept her sense of proportion, common sense, which she did, she would preserve an adequate nest-egg against old age . . . She tucked the handkerchief into her cuff and shut the wardrobe door. She'd never – well, not yet – been invited to Outwick House, though. Perhaps that lay with Mrs Coverdale?

She regained her room without having met anyone except Mrs Dunkerley, who had asked her if she'd had a nice time and to whom she had gaily and spontaneously replied, 'Oh, yes, thank you! Lovely!' Well, she decided, setting down her coffee and toast in the hearth, so she had!

The coffee was good. She was herself again. With her feet against the fender and the album open in her lap, she turned the pages of Miss Seton's history in the making. Beautifully done – scores of them too, right back to the 1860s, all labelled in copper-plate hand. A shooting party on the terrace at the Hall, 1877, knickerbockered men, guns crooked – a couple of women with guns too! Tiny waists, perky little hats, four dogs, tongues lolling. Tea on the lawn, 1882, table-linen and fine crockery; maids in dotty little white caps; summer gowns and parasols – and more dogs. Strawberries? She peered. Probably. A brougham drawn up at the entrance steps, a stout old lady in black – surely not! No. Not Queen Victoria, but 'Cousin May on her 75th birthday, August 14th 1885'. She didn't look very pleased about it! Ah! Building work. 'The new summer-house under construction, April 1886'. Wagoner posing at the horse's head, four men in shirtsleeves and corduroys tied with string beneath the knees and wearing caps – everyone always wore a hat of one sort or another! – and work in progress, mounds of earth, a low hexagonal wall and planed timber stacked in readiness, presumably the top structure. And a large puddle, so it had been raining. This is the sort of thing. The boys know the summer-house. Good. She turned the pages, noting items relevant to her scheme – the height of trees now much taller, surfaces once gravel and now tar macadam, the conservatory before extension, the 'canal' being dug for the water-garden, the first appearance of a motor vehicle at the Hall, 1895. And turning further, ah, here! The Diamond Jubilee! The village at its celebrations for that great British event, the Diamond Jubilee of their Queen, 1897; but not in the village the boys knew now, in the old village across the bridge, the place they'd seen from the church tower, now rough scrubland and straggling copses and now just known as Poundell, though then, Miss Seton said, it had been known as Hollisfont – or The Village. Poundell was the ancient name of a couple of acres there, a name from way back when villeins farmed their strips and Hollisfont had been a monastery, its foundations now beneath the Hall. How pretty it looked, the old village on that summer day thirty-two years ago – the year after she was born! An age! There was Miss Seton, surely, in her early twenties, standing with the elegant party from the Hall. Flags and bunting strung between the thatched eaves; the villagers in their Sunday best, men in suits and stiff collars, women in their long skirts and shawls and straw hats, scrubbed children in clean pinafores grinning at the camera, ranged before trestle-tables set for the feast to come under the cloudless sky. A barrel – beer or cider. And the inevitable dogs. Not many of those little boys had survived the war. Miss Seton had told her, 'Most of the little boys you'll see in the Jubilee photographs didn't survive the war – those were dreadful times.' And Grace had seen their names on the plaque in the church. Including William Cox. Mrs Cox's Billy. Grace wondered which of those scrubbed, cheeky, shy faces belonged to Billy Cox. There were more photographs of that day in the village, one with a brass band, clearly amateur and clad in suits and caps, clutching instruments and gazing sternly at the photographer. And children, lots of children. Unlike Hollisfont now. There had been a dame-school conducted in one of the larger cottages; but no new school built with the new village. After 1905 the Hollisfont children went to their schooling in Parvey, an hour's walk in each direction and in all weathers, according to Miss Seton. Now there was a daily bus. Bicycles, too. But apart from the Suttons, no really young families. Mrs Cox's two were now the youngest, twelve and fourteen, only the twelve-year-old still going to school on the daily bus.

She wondered which of the cottages decked in bunting had been the dame-school. Miss Seton couldn't remember the woman's name; but somewhere in the Hall's attics there were still some of the slates the children had used for their writing, and a primer – she was going to look them out for Grace. She was a wonderful mine of material for the boys' history lessons – so was Tom. And they were both so kind and enthusiastic. In fact recently, enthusiasm had escalated to ambition! 'Why don't we gather it all together and make a book?' Miss Seton had suddenly said, eyes alight! She had laughed then, swiftly pointing out, 'confessing', that what she really meant was: 'Why don't you collate it into a book, Tom, and you, Grace, illustrate it?' and she herself would aid and assist as much as she could and finance a 'small edition'! It was indeed a delightful idea – and a challenge. Grace was not in the least sure that she could meet it. 'Of course you're good enough, my dear! Good enough? Your drawings are quite beautiful!' And Tom had urged her, too. She had demurred. 'Tom should certainly do the book, but it wouldn't need to be illustrated –' To which he had promptly said, 'I'll undertake to do it if you will undertake the illustrations, my girl! There now! What do you say?' She had, of course, said, 'Yes.'

She took the jug from the hearth and poured herself another cup. Well, she could not have refused them; nor ought she to, they were both such kind, dear people. And so she could but try her best. And some of her drawings weren't bad. As for Tom's part, he would make an excellent job of that! And it would be . . . good for him. Grace thought it a shame that such a nice man lived all alone in that huge Vicarage; though in truth there was nothing forlorn about him; he was, she conceded, a contented bachelor. Nevertheless, she quite decided, he needed something more – something absorbing and rewarding for himself, besides the satisfactions of his ministerial work. Not being a Christian herself, she was aware that she was not well placed to begin to understand the rewards of a cleric's life. In externals, those seemed available through the meagre means of a minute congregation: if there were two dozen at a service, apparently, this was a 'good turn-out', excluding the obvious festivals – Christmas, Easter, Harvest – when the nave could be almost full; and his pastoral duties couldn't be very exciting! From what she could gather, those seemed to consist in sitting over yet another cup of tea in some parishioner's parlour listening to small-talk! There must be more to it than that, of course, but, well, it didn't seem to amount to much as a way of life. There were the ceremonies, to be sure. From time to time. She'd had a look in the Parish Register one day. Not many entries over the years: once in a blue moon, a burial service; once in several, a wedding. She drank her coffee and set down the cup. No, she couldn't claim to be a Christian herself, not in the proper meaning of the term. She'd been baptized, evidently; attended chapel at school – that had not been optional anyway; and also at school taken scripture, passed the obligatory exams; knew enough to pass on to the boys a reasonable grounding in the well-known Bible stories, Old Testament and New; from time to time – more to please her cousin than for personal imperatives – Mrs Mayendorff attended St Aldhelm's, taking the boys, and Grace would accompany them. She could not subscribe to the tenets of belief – Virgin Birth, Resurrection – but the ambience appealed to that in her which was moved by the sense it gave her of historical continuum, generations of endeavour surviving bitter differences and schisms down the centuries to produce the harmony and order present in the beauty of form, expressed in architecture, music and, of course, ideals. She did, she supposed, subscribe to those, the ideals. They were after all the basis of the moral code by which civilized society purported to conduct itself decently, although as Tom explained to her, Plato's cardinal virtues of Justice, Prudence, Temperance and Fortitude were in there too, with the *Virtutes Theologicae* of Faith, Hope and Charity – a mutual enhancement, he called it. Well, if she could not be counted a practising Christian herself, she certainly admired the two she had come to know in Hollisfont; and working – if such an enjoyable pastime could be called work – to contribute to their pleasure in *The Book of Hollisfont* would be a pleasure in itself. She turned another page in the album: more Jubilee Day; and a youth, a figure slightly apart from the throng, propping up a bicycle. She blinked. Leaning across the album, she retrieved her cup and absently raised it to drink. It was empty. She sat holding the cup, eyes on the photograph. On the figure. The subject that all morning had been seeking prominence, relegated to the side of her mind, broke bounds, and the undigested core of last night presented itself: the Coverdales. The farm-boy with the bicycle. Lilian's brother.

Outside the Royal Oak, leave-taking, making for their cars, lamp-light and headlights, she had not fully met Lilian's eyes, not matched her warmth; had supplied a smile, unspontaneous, to Lilian's whispered giggly innuendo about the car ride ahead. But there had been more to her evasion than momentary embarrassment – if indeed she had felt embarrassment at all, about that. She could not, not last night nor this morning, distinguish what exactly she felt, following upon that revelation about the farm-boy. A shock. Shock, not mere surprise. Disproportionate. Too much champagne? Why such a jolt? No great matter, after all, was it? But her perception of Lilian had blurred and foundered. Was that on her own behalf? Was she . . . offended, did she find it offensive that in a friendship so easy and sewn with intimacies, Lilian had chosen to exclude her from what must surely be of considerable significance to her, such a recent and still present family fracas? Or – or was it on his behalf? The farm-boy's? Was it the dispatch of the farm-boy, his expulsion from the family – was it that which shocked her, chilled her perception of her convivial friend?

She set aside her empty cup, closed the album and knelt to mend the fire. Kneeling on the hearth-rug, the tongs in her hand, she watched the sparks fly upward. And now he was to lose his home again. 'He does seem to have a talent for upsetting people.' 'Blow?' 'No – the boy.' A flame unfurled, leaped after the sparks. She laid the tongs inside the fender and sat back in the chair, her head cradled against the red plush, arms slack in her lap, energy ebbing. For two pins, she could doze off again . . . late night . . . too much champagne . . . a confusion of images, the flaring of the thriving flame, the warmth of his face against hers, the kiss, Lilian's brother . . . the boy with the bicycle . . .

'Grace! Grace – are you there? Cooeee! Grace!'

She jerked awake, bemused, on edge. 'Hello!' She scrambled upright, groped for the door. 'Hello?' she called out into the stairway.

'Telephone, Grace!'

'Oh! Oh – thanks – all right – I'm coming!' Shaking away her impacted dreams, she hurried down the stairs to say 'Yes', to Lewis.

1930

February

CHAPTER EIGHT

Grace and the boys had called in, by invitation, to partake of morning cocoa. From Miss Seton's window the party reviewed the weather. Nicholaus was anxious for snow. There was a toboggan in the attics here; Aunt Honoria had come across it when she was looking out the old school slates and books before Christmas, and had, perhaps unwisely, mentioned it. 'Well,' she said, with an amused smile at Grace, 'it's possible. It's certainly overcast and cold today!' Nicholaus had been demanding snow for weeks, very irritated to find that England did not necessarily provide it in winter: 'We always have snow at home!' He now said, 'Can we get the sledge out?' His aunt again patiently explained that it was a very heavy one, too heavy for them to manage. 'Eeooh!' said Nicholaus; and then, brightening, 'Well, can we *see* it?' The women exchanged affirmative glances, and 'Yes!' said Aunt Honoria. 'Why not!'

'Finish your cocoa first!' said Grace as the boys headed to the door.

These were not musty attics, cobwebby and dark. There was a dry, clean, interesting smell, and silvery February light from the overhead windows set in the white-washed slanting ceilings of the three connected rooms. System and order had not stifled attractions but made them more accessible – and attractions there were, in abundance. 'One thing at a time – one thing at a time!' Grace laughed. 'We came to see the toboggan –'

'A butterfly collection,' said Aunt Honoria as Max

inquiringly slid open a slender drawer in a tall mahogany cabinet.

Max was appalled. 'Oh, poor things!'

'Oh, it's a leopard!' Nicholaus whooped, poking his finger into the open jaws of a rather dilapidated stuffed animal.

'A lynx,' his aunt told him. 'Careful now – don't tumble him over!' She grimaced to Grace and murmured, 'Horrid thing! Nasty idea, stuffing dead animals for ornaments!'

'It's here! It's here!' Cries of discovery from the further attic. The boys had found the toboggan.

'Steady,' Grace intervened as Nicholaus began casting aside parcels and boxes. '*Gently*, Nicholaus!'

It was magnificent, wrought-iron runners painted red, leather straps to hold, stout, varnished slats to sit on. 'It carries two adults comfortably – three less so, and – oh! as many as six children, I seem to recall!' Miss Seton smiled fondly. The boys had clambered aboard, Nicholaus in front, braced and hunched in position and supplying speed-sounds: 'Zzcheeeoow!' Max smiled up at Grace. 'You get on too!' It was the first spontaneous, open joy she had seen on his face for six weeks; since London. Since seeing Herr Mayendorff. 'Move down a bit, everyone!' she called cheerily, settling herself astride, Max between her skirted knees. 'Zzcheeeoow!' cried Nicholaus. '*Festhalten!* Zzcheeeoow!' And Grace held tight, her arms encircling the slight, tense eight-year-old, the vulnerable Max.

The London visit, at New Year, had presented the first hurdle in the course since leaving Germany. 'Why aren't you coming too?' the boys asked their mother. 'I'm looking after the horses!' 'Well, Vati can come here!' 'No – he can't spare the time. He has meetings in London.' 'But you won't see him!' 'I'll talk to him on the telephone!' Though she did not, nor intended to, Grace knew. 'Aunt Honoria is taking you and Grace – you're going to see a pantomime!'

They stayed at the Seton flat in Knightsbridge. Over the five days, the two women, each concerned for the boys, found a rapport and an intimacy. Spades were called spades between them, Miss Honoria setting the style, discreet and gentle but none the less direct; when they were alone together, the boys out with their father or asleep in their beds, they spoke of the rift between the parents, the separation that would never be allowed to become a divorce, of its troubled history and its inscrutable future effect upon the boys. With Miss Honoria Grace could speak and formulate in the manner tacitly agreed as inappropriate between herself and her employer. The sharing was palliative to both. Grace learned that Margaret Mayendorff, though prepared to talk with her cousin of every aspect of the rift inasmuch as it concerned herself and her husband, would not, or could not, bring herself to address the question of the boys' awareness – or lack of it. 'Oh, they're too young. They're all right. Perfectly happy. Well, yes. Some day . . .' resisting discussion. Miss Honoria told Grace, 'Personally, I think Max has guessed – knows that all is not well.' Grace agreed. On the boat crossing the Channel six months ago Mrs Mayendorff had told her younger son, 'I think you'd better be called Nicholaus now. It will be more suitable for your English school.' The abbreviation Klaus, also the name of her husband, was to be set aside. She had spoken without emphasis, almost with detachment, her eyes and seemingly her attention on the waiter approaching their table, as though the matter had little weight but enough to mention. Nicholaus was intrigued. 'What about Max?' 'Max? Oh – Max is a name given to English boys . . .' and Nicholaus was immediately diverted by the arrival of his ice-cream. Max said nothing. He said nothing in such a way as to confirm to Grace that he had understood, as she had, that an embargo had been laid on the name of his father. Later, following the slight, upright figure out of the saloon, she wondered what questions sought solutions in that eight-year-old mind awakening to the complexities of life beyond childhood, of men and women and their secret power to confound each other. And following him, she felt herself as ignorant as he. More informed, but hardly more experienced. Six months ago. Since when, she had crossed the Rubicon. She was recognizably Lewis's lady-friend. But yet . . . less ignorant . . .?

'Zzcheeeo-o-ow!' Nicholaus brought the toboggan to a stop. 'Oh, I want *snow*!' But something had caught his eye. 'What's that?' He was off and away.

'That' was metallic, a cluster of little discs disclosed beneath the dislodged lid of a bandbox, just now shifted from the toboggan. Nicholaus thrust aside the lid. 'Oh!' Miss Honoria recognized with pleasure. 'The bolero!' A fancy-dress outfit from her childhood. 'I went as a gipsy! Hold it up, Nicholaus – oh, I loved wearing that – and there's a red skirt somewhere – and a tambourine – yes, of course, put it on!' The black bolero, the fringe of gilt discs chinking and tinkling in movement. 'The tambourine must be here somewhere . . .' She delved. 'Mm? Tambourine? A tambourine is a musical instrument, a little sort of flat drum with . . . well, I'll find it and show you! Not in this one . . . Max, dear, open that box there – yes – that one . . .' The tambourine was not in that one either, though other treasures were revealed. 'That was my father's – it's a gentleman's travelling-set!' A mahogany box inlaid with mother-of-pearl and lined with plush and fitted with compartments holding hair-brushes and a boot-hook and nail-clippers and a rack of little bottles. 'Quinine!' said Aunt Honoria. 'Macassar – gooey oil men used to smooth their hair down!' There were several small cartons too. 'Ugh!' she recalled. 'Gregory powders! For upset tummies – dreadful stuff,' she laughed across to Grace, 'guaranteed to *give* you a poorly tummy, never mind cure one!' Miss Honoria had shed years, her face childlike, eager, as she joined the boys, led them in absorbed and joyous foray through boxes and chests, portmanteaux and brass-bound trunks stamped P & O Line or Cunard and bearing faded labels: Marseille, Cairo, Bombay, New York, Trinidad. 'Oh, yes,' she told them, 'the Setons were busy travellers – well, two of my uncles were in the Indian Army, always to-ing and fro-ing, and then there were business connections in America and the West Indies – still are, of course.' They found the tambourine; the boys derived as much noise as possible from it until other delights drew them on. Somewhere along the morning Aunt Honoria said, 'Switch the lights on, dear, will you?', the day having subtly darkened. 'That's better! Now, what's this? Oh – aah . . . Mother's wedding-dress – I think *I'd* better do this, the material is quite delicate . . . Grace, could you take that end, there are yards of it . . . well, perhaps it would be best if we spread one of those sheets on the floor first . . . there, that's right! Now then!' And stepping on to the sheet, she let fall the cascade of pearly silk, tumbling from hands held high to reveal the bridal gown. A waft of lavender scented the air. There was a reverential murmur, even from Nicholaus. Max said, 'It's beautiful!' and stooped carefully to release a crescent of silken hem caught on the tulle underskirt. Aunt Honoria lowered her arms, held the dress against her, looking down upon the décolleté bodice and the handspan waist incongruous against her own sturdy form. 'She was a very dainty woman, always. Delicate,' she said softly. 'Wonderful work, isn't it?' And it was. A confection of swathes and frills, crystal beading, satin ribbon, seed-pearls, rosettes and tiny tassels, but withal, ethereal. Miss Seton sighed. 'They don't make them like this any more! Every stitch hand-sewn.'

Grace was impressed, enchanted. 'It's straight out of a fairy-tale!' She leaned close, examining the work. 'There are several underskirts, you see,' said Miss Honoria. 'Well, it was virtually a crinoline, 1869 . . . Here, Grace, do hold it – then I can stand back and look!'

Taking it, Grace thought of Lilian's dress, the drawings from the designer who was to start work next month; à la mode, 'slinky!' was Lilian's description, a satin sheath belling below the knees and cut away at the hemline in front to reveal the bride's slender ankles and feet in matching shoes buckled with diamanté. The height of fashion and of elegance and chic, and certainly the best that money could buy . . . and yet . . . well, by no means fairy-tale; another era . . .

'Here's its hat!' said Nicholaus, reaching into the trunk and coming up with a coronet of pale silk flowers, its shoulder-length veil floating beneath. Still in thrall to the reverential atmosphere, he handled it with care, carrying it gingerly. 'Put it on!' he said to Grace, and his aunt laughed and said, 'Yes, put it on – here! Let me . . .' and she took it from Nicholaus. 'Duck your head – that's it!' She set the coronet on Grace's hair and deftly arranged the veil. From behind it Grace emitted an unsure laugh. Nicholaus said, objecting, 'It's all over her face! You can't see her properly!'

'Yes, dear,' his aunt told him, 'when the bride comes *into* church she wears the veil down, and then afterwards, when she has been married, she uncovers her face!'

'Why?'

'Well – it's just the way it's done, dear!'

'Oh,' said Nicholaus, unimpressed; and then declared, 'Berthe didn't,' recalling a wedding in Germany. 'Berthe wore a big round hat!'

'Yes, well, Cousin Berthe had a different kind of wedding, dear – there are different kinds . . .'

Max spoke. 'Mother wore a veil. There is a photograph at home. In Father's study.'

'Mm! That's right!' Aunt Honoria agreed; bright and brisk, and matching action to tone, stepped on to the sheet and relieved Grace of the dress. 'Back into its wrappings!' she said cheerfully. 'Open that other trunk, you two! Lots of interesting things in there! That was Uncle Sacheverell's, and he was at the Battle of Balaclava, aide-de-camp to someone, one of the generals – no, no, there won't be any guns in there, dear, but lots of interesting things – that's it! Carefully does it! . . . now, then, where's that tissue-paper? Oh – can you manage?' as Grace detached herself from the bridal veil.

'Yes, thanks!' Shaking her freed hair, like a dog emerging from a burrow, she carried the coronet back to the bridal chest and with deliberation, keeping her glance from Max, laid it away. Busy noises from the military trunk suggested the success of Aunt Honoria's cunning decoy. 'It's got medals!' 'What's this for, Aunt Honoria, what's this?'

'Oh – that will be the cord to carry the sword, I think! Yes, yes, there is a sword but I don't quite know where it is, it *might* be at the bottom of that trunk but if you come across it you must let me get it out, please!' More discoveries, more questions, more answers to and fro, cheerfully sustained by Aunt Honoria's fund of memories, as the two women restored the dress to its wrappings, kneeling together on the sheet, folding its glories away. Miss Seton caught Grace's eye and smiled, offering a quiet observation: 'It suited you!'

Grace flushed faintly, and again came that involuntary, equivocal laugh; but she found to say, 'Oh, veils are very flattering, aren't they!' her tone more spry than she intended, perhaps even a trace brusque; but if so, Miss Seton did not notice. She turned the full warmth of her kindly regard on Grace and softly told her, 'He's an admirable young man – and a very lucky one too, my dear.'

Triumphant cries from the military party intervened; Aunt Honoria was called to extract the sword.

One more layer of tissue-paper, two more skilful folds. Grace was good at packing, she knew. She sat on her heels: '. . . and a very lucky one, too, my dear'. It was expected; awaited; by everyone, herself included. The natural consequence of six amiable months together, six wonderful months: '. . . a very lucky young man'. A very lucky young woman, certainly. Young? Well, just about! Lucky – certainly. 'Admirable'. If 'admirable' was commodious enough to express kindness, patience, humour, honour, then 'admirable' would do. A gentle man, a gentleman. Lewis Gower. Generous, patient and respectful. 'All right, my darling – ssh – all right – ssh – I'm sorry – you're right – it's just – oh – Grace! You're so lovely!' And never since, though they had often spent the evening alone in his house again. 'What's the matter with him?' Lilian had complained. 'Still not popped the question!' They had seen less of each other, much less recently, she and Lilian. A natural consequence of more time spent with Lewis. But also acceptable, seeing less of Lilian. Rapport, such as there had been, had somehow, somewhere foundered; perhaps she had misjudged the degree of rapport to begin with. Perhaps she expected too much, not being wise in such matters, unfamiliar with the ropes. Or perhaps she had simply found her less likeable than she had at first supposed. Less what? Warm? Sensitive? 'Here!' plonking down a green-backed book. 'High time you read this!' A book called *Married Love*; but she had not intended counsel strictly for the marriage-bed. 'All those cosy evenings round at his house!' and her gusty laugh. That was the time, the once, when she had been invited to Outwick House; when Mr and Mrs

Coverdale were away for the weekend. 'And this is the Holy of Holies!' Mrs Coverdale's study: like everything else in Outwick House, immaculate, impeccably tasteful; opulence avoiding ostentation. The desk, an edifice in itself, the ranks of silver frames. 'And that's Bertie getting his boring prize – frightfully clever, the youngest ever to get it, dear old Bertie!' But no sign, there or anywhere in Outwick House, of the outcast. Nor ever a word from his sister. 'Spare room.' She had perfunctorily opened and reshut one bedroom door in the course of the conducted tour, and Grace knew that it was his. The farm-boy's. Downstairs again, coffee delivered by a maid, a fire bright in the Adam fireplace. 'Not a bad old dump, is it?' 'It's beautiful!' And a far cry from a bothy. 'Here – look!' The designs for her wedding-dress, spread on the carpet; an excitement, quite endearing, almost childlike, as she pored over them. 'What do you think? You've got such wonderful taste! No – I really want your opinion. Mother wants that one but it 's *so* fussy, don't you think? *This* is the one – really gorgeous – slinky, hmm?' Then: 'Not sure about the colour for the bridesmaids yet – style, too – have to be the same type of thing as mine, of course. Anyway, *I'm* having that one!' The slinky one; *ergo* slinky bridesmaids. No direct mention that day of the proposition that Grace should be one of the bridesmaids – maid-of-honour, the term had been initially; but no suggestion either that a change of mind had taken place. Only one of Lilian's references to Lewis's prospects: 'If he'd just get a move on, we could make it a double wedding, eh!' Followed straight by 'More coffee? Oh, *when's* this filthy weather going to clear up – look, it's started *again* – does such frightful things to one's hair! . . .' And a change of subject, the double wedding having been, Grace knew, one of Lilian's impetuosities; but this one had to be tidied away, and Grace, after a morning in Outwick House, and one selected for the absence of its owners, thought she knew why. She thought she now knew that Lilian's audacious confidence was more apparent than real. A morning in Outwick House made plain where authority lay. Splashing back to the Dower House, she had thought that perhaps after all a bothy was no bad exchange! And had wondered again about the details of the fracas . . . Not that he'd have his bothy much longer. Coming down next month. And the Poundell cottage, some time this spring, the old man having died. She and Tom Opie now sure to be able to see the place before that happened – genuine wattle-and-daub, take the boys to see, before the demolition. Great year for demolition in Hollisfont! Still, the church tower was repaired – beautifully done, too. Lewis made sure of that – you could see no sign of newness, not so much a repair, more a restoration. Safe and sound for another five hundred years. And meantime she can have her full peal of bells in May . . .!

'Yes, all right – show Grace, and then back in its scabbard – yes, it is a funny word, isn't it? Now, then, come along, everybody! Time to pack up – well, it's almost time for lunch and you don't want to be late – and anyway it's getting chilly – well, *I'm* getting chilly! Not as young as I used to be! Yes, of course we will – there are lots of other things to see, but that's enough for today, and I want everything put back "just so", please – just as you found them . . . Mm? What, dear?'

'Can I keep it, please?'

Max held in his hand a cap, curious headgear, dark blue, a soft pouched crown on a pill-box rim banded in red and with a snub, shiny black peak, above it a metal badge. He was entranced. With slow ceremony he placed it on his head. It sat down round his ears, fell forward over his eyes. Nicholaus yelped and, giggling, snatched at it, clapping it on his own head. Quick as light, Max snatched it back. 'It's mine!'

'Boys!' cried Aunt Honoria, astonished. 'Boys! Now, now . . .' She physically intervened. 'Goodness me! Now stop it!' She made to take the cap from Max, but he swerved away, clasping it to his chest. 'I want it, please. I mean, I want to keep it.' He was not smiling, most solemn.

'Keep it . . .?' Aunt Honoria was nonplussed. 'Well – I –' She looked round at Grace, seeking direction in this odd turn of events. 'Well – I – suppose . . .?'

'*I* want it!' Nicholaus howled.

Grace stepped in. '*Don't* start again – *either* of you!'

Nicholaus thrust his face at Max. 'It's too big for you anyway!'

Max ignored him. Looking first at his aunt and then at Grace, he said quietly, 'Please can I keep it?'

Still bemused and rather out of her depth, Miss Seton raised eyebrows at Grace. 'Well,' she said helplessly, 'as far as *I'm* concerned . . . er – why do you want it, dear?'

'I like it.'

Pre-empting Nicholaus whose mouth was on the move, she said, as though the information might defuse the tensions, 'There isn't another one, I know – it's just some old souvenir brought back – not part of Uncle Sache's uniform, you know! It's only some old army cap – foreign!'

'I like it,' Max told her.

'*I* want one!' Nicholaus wailed. Grace laid her hand upon his shoulder and looked into his face, or tried to, as he sulked it aside. 'Now, come on, Nicholaus, don't be a goose. You heard what Aunt Honoria said.' Aunt Honoria, whose reunion with the joys of childhood had not anticipated its deficiencies, cast round for retrieval: 'You can have something else, Nicholaus!' her tone jolly. 'How about the bolero! You liked that!'

'It's for a girl.' He dismissed the offer with disdain.

'There's no need to be rude, Nicholaus,' Grace told him with asperity. He shrugged her hand aside.

'The tambourine, then!' Aunt Honoria brightly pursued, catching sight of it lying nearby.

Carefully conserving his injury, pout in place, he grudgingly gave it a glance. 'Can't wear that,' he grumbled, but his aunt sensed his hesitation and pressed: 'You played it very well!'

He took his time. He slouched across to where it lay and regarded it stonily. Its charms defeated him; he picked it up. 'All right,' he said, not quite ready to relinquish martyrdom, still pouting.

Grace briskly prompted him: 'Thank you, Aunt Honoria!'

He wrung the last moment of persecution from a silence before intoning, 'Thank you, Aunt Honoria.' But the tambourine, jingling in his hand, got the better of him and a smile reversed the pout as he shook and biffed his consolation prize, ill-humour vanquished.

Miss Seton, with relief, beamed approval and called encouragingly, 'Now, come on, everyone! The packing – on with the packing!' and bustled into action, firmly relegating the disruption to wherever bygones go. But as the last trunk was closed upon its treasures, she could not forbear to murmur to Grace, 'That was *very* unlike Max! What was it all about? Too much excitement, I suppose! Anyway,' she smiled, 'they seem quite happy now!' She fastened the final clasp. 'All finished!' she called. 'Well done, boys! Come along!' and led the way.

'*Snow!*' Nicholaus yelled and pointed with his tambourine at the skylight. It was true! First flakes lay starred and thickening there. 'Yeeeooow!' and he and Max, joined in ecstasy, whooped across the attics making for the stairs.

'Ah!' said Miss Seton equally delighted. 'All *quite* happy now!'

Following her, Grace thought, 'Almost quite happy . . .' She closed the last door behind her and started the descent. Below her the boys thudded ahead, clutching their trophies. Grace knew why 'some old army cap' had such imperative importance for Max: in another photograph in Berlin Klaus Mayendorff, as a young cadet in his university Military Corps, wore just such a one.

The opportunity was there later, to share this explanatory information with Miss Seton; but Grace, for some reason, didn't take it. Somehow it was muddled in with complexities less explicable, indeed barely identifiable, but vaguely related to other findings that morning in the attics; possibly inclusive of a wedding veil?

CHAPTER NINE

'Perhaps it's just too soft,' said Grace sorrowfully. The toboggan had again ploughed to a halt in the snow. 'Perhaps we'll have to wait and hope it freezes a bit more!'

Two dismayed faces looked up at her from under woolly hats and down again at the foundered toboggan. Max said, 'It might just be this bit? Look – it's up to my knees and it wasn't when we were up there!'

They all looked back up the slope to the top of Chilley Hill. 'That's true,' said Grace, brightening. She wished she knew the terrain better, the bumps and hollows effaced beneath the snow. 'Well!' she said. 'We can but try! Come on – we'll have another go on a different bit. Now – like before, I'll pull, you two lift and push from behind!' It was a magnificent toboggan, but it certainly was heavy. 'Right! One – two – three – GO!' A lurch, movement, and off they trudged.

Nicholaus had his snow, and quite up to German standards too, though as was explained, it could disappear as quickly as it came; in England it did not necessarily stay put. Which was why today, Wednesday, they were playing in the snow instead of doing lessons, a special dispensation fortified by the telephone message from Mr Hatherway reporting that the roads were blocked and he could not make his journey from Hestonborough to Hollisfont to teach the boys today. No maths, then, and 'Grace says you may have the day off from her lessons too, this once,' their mother told them, 'and I've spoken to Aunt Honoria on the phone and she's having the toboggan delivered to the

Hall gates . . .' And high jubilation and optimum co-operation in 'being very good and sensible', eating a proper breakfast and putting on suitable clothes; only a moment's quavering, from Max: he baulked at the woolly hat. 'It itches!' He wanted to wear his trophy from the attic, the shako; he had solved the size problem by stuffing it with handkerchiefs. He had worn it indoors and out throughout the three days; at night it rested by his pillow. His mother had made no comment, beyond the initial 'Oh, very nice!' acknowledging the cap and the tambourine together, with some reference to Honoria's kindness, and an abstracted air, detached. Like on the boat, thought Grace. For sure, the relevance to Klaus Mayendorff was not lost upon his wife; even had she not been reminded of the young cadet's military headgear, no blinkers could suffice against the striking resemblance her son bore to his father under the peaked cap. She had evaded the moment this morning by suddenly remembering something urgent about the horses, leaving Grace to cope. 'This one's better for tobogganing, Max, your smart cap would come off when we're swooshing down the hill and it'd get wet – and it won't keep your ears warm!' And, brightly, 'Well, if it itches you can always have a scratch like you usually do!' Both logical observations were obviously true and Max duly relented. He took the cap up to his room where no doubt it lay in state upon his pillow.

How, Grace wondered sadly, do you explain parental antipathies to a child? How and where do you begin? How was anyone to tell a Max and a Nicholaus that their parents had never been happy together? The marriage had been a business contract, the bride the daughter of a shipping magnate, the groom the son of a steel baron, the vested interests of the families enhanced by nuptial union in the time-honoured manner of those intent upon consolidating empires. How explain that once co-opted, the bride discovered that she had no place in her husband's interests, least of all in bedrooms, where her function was merely to produce heirs. How convey that the father they infrequently saw but who then treated them with avuncular indulgence was a man of arrogant self-assertion, ostentatious in his love of power, personal or public, cold and implacable when crossed, ruthless in his own pursuits; and that though their mother learned to bear and contain personal humiliations, her moral sense could not accommodate more sinister developments: there were things going on, forces accelerating in Germany, not even below the surface any more, indecencies – not everywhere, but spreading – potent and disturbing. Grace had never seen, actually seen, the bully-boys in brown shirts raising their racist hell, but one night she had heard them. And next morning no one would speak of it. Not in Herr Mayendorff's household. Herr Mayendorff, along with other rich industrial barons, kept the Nazionalsozialistisch Deutsche Arbeiterpartei in funds. That had dawned on Grace by degrees, confirmed one day by the hallful of departing visitors, all male, some uniformed and wearing armbands carrying that appropriated and perverted insignia, the swastika, once the innocent emblem of good fortune, now the mark of misrule. In a cloud of cigar smoke released with them from their meeting in the library, there was a shaking of hands, confident laughter, mutual satisfaction. Mrs Mayendorff did not appear at lunch that day; the following day she took Grace and the boys away to Reissen. On reflection Grace saw that as the morning on which Margaret Mayendorff moved from compliance to resistance. She did not know the minutiae of the subsequent developments, how explicit or otherwise the reasons given in the confrontations behind closed doors; who among those involved, including shortly the shipping magnate and the steel baron, formulated the euphemisms to cover the separation, or how final anyone acknowledged it to be. But she did now know that Max had intuited a division that was not admitted. Perhaps the fact that he kept silence was an indication of how accurate he feared his intuition was, and how much he did not want it confirmed? But also, perhaps, he would one day ask – ask her; and what was she then to say, she, who had never knowingly lied to Max? Perhaps it was this prospect, never far from her consciousness in recent weeks, that had produced this odd unease in her, almost an edginess? Or . . . perhaps it was a manifestation of pre-betrothal nerves? Because she did know Lewis was going to ask her to marry him. She knew when he would ask, too: this coming Saturday. The Valentine Ball. Just the two of them. Not a party. And she guessed, knew, that he had bought a ring. And 'Yes!' she would say. And this time next week she would be Lewis Gower's fiancée, and Lilian would have said, 'And about time too!' and Miss Seton would have warmly congratulated her and Mrs Mayendorff would have told her, 'I'm delighted, Grace – and you must be married from here!' And the odd unease would be gone . . . except for that residual core of tension about, about . . . Reading – well, not exactly reading yet, but glancing at, Lilian's book had . . . well . . . it hadn't alleviated . . . well – she could not say that she was looking forward to the – physical side of things. Of marriage. She had put the book aside. Love? Married love? *That* part . . . How did people face it? Women. How did they manage to . . . to . . . Did all women feel as she did at some stage in courtship? Had Lilian ever felt . . . apprehensive? Depressed? Had she? That gusty laugh . . . It seemed not. Was she, Grace, not normal? In her musings she managed a smile from time to time, thinking, 'What a pity babies are *not* delivered by a stork or retrieved from beneath a gooseberry bush!' How much nicer that would be! Then all the good things between men and women would be so much better – the shared interests, the mutual affection, the companionship would be clear to see and evaluate, not all sort of muddly, muddled up with this . . . physical thing, the brutish thing. The price you had to pay for the good things, which certainly included children. Well. Mrs Mayendorff had 'coped' – she surely hadn't liked it, but she'd coped, like millions of women – and after all, Lewis was no Klaus Mayendorff, he was kind and gentle. So, she'd cope. He was a nice man and she was a nice woman and this . . . physical thing was after all not the *main* thing. Don't let it get out of proportion! Goodness me!

'Phhooof!' she gasped, heaving the toboggan to a halt at last and grinning at her panting assistants who flopped down and sprawled in the snow. 'Get our breath back a moment – then have a think. Pity about those gorse bushes – that looks quite a good run further down!'

Nicholaus ate some snow and observed that it tasted funny. Max tried some and agreed. 'It ought to taste like water but it never does.' They made grooves in the surface with their gloved fingers, Nicholaus drew a round face. Grace sat on the toboggan and surveyed the world. It was a world of silvery, soft beauty and total silence. No sound under the low grey sky, no movement, no trace, beyond their own, of animation across the wide immaculate tranquillity; '. . . chaste as unsunn'd snow . . .' Now, where did that come from? Shakespeare. Fifth form. *Cymbeline*. Yes, *Cymbeline*. 'If you approach this play as though it is a fairy-story, you will find no problems with its logic,' Miss Bowlby told them. 'In this late romance, accept Imogen as a fairy-tale heroine; put aside the human logic of, for instance, *Othello*, for this piece is, as I say, a romance, and, you may be pleased to hear, has a happy ending!' Eighteen years ago! Can I remember? 'Me of my lawful pleasure oft restrained – did it with a pudency so something something sweet – erm – that I thought her as chaste as unsunn'd snow.' That's it! Something near it anyway – not bad after eighteen years! Rested, she stood up, taking a last look across the flawless world at her feet, and turned to address the boys. Beyond them, cresting the hill and approaching, a figure paused and spoke: 'You're in the wrong place.' It was the farm-boy.

'It's the man!' said Nicholaus.

'Other side of the hill's the best place,' the man told them, advancing again.

Nicholaus ran to him. 'Where?'

'Back there. You'll do no good on this side. I'll show you.' He had arrived at the toboggan and took hold of its strap. ''S not far,' he said. He glanced at Grace now. 'Right?' It was hardly a question, more a passing formality as he set the toboggan in motion and turned, towing it, retracing his steps.

'Er – well –' Grace mobilized herself and found voice. 'Oh, we can manage!' she said to his retreating back. It was red and black, big checks, a thick jacket to the hips over dark grey corduroys tucked into black leather knee-high boots. The curly hair was enclosed under a brown leather cap with ear-flaps hanging untied. No gloves. He looked like a lumber-jack in the photographs of Canada in the encyclopaedia. He strode ahead, the boys bouncing beside him. She followed.

'. . . the north side. Where the wind's sheared the loose stuff off. Colder there too – harder, better surface,' he told his eager attendants, '. . . been watching you.'

Grace, hurrying but falling behind, thought, 'Been watching us!' and frowned a sideways glance at the farmstead below; like everything else it was snowbound, of course – no sign of life, no cattle, all the livestock under cover presumably; she slithered hastily on. Surely there's always plenty to do on a farm whatever the weather, she told herself with disapproval. No need to be standing round watching people! She skidded, almost lost her balance, flushed crossly. But no one was looking; indeed, they were out of sight; gone. What a cheek! Barging in . . .!

The two boys were on the toboggan, ready; the farm-boy was adjusting its position. It stood on a small, level promontory, perfect for the purpose, above the long, smooth decline, equally perfect.

'Come on, Grace!' yelled Nicholaus, and Max, eyes shining, called, 'Come on! Mo's going to take us!'

She halted. The youth regarded her and with a sweep of his arm ushered her to join them. She stayed where she was, slightly above them. 'I'll watch!' she called. 'There's not enough room anyway!' She smiled cheerily at the boys craning up at her.

'Yes, there is!' they chorused. 'Come on!' urged Nicholaus.

She held her smile in place. 'Off you go! I'll watch – I'd really rather watch!'

With a shrug the youth climbed aboard behind them. 'Hold tight!' He gave a deft swing with his body, weight forward, feet thrusting them into motion, and they were off. The toboggan sped smooth and fast as an arrow. Zzcheeeoöw! as Nicholaus would say. Was saying – delighted cries carried back to her where she stood. She thrust her hands into her pockets, hunched her shoulders. It was colder here, he was right, with his north side and his better surface. She sniffed irritably. There are, however, ways and ways of going about things. No need to be rude – yes, downright rude! Unmannerly. A touch too much confidence, to put it mildly! Like in the yard that day, only this time without the diverting effect of the angelic smile. Just too much confidence this time, and not in the least beguiling. Like mother, like son. And sister – well, to a lesser extent; Lilian on a bad day. But he looked more like his mother this morning. Didn't sound like her. Didn't sound like a Coverdale at all, with his vernacular mode. Consciously applied? She hadn't noticed it that time in the yard. Part of an act this morning? She sniffed again. One way and another the excess of that fracas at Outwick House was intelligible this morning. As Lewis said, 'Silly business – too much alike, perhaps – rub each other up, though she should know better – he's just a kid.' And bumptious. Time he grew up.

'. . . oooaaay – Gra-aace!' the boys called to her, arms waving in victory, they had arrived, a perfect controlled stop. She waved back. Coverdale did not look up, busy reversing the toboggan, swinging it round to begin the ascent. Then a short consultation, evidently; then Nicholaus climbing aboard, Max walking, Coverdale leaning into the incline, pulling the load. In conversation with Max. Coverdale made a zigzag route, climbing steadily, Max plodding beside him. What were they finding to talk about? Something amusing, apparently: a shout of laughter from Max, animation in every line of the small muffled form. And as they drew closer, that animation was visible to her on his glowing face; on all three faces. What was it Max had called him? Mo? Mo. Oh. Yes, of course, a diminutive for Maurice. Like Maureen, a girl at school. Pet-name Mo.

'Oh, Grace!' Max scrambled on to the promontory. 'It was spiffing!' He grinned; he flung out his arms and hopped about her. '*Spiffing!*' He laughed. 'That means very very very good!' He beamed at Coverdale, who hauled the toboggan to a halt and, releasing the lead, pushed back his cap and wiped at his forehead with the back of his hand. He was smiling now. 'Yep. A good first run, that!' He addressed Grace. 'It gets better of course – faster as it firms down!'

'Faster!' Nicholaus chanted, bounding round the promontory. 'Faster, faster!'

'Yes,' said Grace, 'I suppose it must!' She would have smiled anyway, a matter of politeness, but the smile she returned broke the bounds of civility. He was being very . . . nice. Very nice with the boys . . .

Coverdale scooped up the strap and set the toboggan in position again. He stepped back, hands in pockets, and nodded. 'There y'are,' he said to Grace. 'Have a go.'

'C'mon, c'mon!' The boys climbed aboard. 'C'mon, Grace!'

As she moved to comply she was suddenly conscious of her skirt. She wished it was longer. She held it about her knees as she swung astride, behind Max. She positioned her heels, dug them in and made the initial thrust. The toboggan, being on the level, hardly moved, it needed the extra impulsion of a jump-start – unless . . . 'Could you give us a shove?' she called to Coverdale. But Max had not realized that Coverdale was not aboard and slewing round told him, 'Oh, you come too – you come too!'

'There isn't room, Max!' Grace protested.

'Yes there is, there is!'

'Oh, come on!' Nicholaus urged. 'Come on, Mo!'

'Hutch up a bit,' Coverdale's voice said calmly, and she felt him arrive behind her. 'Hutch up.'

She hutched, close against Max who eased closer to Nicholaus. 'Ready!' announced the voice at her ear. 'Hold tight!'

It was wonderful – wonderful! That *soupçon* of piquant fear, breathless, mindless, reckless – wonderful! And swoo-oo-ooshhh . . . they had arrived. 'H'raaay!' from Nicholaus; laughter; Grace gave Max a hug. 'Wonderful!' she cried. 'We went further, look!' said Nicholaus, pointing out the tracks.

'Y'll go further yet,' said Mo. 'Like I said, it gets better!'

It did, too. By shrewd placement of the runners at the start of each go, the pitch was extended so as to avoid creating furrows too narrow. 'Don't want tramlines, see,' Mo explained. 'Want to pack the surface but widen it too. Get bogged down otherwise.' There was no bogging down; quite the reverse. Faster, faster, like flying, no, not flying – not like a bird flies – like being fired, shot from a bow, not a gun – pure, soundless flight – like high diving, elemental. Absorbed in refining technicalities, physically extended by the breathless descents and the resolute uphill slogs, intent on more and better and faster flights, they were at one, as one, bonded in simple purpose. They tried redistributing the load; and found that with Mo at the front, the boys in the middle and Grace at the back, the impetus improved – and furthermore they could start the run on the incline because Mo, up front, could sustain the dead-weight by bracing his legs, heels dug in while the team climbed aboard: he just lifted his heels clear for take-off. And at the bottom, each time, they covered more ground. They set a target: Max drew a furrow two yards short of the hedge; panting back, zigzagging upwards, they discussed and argued as to how many more goes it would take for them to reach their target. 'Four,' said Mo. 'Three!' said Max and Nicholaus. 'Five!' said Grace. 'The snow's deeper near the hedge!' 'Three, three!' the boys insisted. At the end of the second run, 'We will, we will!' cried Max. 'Look! – nearly, nearly!' And three it was. 'Yeeoow!' The boys pranced around, triumphant. 'Make another, make another!' said Nicholaus, setting about it, furrowing with the heel of his boot. 'Too near the hedge!' said Grace. 'Come back a bit!' Mo, examining the lead-strap as he bent to move the toboggan round, said, 'Hmm. Needs some linseed. Dried out, cracking, look. Oil or a bit of saddle-soap –'

'Oh, we've got saddle-soap!' the boys told him, examining the problem.

Beyond them and beyond the hedge a movement drew Grace's eye. Someone at the farmyard gate was observing them, a man in a cap and muffler. 'I think somebody's looking for you,' Grace said to Mo. Mo cast a glance over his shoulder. 'Only Arnie,' he said, bending again to the strap. 'He's – well – I think he's waiting for you,' said Grace. 'Mm,' grunted Mo without interest. 'Really,' he said to the boys, 'this strap wants taking right off and resetting – cut off the perished bit at the end, look.'

Grace said, 'Ought you not to go?' and sounded less like a tobogganer, more like a governess. The man was still there. Emerging from suspended time, she blinked and looked at her watch. Twenty to one!

'It's twenty to one!' she cried. 'Heavens! We – golly! It's lunch-time! We're late!' Governess-galvanized, she summoned the boys. 'We must go – I'd no idea!' She said to Coverdale, 'I'd no idea it was so late! Look – thank you, thank you very much – it's been really grand!' – a phrase from Yorkshire childhood surprising her – 'but now we have to go,' she hurried on, 'it's your lunch-time too, I expect – I expect that's – er – he's calling you in for lunch too!' She smiled briskly. 'Come on, boys – best foot forward! Say "thank you" to Mo . . .' And she bustled to take the lead-strap into her own hand.

Mo said, 'Y'can leave it with me. I'll mend the strap.'

'Oh!' said Grace. 'No – really, I couldn't put you to the trouble – and we'd better take it anyway, it's not ours, you see . . .'

'No, I know. It's Setons',' said Mo. He was standing easy, arms folded, regarding her.

She suddenly saw herself to be blithering, wittering like a wet hen; and she laughed. 'Well,' she said, 'that would be very kind – thank you – and without it we can run – which we'd better! So, yes, thank you!' She handed the strap back to him. 'I'll see it's collected by the end of the week,' she said, but was at once assailed by cries from the boys: 'Come back tomorrow – oh, Grace, tomorrow – we –'

'Tomorrow is lessons!' Grace declared, and cut through the protests. 'Enough! Thank Mo, and come on, we must run!' Towing the boys away, she said to Coverdale, 'Thanks again – and that chap's still waiting for you!'

'He's not waiting for me,' said Mo. 'Just nosy.' He nodded briefly. 'Bye.'

Nicholaus had his last word. Over his shoulder he called to Mo, 'See you tomorrow!'

Panting along, Max said, 'Can we, Grace? Please? Because the snow doesn't last long in England!'

'We'll see!' said Grace.

Max seized her hand. 'Oh, thank you, Grace!'

'I only said, "We'll see"!' said Grace.

'I know!' cried Max happily. 'Oh, isn't he *nice*, Mo!'

'Mo Mo Mo!' carolled Nicholaus. 'Isn't he *nice*!'

Grace merely said, 'Race you to the gate!' and ran ahead.

CHAPTER TEN

Honoria saw the toboggan off on its way to the main gate as arranged and, gathering her commodious cardigan closer, scurried back through the chill high corridors to the cosy seclusion of her drawing-room to begin her morning's desk-work.

Her brother, in his own domain, stood hands in pockets, bleakly assessing the snow. Here to stay. Thick, very. And not about to thaw. Terry had cried off; on the phone just now: 'How is it your end?' And the fact was that even if the railways remained in service, the road from Hestonborough was closed. 'Well – have to leave it this weekend, Spen. Damn shame.' Neither Terry nor Martin, then, nor anyone else. More phone calls from the metropolis any moment now. Weekend 'off'. Never an acceptable prospect, this particular weekend even less so. They were in need of emollient company, he and Archie, plenty of amiable diversion, congenial cover within which to regain balance, restore communications, heal the breach. Not for the first time. Nor, life and love being what it is, the last, he glumly observed, but with a degree of resignation, recognition in his mid-fifties of the treacheries of Eros. He ruminated on his findings. There is love; and there is sex. Sometimes, in rare, felicitous circumstances, the two not only appear to belong together, but do, each enhancing the other; felicity indeed. One, however, even while it is, gloriously, enhancing the other, remains a wild card. Sex, sexuality. It's a wild card. And God knows, he should know; he whose sexuality arrived with him in his cradle in deviant form, deftly placing him beyond the pale; and in the process ensuring that his sex and sexuality should dominate his living and his life in a manner and to an extent beyond the comprehension of those within the pale, snugly entrenched in what they claimed to be Decency. Within the Holy Pale, no love of his could be deemed to have virtue, no sexual desire be other than disgusting. How ingenious we are, the human race, at building barriers, how energetic in founding factions, how good at ghettos . . . He sighed a small, involuntary sigh. He did not exclude himself from the universal failing, committed ghetto-dweller that he was.

Into the quiescent world beyond the window a figure trudged, emerging from the side of the house, muffled, brown, Bruegelesque against the snow, and – towing a toboggan! That old sledge! How extraordinary! What could that be about? Some philanthropic scheme of Nonni's, presumably – but on whose account? Oh – of course. The Mayendorff boys. Nephews. Second cousins? Something more obscure than nephews since Margaret was the actual cousin. A good sort, Margaret; always was. Unjudgemental, though with a mind of her own; easy, straightforward in his presence, not swivel-eyed or condescending. Not Pale-minded – though about to encounter the hazards of fiddling with the rules, perhaps. Depends. Nonni says a divorce is out of the question. Margaret is not to be allowed to dishonour the families with public exposure of marital failure. Perhaps she doesn't really mind – she'll certainly not be contemplating marriage again. One was more than enough. Quite right, poor girl. Fancy drawing that arrogant cold-hearted bastard in life's lottery! Well. She may not have got clean away, but she gave them a run for their money! And she's all right here, gone to ground in Hollisfont, and very welcome. Nice for Nonni, too.

The Bruegel figure plodded on, tubby old Dixon, winkled

out from his boiler-house this inclement morning and no doubt muttering some ripe Anglo-Saxon. He surely can't be lugging that thing all the way up to the Dower House? A mile and a half? No. Nonni will have some reasonable compromise arranged. The figure toiled out of sight beneath the arching limes, graceful, delicate vaulting etched upon the tranquil, albescent air. Beautiful. Snow is beautiful.

But a wretched nuisance too.

He shifted himself. Hyacinths flowering in their delftware dish scented the air. He snuffed them, lightly touched the sculpted waxen blooms in passing; white hyacinths, his favourite colour in flowers – or non-colour. The fragrance followed him, yearly antidote to midwinter, February glooms, the sight and scent of ascendant white hyacinths. The fire, lit by other hands before breakfast, flared cheerfully in the handsome hearth. He squatted and fed it another log. Archie was susceptible to cold; loved hot sunshine, glowing fires. Not that it was cold in here, large though it was, this elegant room with its six wall-high classical windows. The central heating, discreet and effective, designed by his father, was one of his more successful ventures; unlike the ghastly model village. Spencer took the poker and settled the log to advantage and considered adding another. He decided against it for the moment. He set down the poker, wiped his hand against his trousers and stood up. He well recognized restlessness in himself, knew it would not be mastered by inventing something for himself to do. The pretty chiming clock on the marble mantel prettily chimed. Ten o'clock. Archie tardy this morning. Withholding his presence intentionally. Punitively? Loftily? Guiltily? Angrily?

He wandered about the room. Those hyacinths again – heavenly smell. He stood by the piano, its keyboard open from the evening before, Ravel on the music-stand. 'Pavane pour une Infante Défunte'. Melancholy-sweet, it was the piece Archie had been playing; prelude to distress. Anger. By the sinking fire, from his armchair, Spencer had idly picked up the book. *Crome Yellow*, Huxley; Archie's current reading. Markered by the card. It was beautifully executed, exquisitely painted, a pastiche of a Persian miniature of entwined lovers garlanded in flowers and attended by gazelles and oblivious to all except each other, in embrace, the two young men. Across the lower margin in unsophisticated hand at variance with the artistry of the painting: 'From your loving Valentine, I am yours and you are mine!'

Spencer softly closed the piano lid, and wandered on. He felt old. He was too old for these . . . upsets. Peace, now, please. Placid, middle-aged contentment. No more highs, no more lows. No more wild, exultant passions; and no more anguish, no more of that most poisonous of afflictions, sexual jealousy. His degree of resignation had been several degrees deficient, come the moment, the shock, last night. He'd thought all that was done with – all passion spent. Not so, evidently. He could hear himself now. Enraged, vindictive, shouting. Not resigned. The servants, thank God, had gone to bed, did not therefore hear. Archie heard. And made reply. No denial; no plea for pardon, no exonerating explanations, but: 'Who the hell do you think you are? Do you think you own me? Do you? Lord of all you bloody well survey, Master of Hollisfont, Divine Authority!'

All passion spent this morning. His, anyway; or most of it. Still a lingering, lurking twitch. Resignation not quite out-flanking passion. And Archie? What remained for him this morning of the row last night? Of his transient passion for the trivial little protégé? Mother Greek, father Brazilian or something Latin, exotic equation, producing the olive-skinned, sly-eyed, plausible and, alas, genuinely talented Xavier Cassiani, twenty-two years old and often been kissed. Slender young Adonis, bred in the Casbah, blossoming in Bloomsbury.

Archie – sane, sound, funny, serious Archie – had once been young, never been slender nor ever been anyone's idea of an Adonis. Not a 'beauty', no oil painting; though actually very like Rembrandt's self-portrait in the Uffizi. Archie's magic was nothing to do with a pretty face or sleek limbs. Mental energy, humour, doubt, generosity of spirit, housed inelegantly in a shambly frame. Spencer reckoned his adulthood, the beginnings of maturity, from the day twenty years ago when he met Archie and together they found the makings of an enduring relationship, something not merely physical, though also that. The war had separated but not divided them. Both in uniform, neither at the Front, thank God, since a combination of age and background placed them in administration, in England, though in different regiments and different places. Both deplored the war, hated army life; and in that aggressively heterosexual ambience perfected the dubious arts of dissembling while full well knowing how most vociferous pansy-punchers were themselves indifferent oaks. Post-war, the social revolution had not extended to the toleration of overt homosexuality; one day, perhaps. Not yet by any means. Unable to make a common home, they saw each other most weeks, here, or in London; and, bowing to social mores, almost always within the acceptable camouflage of mixed company, parties including women – a ludicrous charade, since those women by definition knew and accepted the realities: some indeed were married to homosexuals, and mothers to their children. A charade he had himself fiercely resisted, losing in the process the remnants of affection and regard from his father and, ultimately, his mother, who had moved out of the Hall, widowed, taken herself off to the Dower House, withdrawn herself from him. Yes. Little did the world understand of the daily price exacted from those delivered to their cradles in deviant form.

The telephone rang. Violet Crashaw: '. . . well, the streets are all right, traffic running – I've just been round to Cadogan Place – but it's the trains! Such a shame, Spen. Oh – I've got that Garnett book you wanted – shall I post it, or bring it next time? Sure? Well – keep warm! I bet Hollisfont looks gorgeous all the same! Give my love to Archie.'

Half-past ten. Really drawing it out, Archie. Captive, unable to drive away from the conflict. They were stuck here with it, two middle-aged, upset people, with no ameliorating company. On the other hand, and comfort of a sort, neither could he drive back to the blandishments of the tawdry Cassiani. Cassiani of all people! A flirtatious, mindless tart. An impressive facility with a paint-brush, but a commonplace trollop. He stared glumly at the fire; exerted himself and fed it another log. Such is life. Such, certainly, is sex. Our old treacherous travelling companion, the wild card.

Honoria paused in her progress towards Spen's drawing-room and looked with contentment at the snowscape beyond the landing window. Beautiful. And also an answer to an old maid's prayer, for her nephews. She noted with approval that smoke was rising from the boiler-house shed's chimney. Dixon had not exactly welcomed being enlisted to take the toboggan to the main gate – inveterate old grumbler! Old Enoch Dixon, as much a part of the place as the stone walls his personality resembled! Perhaps she should not be quite so pleased as she was with the snow, since obviously it was an inconvenience and hardship to most people, but now it was here, by divine intent or freak of chance, she felt free to enjoy her enjoyment of it, and did. She adjusted the sheaf of papers in her grasp and continued on her way. An odd and welcome development, Spen's summons. Just right! She had been sitting there with the results of her morning's deliberations, some of which needed Spen's signature, some, consultation, when the blooper had blooped; the internal communication system devised and installed by Papa, a private, idiosyncratic and very useful telephonic network with its own distinctive blooping voice and its own rather austere equipment, the fittings suggestive of safari or military operations. Papa's inventions were strictly practical and frequently presented that impression. Spen had housed his bloopers within beguiling decorated boxes. She'd left hers as they were; whether from some whimsical notion of respect for Papa or from inertia, she had never discovered. She mused upon this morning's summons – well, invitation: 'Come and join us for a sherry, Nonni – about half an hour?' 'Oh, I'd like that, yes!' she'd told him, and then, directed by some inner need for candour in her dealings, 'I need to see you, actually – a couple of things for your signature and that business about the bothy.' Instead of the statutory groan, he had responded cheerfully, 'Fine!' An indication of unusual high spirits this morning; or something more elusive. Whichever, she knew that she had been recruited, was needed this morning for some emotional necessity of his. She didn't mind. She loved Spen, if that was not too grand a claim. What she felt for him was more than tolerance, more than affection, more than a sibling bond. It had not always been so.

At a very early age – she could not have been more than three – she had picked up unease among the adults, a quality of distress, dismay triggered by her elder brother. He had hated riding. 'Oh, pull yourself together, boy!' She could remember the scene. If she was three then Spen was seven. He had fallen at the little jump in the paddock, the pony had jogged on and was jittering about near the hedge, its reins dangling, and Spen lay weeping, sobbing on the grass. Papa's rebuke had an angry ring, but something else too, which at three she had intuited without knowing its name: embarrassment. She had at that moment understood without knowing that there was something unacceptable about Spen. He went away to school. She saw him only in the holidays. He seemed happy, happier than when he had lived at home. He was no longer reduced to tears by Papa's irritation. She became aware that Papa chose to avoid Spen's presence; and that Mama was nervy, *distraite*, during the holidays. There were mysterious sessions behind closed doors following upon communications from the school. A sort of embargo fell upon the subject of Spencer in term-time. Around the age of twelve she had begun to piece together the nature of the problem facing all of them. Over the ensuing years she watched her parents' deepening dismay, watched them riding out the social ground-swell, and at last grimly submit to Fate that assured them no heirs to carry the name. No heirs on the distaff side either. Both parents died resigned to that. Honoria's experience of sexual encounter had remained the secret single occasion as an eight-year-old when Spen and a pre-pubertal prep-school friend had trapped her in the summer-house and demanded to 'see'. Protesting, weepy, threatened and afraid, she had pulled her knickers down. 'Off – right off!'. She had to lie down then, and open her legs. They had not touched her. Only looked, and sniggered, and with secrets of their own to share had bundled her and her knickers out and shut the door. The nightmare had lingered long. Perhaps it would have been exorcized by beguiling suitors, but life brought no beguiling suitors. No suitors, beguiling or otherwise. Spen got the share of family beauty; no suitors for thick-set, plain Honoria. She would have liked to have children. Would have braved the undoubted horrors of physical union willingly, to have children. At the time of Margaret's marriage she would gladly have settled for one such herself – arranged. She would have given her eye-teeth to be the fairy princess, perfected artefact in silks and pearls and drifting veils. She had been thirty-five then, still with dreams. The next few years had shown her that the hour of glory was not necessarily the harbinger of joy. Margaret's reality had soon tempered Honoria's dreams. And in those years also, Mama died, and the war came, and Spencer went and the management of Hollisfont passed unequivocally into her hands, if not under her name: Spencer remained nominally in charge, of course; she would not have had it otherwise, then or now. Spencer had never taken to the role. Why should he? How could he? Always subtly excluded from policy decisions by Papa, never at ease among the villagers with their ill-concealed smirking disdain for the pretty-boy. She took naturally to the role. She loved Hollisfont – and that was not too grand a claim. Hollisfont had absorbed and rewarded her increasingly; she found fulfilment in its service; perhaps – what was the jargon these days? – sublimating therein her maternal instincts? And ever supported by the sacraments, the rites and ceremonies enshrined in St Aldhelm's, and her own personal dialogue with God, who may or may not be the same Being as understood by the hierarchy of Churchdom, but through whom she had learned that sainthood was not expected or required, that the daunting difficulty of human affairs was totally recognized, and that if you could muster Charity, it began at home.

She arrived at her destination, gave her customary knock and let herself in. She stood a moment, adjusting. There seemed to be nobody present. But then she discerned Archie, part-visible in a wing-chair away at the far end of the room; not ensconced in his usual place by the fire. She closed the door behind her and crossed to the hearth, laying her papers on a low table. 'Hello, Archie!'

He looked up from his reading. 'Oh!' He evidently did not expect her. 'Honoria!' He stood up, book in hand.

'No – don't get up, please!' She smiled. 'I – er – brought some papers for Spen to sign!' She did not mention the invitation. 'Please, don't let me disturb you! Spen just popped out?' Should she pick up her papers and depart? Something afoot here. Quietly leave – or was this the reason for her being here?

'Um. I s'pose so. I've been reading.'

He was not his candid, relaxed self this morning. What was the best thing to do? To give herself a little time she said, 'Beautiful, isn't it!' indicating the white world beyond the windows.

'Yes,' he agreed, without enthusiasm.

It was time enough, since the door opened and Spen strode in. 'Ah! Nonni!' His tone could have conveyed surprise or simply greeting. She took her cue. 'Some papers for you, Spen – and if you have the time, a word about the bothy!'

'Right, right! Yes, certainly!' He slid her a conspiratorial smile. Then: 'How about some sherry to sweeten the pill? Sit yourself down!'

Archie had retreated behind his wing-chair and his book. From her fireside seat Honoria saw that he did not look up when Spen placed a sherry at his side. Alas! That was why she was here. They were at odds. And marooned by snow. And Spen needed her presence. She sipped her sherry. It was a long, long time since these two had fallen out. Nine – ten years? Over a protégé of Spen's, that summer, 1920.

The athletic young man almost permanently resident as Spen's tennis partner and 'coach'. Poor Archie. Poor Spen. Poor young man – though actually he was rather an unpleasant youth, very narcissistic . . . She sighed to herself. What now? Sex? Again? Probably. Sex or money seemed to be at the root of most human unhappiness. And it wasn't money, surely? And this time it was not Spen, she knew. Spen was in these recent years contented, at last; and how well contentment suited him! Oh dear. What now?

'To business!' Spen declared. Beneath his assertively cheerful manner, now that he sat opposite her, she saw the strain, the tightness round the eyes, the deepened hollow beneath his mouth. 'About time!' he jovially observed, appending his signature to the document sanctioning the road scheme – and indeed, the matter had dragged on for months, years almost, the sale to the Council of a slice of boundary land to take a new road to a factory development outside Hestonborough. Petty legalities had drawn the business out. Petty legalities kept alive by petty officials in Spen's view, and hers too. A signature to endorse the drainage work in the land below the water-garden. Signatures on cheques, one for payment for the garage extension in the stable-block, one for coal and coke supplies to the Hall.

'Not that they'll go in the post today, what with the snow,' said Honoria, collecting up the various papers. 'And Enoch assures me there's more to come – "Aarh!" he said in that doomy voice, you know?' she grinned at her brother, '"we ain't seen the worst of it yet, missus!"'

Spen's smile flickered and vanished. He stood quickly up and went to the side-board. 'More sherry?' He poured himself another.

'No, thanks.' She still had half a glassful.

He paused, glanced at the distant wing-chair, decanter

in hand; but replaced it and returned to his seat. He drank deeply of his sherry. 'The bothy,' he said.

'Well,' she began. 'This policy decision to demolish it. I daresay the legalities are correct – Lionel Blow will have checked every detail of the by-law to the last syllable, stickler that he is.'

Spen uttered a brief groan and nodded. He did not like Blow, nor did he delude himself that Blow liked him. He swigged his sherry.

'But it's my opinion that it's not as straightforward as he'd have it look. I'm afraid he's using it for . . . well, personal reasons.'

'Personal reasons?'

'He's never approved, you know, of young Coverdale –'

'Oh, *that*? I thought all that had fizzled out ages ago.'

'No,' said Honoria. 'I have to say that Maurice goads him. Goes out of his way to – well, tease him –'

'Good,' said Spen.

Honoria waved aside the red herring; she was aware that Spen's attention was adrift, focused on the wing-armchair really, but now that she was here she was going to make him listen. 'Not good – silly, actually. But something else has now come into it. It seems Maurice has joined the AWU – become a Union member –'

At this Spen gave a barking laugh. 'Better! When was this?'

Honoria said reprovingly, 'It does have implications, you know – for the estate.'

'What implications?' He was amused, off-hand. He drained his glass, got up and went to replenish it. Again, holding the decanter, he looked at the wing-chair. He fractionally paused and then called, 'Come and listen to this, Archie! Insurrection! The Revolution come to Hollisfont!' And then swiftly, 'Tell him, Nonni!' he added loudly.

Archie, perforce, approached. He carried his glass, laid aside his book.

Honoria, perforce, resumed, recapitulating the story thus far. Archie, who was fairly familiar with life in Hollisfont, did not need the *dramatis personae* to be explained. He stood on the hearth-rug, looking at Honoria, listening to her account. Spen, returning from the side-board, put his hand on Archie's shoulder in passing, and reseated himself. Archie hesitated. He sat, on the sofa, studied his glass.

'So – what implications?' Spen pursued, lightly derisive, smiling.

Honoria said, 'He is apparently asking for a wage-increase –'

'Is he, by Jove!' Spen chuckled.

Honoria ignored him, '– and apparently asking for shorter hours in line with the AWU and encouraging the men to do likewise.'

Spen let out a bellow of laughter. 'I like his style – but I don't fancy his chances! What? With the Hollisfont zombies!' He laughed again.

Honoria was regretting her choice of moment, sorry she'd begun now. The issue was important to her, she felt much in need of intelligent support and advice, and she was reaping the side-effects of some sorry discord here, fortified, alas, by unaccustomed quantities of sherry – Spen was not much of a drinker.

'The point is,' she said, trying to order and if possible conclude the interchange on the serious note it deserved, 'that this lends some credence to Blow's contention that the boy's a trouble-maker, and some substance to his view that Hollisfont would be better off without him.'

'It doesn't!' cried Spen. 'Credence and substance? It doesn't at all! It simply tells us that Blow, little martinet that he is, wants to be shot of Coverdale – which we know already – eh, Archie?'

Archie addressed Honoria, and markedly chose her tone rather than Spen's. 'Where,' he said soberly, 'where exactly does the bothy fit into all this?'

'Ah – you see, with nowhere to live, he'd have to go!'

'But he could find lodgings, couldn't he?'

Honoria shook her head, 'Not in the village.'

'Still like that, is it?' Archie raised his eyebrows.

'More so since this Union business.' She was exasperated: 'He *is* a silly boy!'

'Why did he join? Is it known why?'

'At a guess I'm afraid I should say that it was to make a stir . . . it's his temperament, you see. Maurice always was a . . .' She cast round for a suitable epithet.

Spen, languid in his chair, glass empty, said, 'Wild card?'

'A bit of a show-off,' said Honoria. 'I mean, he likes to be the centre of attention. Such a pity,' she observed sadly. 'He's intelligent – clever – but he has this streak. Such a pity he didn't stay in the navy. I feel that there he might have learnt some self-discipline; taken in hand, he'd make a fine young man.'

Archie said, 'Perhaps this little *crise* is a blessing in disguise – if he has to go, he may come to his senses and find a proper career for himself.'

Spen said, addressing mid-air, 'Loss to the neighbourhood. Quite the most interesting member of the work-force. And far the best-looking.'

There was a resonant, brief silence. Archie had not once looked at Spen nor did now, saying to Honoria, 'I don't think you should worry yourself about his future, he sounds the sort who falls on his feet. And who knows – he may even privately be glad to go. Farm-labouring must be fairly boring for an intelligent man.'

'It's Blow who needs to go if anyone,' said Spen, unwinding himself from his chair and heading for the decanter. 'Hollisfont can well spare *him*!'

Archie, still resolutely addressing Honoria, said, 'Well, Honoria, I should let things take their course – and not worry. It sounds as though in the long run Hollisfont might be happier without him?'

Honoria gazed sorrowfully at the fire. 'You may be right,' she said. Then, 'But there's a *principle* here. The boy is not *choosing* to go – indeed, he claims to be very happy where he is – and to enjoy farm-work – and he *is* very good at it – and that's another thing, Sutton, the farmer, says he's the best worker we've got – not to mention the only one who can properly handle the tractor! The others don't like the tractor – new-fangled . . .' She tailed off into a sigh.

'If he goes,' said Archie comfortingly, 'that'll be the end of it, surely. There's no proper future for the boy as it is. And they'll find someone else to cope with the tractor. And Hollisfont will be restored to peace and quiet!'

From the side-board Spen declared, 'I agree with you, Nonni! There's a principle at stake! Let us not betray our principles! Happily, we have no need to.' He fitted the stopper back into the neck of the decanter with absorbed attention, and gave it a parting pat. 'A solution is at hand.' He smiled with satisfaction, strolled to his chair. Seated, he said, 'Coverdale can have Poundell.'

'Poundell?' Honoria gazed at him in alarm and perplexity. He was clearly a little drunk.

'Yes, Poundell.'

'But it's coming down – it's being demolished! It's not habitable, Spen!'

'It can be made so.'

'Of course it can't, Spen!' Irritation spiked her alarm.

'It's been deteriorating for years – no repairs and marked down for demolition since goodness knows when –'

'Since 1905 when revered Papa built our hideous village,' said Spen.

'Spen!' she demurred. Rallying, she said, 'Well, there you are, then! And there's certainly no money to finance such a thing!'

'I shall pay for it,' he replied tranquilly.

'You – ?'

'I,' he said. Sweet reason in his tone, he said, 'There can be no objections, no entangling legalities to excite our friend Blow. Yes – quite a coup, when you think about it! A building of historic interest and undoubted charm restored – reparations to a vandal past. And a principle preserved! Let us not betray our principles! Furthermore,' he added, 'one in the eye for all those who deplore the exercise of independence and find the wayward spirit odious – which includes Coverdale's grotesque mother! No! Beauty *and* talent – we can't afford to lose him! Quite a coup, one way and another!'

Into this vibrant moment Parker stepped. From the door he announced, 'Luncheon is served, sir.'

'Ah!' cried Spen. 'Lunch! Good! Set a place for Miss Honoria, will you, Parker? You'll lunch with us, Nonni, won't you?' he beamed, taking her by the elbow and leading off towards the dining-room.

1930

March

CHAPTER ELEVEN

'It's absolutely sweet! One of those little flower ones – sapphire centre and teeny diamond sort of petals round it. Top marks to Lewis! Blue's very much her colour and for a wonder there's a man who's actually noticed! Or perhaps it was good luck more than good management – anyway, it's *sweet*! He couldn't pop the question on St Valentine's Day – well, at the Valentine hop – because of all that snow – top marks again, though – such a romantic idea! Anyway, better late than never – I'd almost given up! Crikey – talk about dither! I began to despair! After all the trouble I took!' Lilian studied herself in her bedroom mirror and frowned. 'Take it in a bit – round the hips – here!' she told the seamstress who was pinning, on her knees, settling the length of hem.

Mrs Coverdale spoke, addressing the seamstress: 'The hips need no alteration.' She said to her daughter, 'The line is quite sufficiently defined.' She failed to catch Lilian's attention, meet her eye in the mirror, arrest the indiscretions flowing about the ears of the seamstress.

'They're thinking of October – well, *Grace* is thinking of October – Lewis says that's ages away but Grace says it can't be before then because of the boys . . . I s'pose that's right, actually, they'll have gone off to school then, going in September –' She broke off. 'Wider there!' she told the seamstress, 'I want the shoes to *show* – oh, much wider, like in the *drawing*! Another six inches at least! So it looks like October – another wedding for Tom! They haven't decided on where to go for the honeymoon yet except there's some talk of Cornwall – *Cornwall*, I ask you! In October! And anyway it's a hopeless idea for a honeymoon – it's where Lewis's parents live, hardly the ideal spot for honeymooning! I said, "Why don't you go abroad? Get a bit of decent weather!" A word in Lewis's ear about that! Nought out of ten for Cornwall! Oh, yes – that's better!' she told the seamstress. 'That's the ticket!' The seamstress sat back, Lilian swirled her belling hem-line: '*That's* better, isn't it – see? Heavenly material, this satin!' Satisfied, she rewarded the seamstress with a smile. 'I've recommended the firm – another client for you! My friend, who is to be married in the autumn! Well – she's one of my bridesmaids, so you'll have her measurements already!'

Mrs Coverdale moved forward. She said to the seamstress, 'Thank you. You have finished for today, I think? It looks very well, though perhaps there's a tendency for the panel to pucker here below the bust.' Better placed to catch her daughter's eye, she now did so, and the flow was duly arrested. Lilian, inside the satin tube being eased over her head by expert hands, had time to absorb the implications of that iron glance and to be irritated and piqued. Jolly good thing when she was married and on her own ground! Enough of being treated like a child all the time! But she was not entirely composed as the seamstress departed, leaving them unattended.

'What,' said Mrs Coverdale, 'could you have meant by that last remark, Lilian? For the moment I will leave aside the impropriety of your earlier chatter which you are perfectly aware was totally inappropriate in front of an employee. I wish to know what you meant by your last remark concerning bridesmaids.'

Lilian, stung by the pejorative 'chatter', countered: 'You wanted to know where I'd been and I *told* you! Really, Mother! We aren't living in the Dark Ages, and anyway she doesn't know who or what I'm referring to and if she did it hardly matters – it's just what everybody knows anyway!'

'Answer my question,' said Mrs Coverdale.

'What question?' Lilian drew on her tweed skirt, busied herself buttoning the waistband.

'Regarding the bridesmaid.'

Lilian picked up her jumper, turned it right way out. 'Well, now Moira's pregnant again *she* won't be one and I've always said about Grace, from the beginning – it's obvious!' She thrust her head into the jumper, pulled it on, attended to adjusting its cuffs.

'Am I to understand that you have approached Miss Moon on the matter?'

Lilian flushed, cross. 'I asked Grace ages ago! You know I did! Last year!'

Mrs Coverdale almost flushed, herself. 'Since then,' she said evenly, 'other arrangements have been made, as you well know. The bridesmaids have been chosen.'

'Yes, but *now* we know that Moira's out of it! She's said so – *you've* said so!'

'And there are to be three bridesmaids.'

'Three's hopeless! I've always wanted four, it's what's planned!'

'I see. I am to take it that you have officially enlisted Miss Moon, this morning?'

Lilian brushed furiously at her hair. 'Her name's *Grace*, Mother, and it's *my* wedding and she's my friend just as much as Thelma and Jean and Liz!' She glowered at her reflection, fed up with being yet again spreadeagled between defiance and defence and, seemingly, unable to break the mould; and was entirely unprepared for, not to say bewildered by, her mother's response:

'We must lose no time in arranging a fitting,' she observed

pleasantly, 'as soon as Moira returns the material we sent her.' She withdrew towards the door. 'After lunch we can check the guest-list and begin to write the invitations – the cards have been delivered this morning.' At the door she turned momentarily. 'And do bring . . . Grace to tea. Next week?' She endowed her daughter with a parting smile. And left her staring at the softly closed bedroom door, hairbrush suspended, temper capsizing, with nowhere to go.

Before her own dressing-table mirror, completing her toilette prior to lunch, Mrs Coverdale assessed the field, and found herself satisfactorily placed. To give ground was, on occasion, to move to advantage. She gently pressed fresh powder to her cheekbones, added a touch to her finely modelled nose, the Courtenay bone structure still and ever sustaining her acknowledged beauty. She ran a practised finger along smooth eyebrows and met the calmly reflected eyes beneath. Yes. Had she had choice, she would have directed otherwise; but choice had been pre-empted. So. *Il faut marcher quand le diable est aux trousses.*

Developments had taken place recently. While she found no cause or inclination to revoke her personal evaluation of the governess, certain developments invited a degree of appraisal.

The winter season's activities had taken their customary course for Mr and Mrs Coverdale, the month in Rimini, the visit to friends in Paris, engagements in town and so on; a period of the year when Hollisfont and its affairs necessarily received only distant attention, though Mrs Coverdale kept herself informed. She had her methods. So that she was quite aware of the continuing connection between Lewis Gower and the Moon woman. She noted with satisfaction that Lilian's interest in that quarter had lapsed, as intended: Lilian this year accompanied them to Rimini, a move accomplished by the simple expedient of inviting Frank Bellinger. And the 'friendship', together with the 'maid-of-honour' nonsense, had duly lapsed. The governess had received barely a mention since Christmas.

Mrs Coverdale anointed her hands with lotion and restored her rings to her fingers.

The news of the engagement had not had the power to surprise. Mrs Coverdale had recognized that it was not beyond the bounds of possibility that Lewis Gower could make a proposal. He had shown himself to be unreliable in the matter of Charlotte Inglesby, and latterly shown himself less endowed with discrimination than one had supposed; furthermore he was at a certain age, a vulnerable time of life in men. No, she had not been taken by surprise that he had made a proposal, and clearly, such a proposal would be accepted. For the governess Lewis Gower would be 'quite a catch', as the vulgar expression went. No surprise there. So Mrs Coverdale had received the news calmly, and had not passed it on to Lilian, time enough for a revival of that subject when they should return to Outwick. Her own return had been a week ahead of Henry and the young people, who had arrived from Paris late last evening. The telephone, Mrs Coverdale reflected, was a dubious benefit of modern life. It was by telephone from friends whom Lilian had immediately called, in Hestonborough, that she had learnt, sooner than Mrs Coverdale had anticipated, of the engagement, and had reacted with a lamentable display of boisterous excitement. Mrs Coverdale reproached herself that she had not been duly forearmed against this morning's escapade . . .

However. She had in other respects been forearmed. She had in the past week learnt of developments which had indeed threatened to surprise her, developments revealed at

Thursday's quarterly meeting of the committee. Anthea Bruce-Duff had set the tone, and it was the tone quite as much as the content which might indeed be said to be unexpected. With undeniable warmth of inflection Anthea Bruce-Duff had told her, 'Grace by name and Grace by nature, as Honoria says! You've met her, of course? So good for Lewis Gower to be settling down at last – never seemed the bachelor type to me!' It then transpired in an exchange with Cecily Margolies that Honoria Seton was on close terms with the Moon girl, something apparently to do with a book, though what, exactly, was unclear. What was clear, however, was that the girl had been introduced to some of their circle, and that presently she was attracting favourable attention, especially, it seemed, from Honoria Seton. *Alors! Il faut marcher quand le diable est aux trousses.* Had she had choice . . . but Lilian's impetuosity had pre-empted that. *Alors!*

She rose from the dressing-table. She adjusted the set of her dress in the cheval mirror. Lilian would have her fourth bridesmaid. Her ill-considered chatter before employees was another matter. Of that, she had more to say. Mrs Coverdale frowned momentarily. From her behaviour these past few months, it had seemed as though Lilian was learning a little restraint . . . was becoming a little less unlike Moira. Moira, and Bertie, who could always be relied upon . . .

The luncheon-gong sounded from below. Dispatching the frown, she descended to the dining-room. 'Pregnant' indeed! The coarsening of Lilian's speech these days! She took her place at table. 'I shall require you here all afternoon, Lilian,' she told her. 'Please make sure that you are available.' And to the hovering maid: 'You may serve now.'

CHAPTER TWELVE

'I should change down for this bend – slow down a bit, and change gear . . .' Lewis spoke slightly from the back of his throat despite efforts to remain calm. He was teaching Grace to drive. He pressed back in his seat, rigid. 'Ease off the accelerator! Ease off!' He was shouting.

'I am, I am!' cried Grace. And so she was; the car stalled, a searing protest from beneath the bonnet, and silence. The near front wheel grounded an inch away from the ditch. Lewis snatched the handbrake on, hard.

Grace, clutching the steering-wheel as in rigor mortis, glared ahead. 'Sorry,' she said shortly.

Lewis summoned an effort at jovial reassurance. 'Oh, don't worry, don't worry – we all do silly things when we're learning!'

He somehow failed to sound quite jovial; and Grace was not noticeably reassured. Still presenting her profile, she said, 'I *was* slowing down. And we're still a long way short of the corner.'

'Yes – yes – er, sorry! I, er –'

'You shouted.'

'Yes. Sorry.'

'No, that's all right,' she said, stiffly.

'Er – ignition,' he said. 'Turn the ignition off, could you?'

She did.

Lewis glanced behind, 'All right, old fellow?' he inquired of Guinness. Guinness, jolted from slumber, was blinking round. Lewis leaned back and patted his head, and the dog grinned, heaving himself upright. 'Not yet, old fella – not yet!' Lewis told him. 'Lie down – lie! That's right, goodog!' Lewis shifted his arm enough to let it lie along the back of Grace's seat. Grace sat forward, her hand plying the door-latch. 'I think you'd better take over,' she was saying as she moved.

He cupped his hand about her shoulder, at once restraining and caressing. 'No, no,' he soothed, 'course not! You're doing very well, darling!'

She said, 'In view of the fact that I've almost put us in the ditch, I think you had better take over.' She did not meet his eye, her tone was crisp and sensible, and she clicked the door-latch, moved to get out.

'Darling!' Lewis protested, and without ceremony hauled her to him, making for a healing kiss. Within an ace of his objective, 'Oh, HELL!' he said; for round the corner, on her bicycle, came Mrs Cox.

Mrs Cox gaily called, 'Oh, hello, Mr Gower!' and dismounting, eagerly wheeled her bike alongside. Her pink perspiring face and busy eyes hove to the driver's window. Grace perforce wound the window down. 'Oo! Having our driving lesson, are we? Doing well, is she? Rather you than me!' she chatted at Grace. 'I wouldn't have the stomach for motors – my bike suits me! Well, I won't hold you up, it's just I'm glad I happened to see you, Mr Gower – you'll be wondering where those two linen sheets have gone and I meant to leave a note, but what with one thing and another . . .! Anyway, I've taken them out – out of the linen cupboard.' She said they'd had their day, they were worn, needed turning sides to middles, that there were plenty of others, so really there was perhaps no need to go to the trouble, they could serve best in the rag-bag for polishing cloths if he was agreeable. While she talked the eyes quartered, assessing the arm now disengaged but lying along the back of the driver's seat, the sentiments accessible in two faces, and the value, pounds sterling, of the ring on Grace's finger. 'Well,' she said at last, 'here's me holding you up with talk about bed-linen!' She flashed Grace a kindred smile, woman to woman. 'Not a man's department, really! We're all that pleased for him – well, for you both, of course!' She nodded reassuringly. She aligned her bike, stepped aboard. 'And I must be getting along or I'll be all behind like the cow's tail! Bye bye!' she called, and whirred away.

Lewis had managed some affirmative 'Oh's' and a valedictory 'Thanks!'; Grace, nothing. In the sudden void, neither seemed to know what to say now, left with a seeming choice between motoring methods and bed-linen. Lewis found himself opting for comedy. 'Not the subtlest of nosy-parkers, Mrs Cox!' He laughed. 'She might have thought of something more convincing than my concern for sheets!'

Grace, still in profile, raised a minimal smile, and said, 'You're not thinking of keeping her on after we're . . .' She lapsed, left the sentence incomplete.

'Married?' Lewis supplied. 'Erm – well!' Having never given the matter a thought he could only say, 'I've never thought about it, darling! But whatever you want! Not if you don't want her!'

She made no answer. Instead, she opened her door, and at last glancing at him, said calmly, 'You take over – we need to reverse anyway. You'd better do it.' And she got out.

There was nothing else for it; cheated of his healing kiss, Lewis heaved himself across into the driving seat, switched on, and angled the Rover back and on course. He failed to persuade her to resume; she had walked round and put herself in the passenger seat. She did smile at him, though, a proper smile, albeit brief. 'No – honestly, I'd prefer it – I'll have another go later.'

'That's it, my darling!' he cheerily agreed. 'You can drive us home after the walk – nice straight run!' He let in the clutch and swung them easily round the corner. 'We'll go by Barley Bridge – all right? – I've to look at some loose coping, so we might as well go that way?'

'Yes.'

She seemed a bit quiet. He regretted shouting. Stupid reaction; you should never shout at a pupil, and doubly never shout at a learner driver in motion . . . Specially if the pupil happens to be your girl-friend. Fiancée. He reviewed the desirability of a further apology; but the moment seemed to have passed; and the silence was of a variety not inviting communication. Leave it be. Let it pass. It would pass. Or there'd be a propitious moment later, to apologize. Or perhaps the shouting had nothing to do with it, this quietness of hers . . . She had, he had noticed vaguely, been somewhat *piano* recently. Since? He cast his mind back. Since the driving lessons began? About four or five weeks, then? They'd started the lessons just after the snow, a few days after they'd become engaged. Perhaps Frank was right! 'Madness, old man! Wouldn't let Lilian within a mile of my steering-wheel! Women and cars – no, *sir*! Strictly for carrying the little dears about in as and when unavoidable. Too much ruddy temperament, the female of the species – asking for trouble, old boy, and I don't just mean the poor old gear-box!' Typical Bellinger, of course. Though perhaps he had a point in Lilian's case! But Grace was no flappy little boss-pot. Grace was a rational, adult woman; and she had asked to learn, she'd been thinking of taking lessons in Germany, but then they'd left. And she'd picked up the rudiments very quickly, as any intelligent being would; but it was true that while he totally approved of the enterprise, he did find these outings a bit . . . taxing. Not as . . . enjoyable as straightforward outings, no lesson included; so perhaps there was a grain of truth in Frank's theory, inasmuch as temperaments were tried when boxed together in a swiftly moving classroom? That must be it! And it was understandable. And unimportant! Really rather comical – even charming. He smiled, flicked a sideways glance at Grace. She was perfectly happy riding beside him, watching the passing countryside. And by way of confirmation a recollection came to him: her high good humour, animation, a few days back, telling him the story of the tea-party – not in the least *piano*! A witty, vivacious account capturing the essence of Outwick House and its *grande dame* manoeuvring amongst the social complexities: Grace was fully aware of those – Lilian had committed a gaffe in enlisting her as bridesmaid, and sat unwontedly silent, smiling a fixed smile, while her mother used her formidable talents to produce a silk purse from the sow's ear with which she had been presented. 'It was a very impressive performance!' Grace had laughed, amused, not affronted, and 'sorriest for Lilian, poor girl – I mean, there we were with our tea-cups, making the best of a bad job, all of us, because Lilian had put her foot in it again! Mm? No – I don't mind being a bridesmaid for her! And I did at last get my official invitation! I've been promoted – *persona grata* at Outwick House!' Yes, an occasion of much mirth between the two of them, she had not been *piano* at all – he was exaggerating, getting this motoring business out of proportion!

At Barley Bridge he pulled on to the verge and parked. Guinness was now in no doubt, up and quivering, bright-eyed. 'Yes!' cried Lewis. 'Walk-time! Goodog!' He grinned, and so did Guinness, leaping from the car and bounding on to the bridge. It was little more than a footbridge, a small stone span wide enough for a pack-horse, one of the locality's many ancient artefacts coming under his surveillance. Barley Brook surged and gurgled beneath it to join the river a mile away at the foot of Chilley Hill. The coping-stone in question rocked a little under his touch. Nothing serious, easily made good; mortar impaired by winter's frosts.

'Celandines!' Grace spoke from behind him. He joined her leaning on the other side of the bridge. She had pulled on her woolly hat, framing her face suffused with pleasure, childlike. He hugged his arm about her and kissed the smiling cheek. 'Yes!' He kissed the cheek again. 'Spring is here!' She was warm, she was happy, and sweet, so sweet.

The wind plucked their coats and biffed the thinning clouds along as they followed the track beside the brook. Above them on the slope Guinness, nose down, coursed for rabbits. 'He'd faint if he caught one!' Lewis laughed. He took Grace's hand and together they left the path, climbed between the gorse bushes. Released sunlight ran down the hill to meet them. In an access of bonhomie, his girl beside him, springtime promise in the air, he halted, surveying the world, and declared, 'Oh, this is a *nice* place to live!' He smiled at Grace for confirmation.

'Oh,' she said, adjusting her attention, 'yes!' She smiled.

There it was again, the *piano* note. He went on, impelled to elucidate, to include her in his expansive moment, 'I mean, I don't mean the hideous village – I'm glad we'll be living out at Fold Cop – not stuck in Hollisfont proper,' he dismissed the village beneath them with a sweep of hand, 'but I mean the – district, all this,' another sweep, embracing the wider view, 'though not to be churlish, I must say people have been extraordinarily nice about *us* – you and me!' He nodded approvingly towards the aesthetically unacceptable village, exonerating its inhabitants, who had, indeed, surprised them both by the generosity of their glad response to their engagement. He seemed to be making a lot of words and she none, though she smiled. He gave a brief culminating laugh. 'I suppose I just mean I'm glad to be alive!'

'Mmm!' She nodded. The smile widened, she looked about her. 'It's turned into a lovely day!' she said. 'Looks set fair, too – should be all right for the boys!'

'Oh, yes!' Lewis cast a judicial eye at the clearing sky. 'Pretty general – and they won't have had any rain today, not that kind of cloud!'

They climbed on, hand in hand, Guinness blundering ecstatically ahead of them. The boys were at some grand hunt today, with their mother, somewhere twenty-odd miles off, the horse and ponies boxed over early this morning. Lewis knew that Grace was concerned for Max. She'd talked again about him today, when they'd started out on the lesson, and again at lunch at the inn. Odd little blighter, Max. She was very fond of him – fond of them both, of course, but especially of Max. 'He's a tender plant, is Max.' She saw him as specially vulnerable. Probably right. Not like his brother – young Nicholaus was a normal noisy boy, nothing odd about him! Poor old Max didn't like hunting. He loved horses and riding, but not going out to hunt, Grace said. He didn't admit it; not, so Grace said, because he was ashamed or anything, but because he didn't want to disappoint his mother, let her down. Grace had a theory that the boy felt responsible for his mother – an odd conjecture to make about an eight-year-old, but Grace, unlike himself, was familiar with the minds of children. And furthermore she claimed that Max felt responsible for the father, which, she said, explained his wearing that hat all the time. A rum business. But she reckoned that the boy worried about both his parents and felt, in some way which Lewis could not comprehend, responsible for their parting.

The rummest thing of all was that the boys had not been told about that – so how could Max be worried? As far as they and the world in general were concerned, Mrs Mayendorff was here to see her sons into public school and the father had to stay in Germany to run the business, see it through the current economic crisis. But Grace said that 'Max knows'. And Honoria Seton thought so too, she said. So perhaps they were right; women's intuition at work. Lewis had eventually said to Grace that it would surely be better and simpler all round for the boys to be told the truth, since they'd have to know it some day! But Grace said that Mrs Mayendorff couldn't face that, it was too difficult. Lewis wanted to know for whom it was too difficult, and Grace said, 'For her!' and that she could understand how Mrs Mayendorff felt. He was blessed if he could! And slightly puzzled that Grace should defend her. Seemed to Lewis that the woman should pull herself together and straighten things out for the boy's sake – at least it would clear the air, give the boy a chance to speak up rather than slope about with it all bottled up under that hat! Still, thought Lewis, it would all sort out some day, and meantime Grace was keeping a caring eye on him and the boy obviously adored her – not such an odd little number after all! He could tell a good egg when he saw one! Holding her hand and climbing the sunlit hill, Lewis thought again what an excellent mother she was going to be; a wise head and a loving heart. And he further thought, again, that begetting children with Grace was going to be . . . wonderful!

It was, to him, remarkable, the serenity with which he had accepted her rule of chastity. He was surprised by and grateful for his own forbearance. He had been momentarily fazed by her resolution, but then at once recognized its imperative for her. It was all of a piece with a clear, strong simplicity in her. A purity. Old-fashioned word, purity. She was not merely shy, though she was physically shy, modest. And she was certainly not prudish, not small-minded or censorious. Nor had she religious reservations – she counted herself agnostic, as did he himself, and indeed neither of them had really wanted the church wedding into which they had been persuaded by general opinion; they'd both intended a Register Office marriage in Hestonborough but finally succumbed to enthusiastic demands from all sides for a 'proper wedding' here in St Aldhelm's. No; her restraint was all of a piece with the value she put on commitment. 'After, Lewis – after we're married,' she had pleaded. 'It's the point – the point of becoming married – the final commitment, isn't it?' And curiously enough he had at that moment felt her to be more completely his than if there on the rug before the fire at Fold Cop she had surrendered to their passion. For she had passion. Oh, yes! Even, in retrospect, that girlish kiss in the car five months ago had signalled that. Not cold, not cold at all! He had encountered cold women. Not reluctant by any means, but cold; their sexuality rapacious and self-centred. Not Grace. Not she! He blessed his good fortune. Good luck rather than good management had kept him single until now. He could so easily have got himself into a marriage on a wave of lust unsecured by affection and respect . . . friendship. How many couples he could think of who as the years went on found themselves with seemingly no more in common than receding memories of a sexual binge. It had occurred to him recently that abstinence was not just 'not having sex'. If he and Grace were now having sex together, they would, he was obliged to concede, know each other less well, not better. Getting to a bed would be the pervading preoccupation; getting to know her, and she him, would be peripheral. And furthermore it was true that they were easy and relaxed together, free from the furtive machinations of illicit sex, specially in a place like this – small community, eyes and ears and tongues on the go, Mrs Cox a prime example! Yes, he was content, they were content. This was love, and it was everything it was claimed to be. He pressed her hand in a surge of satisfaction; but was at once perversely overtaken by restive gloom about that damned trip to Germany – she was taking the boys to see their father in a month; he winced every time he thought of it; he had resolved not to mention it again, but out it came: 'Damn this Germany business!' he glowered.

'Oh, Lewis!' She turned to him, fondly laughed. 'You're not still worrying about that?'

'Well . . .' he grumbled.

'I don't *mind*!' she assured him again.

'But I do!' he said morosely. He drew her to a halt. 'Germany's in a funny state at the moment – and it's a hell of a journey, all the way to Berlin.'

She smiled, her grey eyes gentle, her hand clasping his. 'We'll be perfectly all right! We're used to travelling about, and it was my home for four years, remember.' She said, 'It's only for a fortnight!'

'Two weeks too long,' he said.

'Well, you'll be in Cornwall anyway!'

'Only for a week.' A duty visit to his parents. 'You should be coming with me if you're going anywhere!'

As before, she reminded him, 'But I couldn't do that, could I? Because I'll be on duty with the boys in any case!' She laughed. 'Cheer up – it's nothing to worry about!'

'Oh, Gracie!' He took her in his arms, hugged her to him. 'Roll on October!'

She kissed him, softly. 'Don't worry!' she smiled.

He thought, 'If their mother pulled herself together and took her responsibilities instead of shoving them on to you we'd all be a deal better off!' But this time he kept it to himself; Grace did not see it that way and was discomfited by criticism of Mrs Mayendorff. He just said ruefully, 'I'll try!'

'Oh, *Guinness*!' Grace jumped aside, appalled and laughing, her hand clapped over her nose.

'Oh, my God – what's he found!' Lewis took evasive action as Guinness, well larded with some nameless decomposing sludge, grinned and wriggled about their shins. 'You disgusting old idiot!' Lewis grabbed at the dog's collar and hauled him to a swathe of last year's fallen bracken. 'You horrible dog!' Part laughing, part gagging at the stench, he scrubbed handfuls of bracken at the offence. 'I should think so too!' he scolded as Guinness cowered and whinged in a semblance of remorse. 'Phoo!' said Lewis. 'Well, that's the worst off, but it's the river for you, my lad!' He released the dog, wiped his hands vigorously on grass. 'And for me!' he grimaced.

'What on earth is it?' Grace kept her nose defended.

'Perhaps it's as well we don't know! Come on!' Laughing together, they ran Guinness down Chilley Hill and to the river.

Lewis dried his hands on his handkerchief. 'Wow! It's *cold*!'

'I'm sure it is!' said Grace. 'Guinness doesn't seem to mind!'

'Fortunately!' said Lewis. 'He certainly wouldn't have been allowed in the car as he was! We'd have been asphyxiated!'

'Whoa! Look out –!' Guinness, heaving himself on to the bank, disburdened himself of excess water very efficiently by vigorously shaking and spraying it far and wide.

'Another stick!' cried Lewis. 'Throw the stick!' And Grace

hurled her contribution into mid-stream. 'Fetch! fetch it boy!' And Guinness cheerfully obliged, plunging off again.

'Not a good spot to be standing!' said Lewis, and they moved along the bank away from Guinness's landing place.

'Can all dogs swim?' asked Grace. 'Is it instinctive?'

'I've never heard of one that couldn't – ' Lewis stowed his damp handkerchief in his pocket ' – and no one taught old bugalugs there – he just jumped in and – swam!'

'It's a pity the boys can't have one,' Grace mused. 'They'd love' – she watched Guinness striving nose aloft, ears afloat, behind the retrieved stick – 'all this!'

'Yes, it is a pity,' said Lewis. 'Do them good – take young Max out of himself a bit.'

'But she's right, of course,' said Grace. Mrs Mayendorff had ruled against it. 'They'll be gone, away to their school in September . . .'

'They'll have to leave their ponies,' Lewis pointed out. 'Why not a dog?'

'That's different. A dog's more . . . well, it's different. Horses don't seem to mind who rides them or feeds them as long as it's done kindly – horses don't pine, do they?'

'Mmm,' said Lewis, conveying general assent, judging it wiser to avoid further assessment of Mrs Mayendorff's decisions.

Grace said, 'Guinness will miss you when you're in Cornwall, won't he?' Guinness was to stay with Tom Opie that week. Not only was it going to be a long journey, but the senior Gowers were not keen on dogs anyway.

'Oh, no!' said Lewis. 'Well, he might miss me a bit but he enjoys staying with Tom – like Tom, don't you, old chap?' Guinness, who was ashore again and divested of excess water, was presenting the stick for more action. 'I think that's enough for now, Guinness, we've got to get you dry! Come on – c'mon, boy! No – this way!' He set the pace,

Grace beside him, away from the waterside, on to the lane, Guinness, after a moment's reluctance, cantering to join them. 'Seems to have done the trick!' said Lewis. 'Got rid of the worst of it – though I daresay we'll be glad to keep the windows open in the car!'

Grace suggested, 'You can hose him off in the yard and there are plenty of bits of old towelling around the stables.'

'Oh,' said Lewis. 'I thought – can't we go to Fold Cop first – have a cup of tea, and I want you to see the cooker – y'know?'

'I've got to be back there for when the boys come in,' she said. The tone was gentle, even propitiatory, but also one that he recognized as final. He did not want to start an argument. Disappointed, and a little irritated, he restrained comment, did not say, 'Why on earth you have to be standing around for them when they get back I fail to see, since their mother's with them and Mrs Dunkerley'll have their tea ready!' Nor did he say, 'I'd have thought you'd have been keen to see the new cooker in place!' for of course she was – they'd chosen it together, the very latest, a Belling Electric to replace the fumey old oil-range in his kitchen – their kitchen. She had demurred, been anxious about the expense for him, said there was plenty of time, wasn't there? Anxious for him. She was the least acquisitive woman he'd ever come across! But he had carried the day, it pleased him hugely to be thus endorsing their future; and, once persuaded, she too had been pleased. And it was, he acknowledged, a very amiable 'failing', this commitment to duty in her. He took her hand and just said, 'Yes, of course!'

The hazel coppice separating the lane from the river whispered in the wind, shaking its catkins; a blackbird, startled by Guinness, rattled its alarm and fled upwind over Chilley Hill. 'Nesting, I suppose,' said Grace, watching it go. 'Very likely,' Lewis agreed. 'Very popular with birds, this place – and the spinney at Poundell – we had a pair of stonechats there last year. I just hope the hard spell didn't polish them off – they don't like snow and ice, can't cope.' The lane rounded the coppice. 'Oh, look! That's handy!' said Lewis, accelerating. 'He left a message at the estate office – wants a word.' Coverdale was crossing the farm's yard ahead. 'Hi – hello!' Lewis waved and jog-trotted onwards.

'Hello!' he said, arrived at the gate. 'You wanted to see me?'

Coverdale nodded. 'About the date.' He spoke flatly. 'Second time it's been postponed. What's going on?'

Lewis said, 'Yes, I'm sorry – obviously you need to know –'

'Yes.'

'There's been a hold-up – with planning –'

'I can see that,' said Coverdale. 'What's the problem? You don't need planning to pull a bothy down, do you? I need to know, and so does Mr Sutton. Are we talking about days or weeks or what?'

'Mr Sutton's supposed to have received a letter from the office –'

'Well, he hasn't. Knows no more than me.'

'The office is usually very efficient.' Lewis was puzzled. 'I'll look into it.'

'Well, what's in this letter anyway?'

'Ah, yes. Well, the matter is being deferred for a few weeks while, um, certain legalities are . . . tidied up.' They stood in silence. 'I'm sorry,' said Lewis. 'It's not very satisfactory for you, I see that. Not satisfactory for any of us, actually. None of us is . . . enjoying this, you know, Coverdale.'

'Oh, I wouldn't say that,' said Coverdale. 'I think we

can safely say that Lionel Blow is enjoying it.' He turned to go. 'A few weeks, hm? How long's that? Oh, I know: "How long's a piece of string?" Eh?' He suddenly smiled, and the transformation was marvellous. He said, 'I know it's none of your fault. Thanks for stopping by.'

Lewis warmly returned, 'I'm glad I spotted you – I'd have come over on Monday anyway, but it happens we were just out on a walk . . .' He turned his head, glancing: 'This is my – oh!' Grace was nowhere in sight. 'Oh – she's gone on, with the dog. Well, I'll be off – 'bye – and I'll ginger up the office, tell Mr Sutton, would you?'

Coverdale, departing, nodded and raised his hand. 'G'bye!'

She was well ahead, up the hill among the gorse bushes. 'Gra-a-ce!' he called. She looked round, halted. He waved, ran, losing speed up the incline. 'Phoof!' he gasped, drawing near, 'old age!' He grinned. 'Well!' he said, 'that was just right – saved me a call on Monday, too.' Together they resumed the climb. Lewis went on, 'He wanted to know what's going on about the bothy, quite right too, but I couldn't tell him anything. Y'know,' he said, 'he's not a bad sort – I'd've introduced you only you'd gone – you're the expert in psychology! He's supposed to be a bit of a clown but I must say there was none of that about him just now. He's pretty fed up, it's beginning to dawn on him at last – you can rub folk up the wrong way too often – this Union business has upset the villagers, not just Blow –' He broke off to call Guinness, who showed signs of sidling away to renew acquaintance with his noxious pomade. 'Heel, boy! Heel! Come on – you'd better go on the lead!'

Grace, handing the lead to Lewis, thrust her hands in her pockets. 'He has a right to join a Union, doesn't he?' It was more statement than query.

Lewis gave a short laugh, a touch derisive. 'It's hardly a matter of rights, darling! More a matter of common sense in his position – and he doesn't seem to have much of that!'

'Why common sense? Principle, surely? A matter of principle.'

Now Lewis looked at her, quizzical and beginning to smile. 'Ah! So you've been talking with Miss Seton! Well,' he shrugged, 'so! It's of no consequence – folly, high principle, whatever! If it comes off, that is. It's not certain yet –'

'What? What do you mean?'

'The cottage!'

'Cottage?'

'Oh.' Lewis halted. 'Oh, Lord. I thought you . . . you seemed to –'

'*What?*' demanded Grace.

'You don't know? About the cottage idea?' She clearly didn't. 'Well . . . oh, dear, I got the impression you . . . well, and I'm not supposed to mention it to anyone . . . Still! *You're* not "anyone".' His frown cleared, and he told her about the cottage.

'*Mr* Seton!' Her eyes were wide, intent.

'Yes!' he said. 'Well, it would have to be, he's the one with the clout, not to mention the money, but it's Honoria Seton's idea, for sure. Spencer's never shown any interest in estate business.'

'Yes . . . er . . . no!' she said abstractedly. 'So I understand.' She said, 'So he's not going to have to go, then?'

'If the purchase goes ahead.'

'If?'

'There are difficulties there too, apparently. I don't know the details, something legal. I was just brought in to give a professional opinion about restoration.'

'And that's . . . all right?'

'Restoration? Oh, yes – the ground floor's perfectly

sound, just the roof; though that's a considerable undertaking. It'll cost a pretty penny but that doesn't seem to bother the Setons.' He said, 'I knew you'd be pleased, you and Tom, if it's salvaged!'

'Oh, yes!'

'But Gracie, it might not happen, so don't get too excited!'

'But it's likely?'

Lewis shrugged. 'Many a slip!' he cautioned. 'And who knows, Mr Seton might yet be persuaded to drop the idea. It's not going to be popular in some quarters . . .'

'Mr Blow,' said Grace.

Lewis laughed. 'You sound like Coverdale – he hasn't half got a chip on his shoulder about Blow!' They were descending the hill, almost back at Barley Bridge. He said, 'Anyway, you understand – you're not supposed to know, darling!'

'I understand,' she said.

He said, 'It won't be popular with the village though, I'm afraid. If it happens.'

'Why not?'

'Why not? Well, special treatment – never goes down well; and he's ruffled a lot of feathers with this Union nonsense – and it *is* nonsense in his case, despite the protestations of you two lovely ladies!' He opened the car door, releasing Guinness. 'Hup, boy!' He produced the ignition key, held it out to her.

She glanced at it. 'You drive,' she said.

'Darling!' he said, and hugged his arm about her shoulders. 'You're still upset about . . .! Look, I'm very sorry I shouted, it was stupid, quite uncalled for!'

'No, no really,' she said. 'But you drive. Time's getting on.'

She was quiet, *piano* again, as they drove away from Chilley Hill. He thought: Roll on October! After which, any children in our lives will be our own!

CHAPTER THIRTEEN

Mrs Cox, propped against the draining-board in the Dower House kitchen, cradled her mid-morning mug of tea and observed: 'Still the best remedy! Ordinary household soap and your salts of tartar! They can keep their patent fally-lallies! That carpet's come up beautiful.'

'Old remedies best remedies,' nodded Mrs Burtle and helped herself to another ginger-nut. 'Something smells tasty, Mrs D!' she said. 'Bit of beef, is it?'

'Steak and kidney,' said Mrs Dunkerley. She poured milk into a saucepan and set it on the range. 'Nice bit of flank. Sheep's kidney, of course, not ox.'

'Not ox?'

'Rubbery stuff, ox,' said Mrs Dunkerley. 'Cooks different from sheep's.' She stood two mugs to warm.

'That's right,' Mrs Cox told them. 'Rubbery.'

'I see where the doctor's car was outside Bates's again. When I came by this morning.' Mrs Burtle shook her head, took another bite of ginger-nut.

'Vicar was there last night,' Mrs Cox supplied. 'There an hour. Happen she's failing.'

'Poor old soul!' Mrs Dunkerley reached down the cocoa tin.

'Wonder she came through the winter!' Mrs Burtle sighed.

'Spring carries them off, often as not.' Mrs Cox adjusted her tone, expressing compassion. 'She's been that uncomfortable. She'll be ready for her call.' She took a sip of tea. 'It's Biddy I feel for, all that lifting.'

'Well, that's right,' said Mrs Burtle. 'Though the Vicar's been a real help there. Twice a day these last few weeks, give her a hand with the lifting.'

'He went extra, last night.' Mrs Cox had the details. 'Not for the lifting, last night. Gone nine o'clock. Stayed till gone ten. I expect she's sinking, and what with the doctor there this morning.'

'Tst tst . . .'

Into the comfortable mournful silence came the clatter of advancing, running feet battering along the passage. 'Oh – here they are, then!' Mrs Dunkerley brightened and busied about the cocoa. 'They'll be ready for their drink!'

The door flew open and Nicholaus, followed by Max, erupted into the kitchen.

'Ooo – ginger-nuts!' Nicholaus applauded. 'Are there any chocolate ones, Mrs Dunkerley?' He hauled a chair out and sat himself in readiness at the table. Max closed the door and took a seat beside him.

'Well, now.' Mrs Dunkerley smiled sideways at him, mixing the cocoa and pouring hot milk. 'Have you been a good boy – done your lessons right?'

'Yes!'

'Then I 'spect there's a chocolate biscuit somewhere if I look!' She carried the mugs to the table. 'Get off all right, did she, Miss Grace?'

'She'll be wet through!' said Mrs Cox, glancing critically at the streaming rain beyond the window.

'It's not *far*!' said Nicholaus cheerfully, ducking to slurp his cocoa. Grace was having a fitting for her bridesmaid's dress at Outwick House this morning.

'She's wearing her raincoat,' said Max. 'And she has an umbrella.'

'She could've borrowed my bike if I'd thought,' said Mrs Cox.

'She'd get wet on a bike!' said Nicholaus, helping himself to a ginger-nut.

'I wonder they didn't think to send the sewing lady over here, morning like this!' observed Mrs Burtle, and exchanged sardonic glances with Mrs Cox, eloquent expression of their view of the grandiose mistress of Outwick.

'And what are you two young men going to do this morning?' Mrs Dunkerley opened a cupboard and drew out a large square tin. 'Too wet to be playing out!'

'Oh, we're cleaning tack! Going in the tack-room,' Nicholaus told her. 'And we're filling the hay nets.'

'And Mother says we can watch when the vet comes,' said Max.

'Shenshi's ever so fat!' said Nicholaus. 'And there are five more weeks – it's probably going to be a boy foal.'

'You can hear its heart,' said Max.

Mrs Dunkerley took the lid off the tin. 'There you are, then – just two each, mind, don't want to spoil your dinner!'

Nicholaus dunked a biscuit in the cocoa and deeply sucked the result before dunking again.

'Oh, Master Nicholaus! That's not polite, now is it? Your mother wouldn't want that!' Mrs Dunkerley gently reproved.

'Mo does it!' Nicholaus serenely replied. 'It's spiffing!' He tilted back his head and in one expert move engorged the sodden remains.

There was a moment's intense silence. Mrs Cox spoke. Casually, she said, 'Where d'you see him do that, then?'

'In his little house!' said Nicholaus. He applied himself to biscuit number two: 'He does it with tea, he doesn't have cocoa, we have tea!'

'Oh!' said Mrs Cox brightly, her tone cajoling. 'Go to tea there, do you?'

'Oh, yes!' said Nicholaus airily. 'We sit on the bed because there's only one chair and Grace sits on that, we sit on the bed with Mo!'

Max said, 'We go to the farm to see Hector and the other horses and sometimes we watch the milking. We don't really go to tea.' He looked at his brother, directing the correction at him but failing to catch his eye.

'We went to tea when it was snowing!' countered Nicholaus. 'Mo made bacon sandwiches and sausages, only they burst in the pan! Well,' he conceded, 'that was lunch, really.'

'That was when he mended the toboggan for us.' Max addressed the three attentive faces. To Nicholaus he said, 'Come on!' He stood up. 'Let's go!' And Nicholaus up-ended his mug, draining its dregs, and jumped down off his chair. He wiped the back of his hand across his mouth. 'I'm going to do Villanelle's saddle first!' he announced, heading for the back door. Remembering himself, he said, 'Thank you, Mrs Dunkerley!'

'Thank you,' echoed Max.

'You'll need your wellingtons . . .' Mrs Dunkerley joined them. 'All here in the porch, look!' She bustled out to assist.

'*Well!*' said Mrs Cox.

'Well, I never!' said Mrs Burtle.

The two regarded each other. 'Well, well, well!' said Mrs Cox. She turned on the tap, took up a dishcloth, washed out her mug with firm purposeful movements. 'In his little house, eh? I wonder does Mrs Mayendorff know about *that*!'

Mrs Dunkerley returned, bringing with her a gust of wet March morning. She closed the door. 'Well!' she said.

'Yes!' said Mrs Cox. 'I was just saying to Winnie, I wonder does Mrs Mayendorff know about *that*!'

Mrs Dunkerley was disinclined to allow of any faults

within 'her' Dower House circle and unhesitatingly re-directed censure. 'Him and his wily ways!' She poured herself a mug of tea. 'Oh, I'm sure Missus *knows* – there's no secrets in this house, why should there be? But she don't know what sort he is, that's for sure!'

'Him and his politics!' said Mrs Burtle.

Mrs Cox drew up a chair. 'I expect Mrs Dunkerley means something else than his politics!' She leaned and selected a chocolate biscuit.

Mrs Dunkerley sighed. 'Not the sort of company she'd want for the boys,' she said. 'Not the sort of influence. Ah, well,' she said, 'he'll be gone out the way soon.'

'He was there again,' said Mrs Cox. She took a bite of biscuit and let the moment mature, two pairs of eyes and two pairs of ears in attendance. 'That hussy on the vegetable stall this time – and her with a ring on her finger!' Mrs Cox's weekly visits to Hestonborough market were a cherished source of information and entertainment. 'Not to mention he'd had a few too many as usual – bike all over the road. Bus had to slow up – that nasty corner past Tilbury Hythe. I wonder Mr Sutton puts up with it.'

Mrs Burtle, either from regard for truth or from a need to supply first-hand information of her own, said, 'Oh, I'll say that for him – he never shows his drink at work, Dan says. Whatever he gets up to, he's a worker! His work'll be missed!'

Mrs Cox, having no answer to that, ignored it. 'I'd have thought Grace would see through him,' she mused. 'I'd have thought as she'd have her wits about her, what with living abroad and such – speaking languages.'

Mrs Dunkerley sought to make two corrections. Stressing 'Miss', she said, 'Oh, Miss Grace is a real lady – for all she's a governess, she's quality. She'd not likely have come across his type, the sort of life she's led. And she never thinks bad of anyone!' she stoutly concluded. 'Never crossed her mind to complain, being dragged out in this weather when they could've sent the fitting woman here for her!'

'Or sent the car to pick her up!' said Mrs Burtle.

'Or sent the car to pick her up!' Mrs Dunkerley concurred.

'All the same, those Coverdales,' was Mrs Cox's opinion.

'The youngster's all right, the young one. He's all right?' ventured Mrs Burtle.

'Miss Moira's in for another baby, then,' said Mrs Dunkerley. 'Fell a bit quick, didn't she? How old's the first one?'

'Can't be more than a year,' Mrs Burtle worked out.

'Have her hands full!' said Mrs Dunkerley, shaking her head.

'Not with *her* money she won't!' Mrs Cox took another biscuit. 'Nanny's hands, more like!'

'She was quite nice, Miss Moira. Always quiet and nice,' Mrs Burtle recollected.

'Not like her sister!' Mrs Cox averred. 'Voice like a parrot!'

Full agreement on this assessment was marked by laughter. 'Aye!' said Mrs Dunkerley. 'Nothing quiet about that one!'

'Big do, same as Moira's,' Mrs Cox suggested.

'Well, it would be, wouldn't it?' said Mrs Dunkerley. 'Two hundred guests. Posted at Parvey Post Office, two hundred invitations if there was ten!'

'Same as Miss Moira's,' said Mrs Cox, point proven. She munched her biscuit. 'Mr Lewis's wedding – that's the one as interests *me*. That's the one as *I* shall like to see. I said to him, "A wedding in a Register Office isn't a proper wedding, now is it?" Yes,' she said with satisfaction, 'I told him!'

'Well, and you were right there, Dora – men need telling! And Miss Grace wouldn't have spoken up for herself, bless her!' Mrs Dunkerley smiled benevolently. 'You can tell she's pleased. Nice white wedding, well, it's what a woman wants, isn't it!'

'And it's right it's in the village, not off in some Register Office in Hestonborough!' said Mrs Burtle. 'And what with Mr Opie being Mr Lewis's friend!' She proffered further grounds for acclaim.

'Hmm,' said Mrs Cox, assuming an air at once sympathetic and knowing. 'If it hadn't of been Mr Lewis it'd've been the Vicar, no doubt about it. He took a real shine to her – well, I wasn't born yesterday. A real shine, he took. And she didn't seem to find *his* company too much against the grain – down there many a day!'

Mrs Dunkerley promptly dispatched that line of inference. 'They were busy on Miss Seton's book, Dora! Still are – lovely drawings she does, lovely one of this house she's doing now!'

Mrs Cox demurred. 'Oh, I'm not saying anything but I reckon he fancied himself a wife there – and a vicarage needs a wife, we'd all like to see Mr Opie married, I'm sure!'

'I was saying to Dan,' Mrs Burtle agreed, 'no sort of life for a man really – all he ever does is go down Parvey of an evening sometimes to sit at another Reverend's table. Not but what the Howarths aren't a nice family, but it's not the same as your own, is it?'

'Miss Seton's too,' Mrs Dunkerley reminded her. 'Miss Seton has him along of an evening. But it isn't the same,' she agreed. 'He's a nice gentleman. Shame.' She sighed, levered herself up from the table. 'Well, this won't get my pudding mixed!' she said.

'And I must get on!' said Mrs Burtle, following the lead and rising.

'Aye, time ticks on!' said Mrs Cox. 'What're you doing for pudding, Mrs D?'

'Apple Charlotte today,' said Mrs Dunkerley, departing towards the larder. 'Not too heavy after the steak and kidney,' she explained, disappearing into her store-room.

Mrs Burtle carried the mugs to the sink. Mrs Cox took another chocolate biscuit and popped it in her overall pocket before replacing the lid and carrying the tin back to its cupboard. 'They're off to Germany, then, Grace and the boys,' she said, collecting up her polish and her dusters.

'It's a while yet, isn't it?' said Mrs Burtle, collecting hers.

'Next month somewhen.' They left the kitchen, plodded down the passage together. 'Funny thing, isn't it?' she said, 'as how there's no photographs of Mr M about. You'd think, wouldn't you, as how there'd be a photograph, what with them not seeing him so long?'

'Perhaps he don't like having his photograph taken,' Mrs Burtle suggested. 'I know my Dan won't go on a photograph, not for love nor money, lots of men don't want a photograph.'

'No more did my Billy,' Mrs Cox pointed out, 'but I had one done just the same, with him going away to the war . . .' She sighed heavily. 'And a good thing too, seeing as it's all I've got of him now, all his children know of him . . .'

They had reached the front hall and paused there. Mrs Burtle lowered her head and murmured, 'Aye, Dora . . .' acknowledging the sad loss, and remembering her own.

'Ah, well!' said Mrs Cox, achieving philosophical resignation. 'What had to be had to be!' She flipped out her duster. 'Funny, though, there's none of him about. And I for one have never heard him mentioned, not a word! You'd think the little lads'd say *something* – not even over Christmas!'

'Well, p'raps they did when we weren't here,' Mrs Burtle reasonably offered.

'Boys need a man about the place,' said Mrs Cox. 'They need their father, as I know to my cost! Need a strong hand. It's all very well,' she said, 'but a man wouldn't be letting young Max go round with that hat on day in day out – aside from anything else it's bad for his hair, child needs air about his head! You'd think she'd know that, but there you are! It's horses takes up her attention.' She rubbed absently at the banister with her duster. 'Funny business, if you ask me, him over there and them over here all this while. More to it than's ever said.'

Mrs Burtle glanced about uncertainly, and made no reply.

'Oh, she's not about!' Mrs Cox assured her. 'She's out in the stables, been there since half-past nine. Well!' she said, 'I'd better go and see how my carpet's drying out. Come and have a look, Winnie, when you've done your brass. It's come up lovely with that soap and tartar!'

'I need more saddle-soap,' said Nicholaus, suiting the action to the word.

'If you put too much on it takes too long to dry,' said Max, polishing at a head-band.

'Bubbles and foam, bubbles and foam,' said Nicholaus, gleefully producing froth on the saddle propped before him. 'Ollie calls it dubbin, he doesn't call it saddle-soap,' he observed.

'It's another word for it,' said Max.

'I know,' said Nicholaus. He tucked his lower lip under and practised his ostler's whistle in the manner of Ollie Furber. Ollie Furber was on permanent loan from the Hall's ground staff to assist Mrs Mayendorff with the horses, the obvious candidate for the job, having been stable-lad for the Setons in his youth, his father the coachman there in the good old days before the motor-car ousted horses. There were no horses at the Hall any more. Uncle Spencer did not like riding, and Aunt Honoria had given up ages ago because she didn't enjoy it much either, so Ollie Furber had joined the ground staff. He was very pleased to be back working with horses and Mother was very pleased too, she said he was a first-rate hand and she could trust him entirely, and he shared the exercising with her, riding Villanelle and Burgundy, and even Shenshi sometimes, though no one was riding Shenshi at the moment, she just had to be taken for walks. Ollie knew everything about horses. He didn't talk much, but he whistled a lot, and sometimes smiled. He never minded you asking questions. He looked peculiar because he had only one eye, a horse had kicked him in the face when he was a boy, but he said he got on very well with one eye, thank you, and he reckoned that horse had saved his life because he couldn't go to the war. He was nice, Ollie.

'He said *he* doesn't like tractors, either,' said Nicholaus. 'He said what Mr Williams said, he said tractors are no good for the land, not like horses. I asked him.' He took up a dry cloth and began to mop at the foam.

'You've got too much on,' Max told him mildly.

Nicholaus was not worried. '*I* like the tractor,' he said, mopping. 'It makes you all shiver when it's going along' – he gave an extempore demonstration of vibrating – 'and I like the smell, it's not like car smell. That's horrid!'

'It's because the fuel's different. It's paraffin. I helped Mo put some in.'

'When?' Nicholaus challenged.

'You were still in the bothy with Grace, getting bread for the hens.'

'Oh.' Nicholaus considered the relative merits of putting petrol in the tractor and crumbling bread for hens.

Max, rubbing at the head-band, said, 'I don't like Mrs Cox.'

Nicholaus looked up from his mopping. 'Why not?'

Max didn't reply immediately. He held up the head-band, inspecting it. He said, 'She asks things.'

'What things?'

Max stood up and carried the finished head-band to its hook. 'Oh – things . . .' he said. He took down some stirrup leathers. 'She doesn't smile properly.' He returned to his seat.

'Mrs Burtle's got a broken tooth at the front,' said Nicholaus, visualizing smiles.

'You do these,' said Max. 'I'll finish that.'

'Why? Oh, I don't like doing those!'

'You've got it too wet.'

'I haven't!'

'Oh, all right.' Max proceeded with the stirrup leathers.

Nicholaus took up another dry cloth and attacked the froth. 'See? It's not too wet!' He resumed his ostler's whistle. In a while he said, 'Grace can buy us some more glue this afternoon. And that shiny paper.'

'Cellophane.'

'Yes.' The history class was presently devoted to making a model of Poundell Cottage. Lewis had told Grace how to do it. He had shown Grace how to take the measurements. When he was a student he had made models, so he told her how to set about it. They were going to have real thatch, made out of straw. They had collected very small twigs to make the wattle and used plaster of Paris for the daub. They spread old sheets on the schoolroom floor and newspaper on the table because it all made such a mess. They wore aprons, too. People came in to watch, Mother and

Aunt Honoria, and Mrs Dunkerley, and Mr Opie, and Mr Hatherway had looked in too. He was pleased, he said it made good use of their maths, and he talked about Area, then. Lewis hadn't seen it yet. He was going to see it this afternoon when he brought Grace home from shopping in Hestonborough. He had said it should be at least two feet long on the front elevation, to get everything in, and he was quite right! You did things in inches and feet, not in centimetres, in England. They had to measure all the flagstones on the floor at the cottage. They weren't sure yet what to make the stones of in the model. They'd probably just paint them on cardboard, Grace thought. It was Nicholaus's idea, the shiny paper for the windows. Cellophane. He had told Grace that they could take it with them, the model, to show Vati, but she had said it was too big and it would break, even if they packed it ever so carefully, it was too far all the way to Berlin.

He paused in his whistling to observe, 'Vati can see it when he comes for Grace's wedding!'

'He isn't coming,' said Max, simply. He bent to adjust the leather on his knee and continued polishing.

'He is – I asked Grace!'

'I know. She said, "We'll see."'

'That means "yes"!' Nicholaus laughed, dismissing doubt.

Max did not reply.

From the yard came the swish and throb of a motor-car arriving. 'The vet!' cried Nicholaus, and abandoning Villanelle's saddle he leaped for the door. 'Come on!' he called, pulling at the latch. 'It's stopped raining!' he whooped. 'We can ride without our oilskins today!' The wind caught the door and clattered it wide. 'Come on!' he urged and bounded away.

Max completed his stirrup leather and hung it in its

place. He picked up the rag on the saddle and spread it to dry. Adjusting his cap, pulling it down firmly against the wind, he closed the tack-room door behind him and went down the yard to watch the vet. Perhaps he would let him use the stethoscope again, to listen to the foal's heart.

CHAPTER FOURTEEN

'Oh, the cellophane, the cellophane!' sang Nicholaus, waving the packet as he raced to show Max in the schoolroom.

'Steady on, Nicholaus!' his mother called. To Grace and Lewis, still coming through the porch, she said, 'Wouldn't you two like some tea first? No? You sure? Well, let's go and see this model, then!' In her stockinged feet, riding boots discarded elsewhere, she padded down the hall. 'Oh,' she recalled, passing the telephone, 'Lilian rang, Grace – I jotted it down here.'

'Come *on*!' Nicholaus urged from the schoolroom. The boys were standing almost to attention, anticipation and apprehension equally etched across their faces.

'My word!' said Lewis. 'That *is* good! Very good indeed!' He regarded the model, genuinely impressed. Stepping forward to make closer examination, he glanced at Grace. 'Clever girl!' He smiled, and remembered to add, 'Clever boys!' He said, 'Tom told me it was good, but I didn't expect it to be such a professional job!'

'And look,' Nicholaus was flushed with success, 'that's the chimney pot we're going to put on – show him, Max!' Max came up with it and carefully balanced it atop the stack. 'It's a cork,' he explained. 'We painted it. It's got to be glued on.'

'It looks just like the real thing – goodness! You've even hollowed it out!' Lewis approved.

Nicholaus let out a delighted yowl. 'Oh, you've got a potato!' He was pointing at his mother's feet.

'A potato?' Vaguely mystified, Mrs Mayendorff considered the hole in her sock.

'That's what they're called!' said Nicholaus. 'That's what –'

Grace stepped forward. 'Here – the glue, Nicholaus!' She presented it before his face. 'It's the special glue – Lewis bought it, wasn't that kind!'

'Oh, *thanks*!' cried Nicholaus. 'The paste goes dry, you see!' he told Lewis.

Lewis smiled. 'You need the proper fixative for model-making – I should have thought of it before.'

'Can we put it all together properly now?' Max asked of Grace.

'Almost,' she said. 'We have the windows to do first.'

'Oh, yes.'

Lewis, scrutinizing detail, said, 'It's worked well, the twigs and plaster!'

'The twigs are woven, underneath,' Max said, 'just like they really are.'

His mother said, 'Have you decided yet – how it's going to open?'

'We're going to take the top off,' said Nicholaus.

'It's too big, the front bit, and it would catch on the thatch every time,' Max explained.

Grace said, 'And making hinges secure would be difficult. It's easier just to lift the roof right off.'

'And you can see everything better then,' said Nicholaus. 'And we're going to put a bed in, for the man, and I'm going to make a frying pan and' – he sketched generous dimensions in the air – 'oh, we're going to make lots of things for him!'

'Man?' said Lewis.

'Yes – you know! The man – the old man – the gipsy!'

'Ah!' said Lewis. 'Oh, I see! Old Tully.'

'He had his bed downstairs, well, there isn't any upstairs, so he slept downstairs, in this room!' Nicholaus showed him.

'Uh huh?' said Lewis. 'Yes, I expect that's right.'

'It is!' said Nicholaus. 'Mo told us. Mo knew him, you know, he was his friend, he often went there. He was a –' he turned to Grace, frowned, 'what was it Mo said, Grace?'

Max said, 'A poacher.'

'Poacher!' said Nicholaus. 'That means you steal things!' he said. 'Only things to eat, though,' he pointed out. 'He taught Mo to poacher!'

'Poach,' said Max.

'Poach,' said Nicholaus. 'He told Mo how to do it!'

'Heavens!' Mrs Mayendorff, amused, wryly observed, 'I don't know that I can approve of this! Well, just so long as he doesn't decide to teach you two how to do it!' She laughed.

Lewis said, 'I didn't know you'd met him!' and looked at Grace.

'Oh, we often see him!' Nicholaus assured Lewis.

Grace had stooped over the model, adjusting something. She said, 'Paths have crossed sometimes. We go to the farm, to see the horses.' She continued her adjustments.

'And to watch him milking!' Nicholaus reminded her.

'Oh,' said Lewis. 'I see . . .'

Mrs Mayendorff said, 'He's quite a card – or so I gather. Anyway, he has my vote, as they say. Invaluable over that water business. We'd still be waiting if we'd left it all to thingummy.' She was moving to the door. 'Let's get our tea – I'm jolly parched! Nicholaus – cut along to the kitchen and tell Mrs Dunkerley we're ready now, will you?'

'Eeow! I want to make the windows!'

'Off with you! Windows after tea.' From the door she said, 'Do come through to the sitting-room – you must be longing for tea!' A glance at Grace and Lewis as she departed.

Grace lifted her head and met the concentrated gaze of Max, watching her. She swiftly turned towards the doorway. 'What did Lilian want?' she called to Mrs Mayendorff, and hurried from the room.

'Oh, it's about fittings,' came Mrs Mayendorff's reply.

Grace was a while attending to her telephone call.

'All right?' asked Mrs Mayendorff, pouring tea for her.

'Oh, yes! Just fittings and so on – rehearsals soon.' She smiled cheerily. 'Lilian likes a good chat! Oh – thanks!' She took her tea. 'Sorry – I interrupted you!'

'Oh, I was just telling Lewis about the Furber proposition.'

Lewis said, 'It's a very good idea. You're rather isolated out here, it's a good solution.' The Furbers, Ollie and his wife, were to move over from the Hall mews and into the Dower House once Grace left in the autumn; her room and the three adjoining were to be turned into a flat. 'It's sensible to have someone living in.'

'Oh, I'm not worried about *that*!' Mrs Mayendorff waved a sandwich dismissively. 'But it's certainly right for the horses! I won't have my stable lads after September!' The smile she gave her sons was warmly affectionate but entirely unsentimental. She went on, 'Actually, Ollie's going to camp out here while they're in Germany; Shenshi, you know.'

'The vet thinks it's going to be a boy,' Nicholaus told Lewis.

'Well,' said Mrs Mayendorff indulgently, 'there's no way of knowing, but whichever it is, it should be a beauty. Hoping for great things – brilliant stallion, sired a couple of superb eventers.'

'It's called Maharajah, the father,' said Max, running his finger under the band of his cap and adjusting the peak.

'A right royal name, eh?' Lewis jovially returned.

Mrs Mayendorff said, 'Cake, anyone?' offering a plate. 'Dundee, I think – or the sponge – cut it, would you, Grace?' To Lewis she said, 'So do go ahead whenever you like with the flat. Kitchen'll be the only real upheaval, wouldn't you say? Bathroom's there, nothing much to do in the other rooms – anyway, I'll leave it with you and Grace.' She rose, flexing her back, easing it. 'Look, would you excuse me? I'm off for a bath, dining over at the Hall – all right? No, don't get up, do finish your tea in peace.' Lewis reseated himself, but as Mrs Mayendorff quit the room, Grace set down her cup and murmuring, 'Back in a moment!', followed her.

'Mrs Mayendorff!'

Mrs Mayendorff paused on the stairs. 'Yes?'

'Next Saturday afternoon – that's the point-to-point, isn't it?' Mrs Mayendorff confirmed that it was and that yes, the boys would be out most of the day; and that yes, Grace would be free to partake in the wedding rehearsal proposed by Lilian.

Resuming her ascent, she said, 'We'd manage anyhow. Don't worry about Saturdays for the time being – bound to be wedding palaver for the next few weeks – I recall it well!' she added sardonically. 'By the way,' she turned, 'do invite Lewis to stay on this evening, of course. A word to Mrs Dunkerley – there'll be no difficulty with supper, I'm sure.'

'Thank you,' said Grace.

But Grace did not extend the invitation to Lewis; by the time she had organized the boys through their tea, and dissuaded them from further work on the model, on the grounds that it was too late to start that evening, and then diverted them by suggesting a visit to the stables and Shenshi, to 'show Lewis' – by then her charges were due for baths and bed; and she confessed herself 'ready for an early night tonight, Lewis . . .' The tone gentle, even propitiatory, but also one that he recognized as final.

'Of course, darling,' he complied. He kissed her on the cheek in parting; the boys were still present.

Grace tucked Nicholaus into bed and left him choosing tonight's story from the *Boys' Book of Adventures*, then strode to the bathroom to hustle Max; and walked straight into what she had been avoiding, half-aware, half instinctively, since before tea.

'Grace,' he said, regarding her from his cocoon of bath-towel, 'does Lewis like Mo?'

'What?' She reined in her voice, hearing its edge. She said, 'I don't know – he doesn't know him. Come along now – still not in your pyjamas!' And the edge was still there. Plunging her arm into the water, she pulled out the plug. 'Have you done your teeth yet? You haven't cleaned your teeth?' She addressed herself to towelling him down from behind.

'Will you see Mo, when you are married?'

'Of course not! You'll be at school!' She thrust the towel aside. 'There now! Into your pyjamas quicksticks!'

'Only, you'll still be able to, won't you?'

'Here – let me do the buttons . . .'

He watched her quick fingers. 'Grace, why did you mind when Nicholaus said potato?'

'I *didn't* mind!'

'But – you were cross. Is it rude?'

'I *wasn't* cross! Here – this foot up, please!' She bustled him into his pyjama trousers. 'Well,' she said briskly, 'yes – it's not very polite!'

'You didn't mind when Mo said it yesterday. When Mo showed us his potato, you laughed. We laughed.'

The edge, in spite of herself, intensified: 'I mean, it is not very polite to point out that someone has a hole in their sock in front of other people. There now!' She tied his pyjama cord firmly. 'Teeth!'

'Oh. Would Lewis mind?'

She emitted a brief sigh of impatience. 'Your mother might have been embarrassed.'

'She wasn't embarrassed,' said Max.

She cried, 'Oh, Max, what does it *matter*? Hurry up and get on with your teeth!'

She tried to retrieve the moment, telling him in jollying tones as she spread the towel on the rail that Nicholaus was 'tucked up and waiting, ready for the story'! But the silence between them then had nothing to do with the limitations imposed by a toothbrush restraining Max's tongue.

She took the boys to morning church. It was Palm Sunday; and as Aunt Honoria had pointed out, it would be 'useful' to the boys' education to witness the exposition, Anglican style, of this aspect of the Christian mysteries – and anyway, the church would look pretty with its array of ferns and foliage and potted palms from the Hall's hot-houses. Tom addressed his flock, a 'fairish turnout today', with his usual flair and vigour, commending the congregation to take note, at this season, of the fickleness of human responses: easily moved to adulation by the appearance of triumph; all too easily moved to baying opposition by any subsequent discomfiture. 'It is,' he pointed out, 'the same people who cheer and carpet the favourite's way with palms, who five days later jeer and hiss at the foot of His Cross.' The human appetite for victims, he explained, was universal, rooted in envy and fear, a lust which only God, through Christ and the Holy Spirit, could absolve.

Grace heard, with little real attention. Vaguely she noted the Mystery, automatically relegated it to its customary agnostic corner. She was tired. She had slept heavily but not well. Such attention as she had was preoccupied with Max. She had spent some essence of herself last night; she had jollied on brightly, read the story with animation, 'did' all the voices with gusto, raised ooos and aaahs and laughs; given each his goodnight hug-and-kiss, recited 'Sweet dreams and soft repose!' and duly received their chorused chant of: 'Lie on your back and you won't hurt your nose!'

'Ni-ni, you two!'

'Ni-ni, Grace!' from the two of them.

And yet.

Nicholaus fidgeted a bit during service; he dropped his hymn-book twice, but he was really very good. Max was quiet and still. But then – so he usually was.

Miss Seton joined them in the aisle afterwards, she was coming back to lunch with them. Mrs Coverdale was there. She and her husband and some house-guests. Statutory pleasantries were exchanged, comments on the weather, social smiles, inclusive of Grace who responded in kind.

They rode home in the Seton motor-car. Lunch was of Mrs Dunkerley's excellent best efforts, the afternoon and evening pleasantly diverting, a gentle walk with Aunt Honoria round the grounds before the rain set in and then games of Snap and Ludo after a session making windows for the model, Aunt Honoria joining in, hugely enjoying the mess and quite as delighted as the boys when success crowned their efforts. A delightful day. And yet. Throughout it all a phrase beat in Grace's head: 'Roll on, Germany! Oh – roll on, Germany!' Some space, some solitude, some time to sort out . . . whatever it was . . . It would be all right, once they were married. It would. It was just that, it was all so . . . incessant, so much requirement to be . . . happy and blithe, since the engagement. And she would be, she would be happy and blithe once they were married but – but just now, she needed . . . Oh! Roll on, Germany!

1930

April

CHAPTER FIFTEEN

Spen said, 'All it lacks – apart from a sound roof, of course – is roses round the door! It's charming, quite charming – I'd forgotten how quaint, years since I've been down here.' He smiled round at his sister and Archie behind him on the crumbling brick path in the April sunshine. 'Well, shall we go in? I see our prospective tenant has arrived.' Maurice Coverdale's bicycle lay propped beside the capsizing porch, the elmboard door stood ajar.

There were two shallow steps down. They stood for a moment adjusting to the half-light. It was a big room, low but long, its flagged floor smooth with the wear of centuries. Honoria, inspecting that, declared with some surprise: 'Dry as a bone!'

'Splendid inglenook,' observed Archie, going to examine it.

Spen said, 'He must be out there somewhere,' and stooped through another door to peer through a low window in the slot of a room beyond. 'Yes,' he said, returning, 'he's out there by the well.' He reached up and touched the ceiling, running fingertips across the tongue-and-groove boards. 'Tarred, apparently – on the upper side. In Gower's report – it explains why the place is tight and dry despite the roof. Clever.'

'Look at this!' Archie had partially disappeared within the cavernous chimney. Honoria and Spen joined him to stand in the ashes of Old Tully's last fire and peer upwards to the disc of blue sky ten feet away. 'Primitive, eh? But obviously effective – just this one break in the shaft – and built to last, by Jove – just look at the size of these rocks!'

'As of Gibraltar!' Spen agreed. 'Mind your jacket, Nonni!' He fended her shoulder from the soot-lined stack, and they ducked out, back into the room.

'Ah! There you are!' Spen acknowledged Maurice Coverdale arriving from the lean-to kitchen. He held out his hand which Coverdale duly shook, and then gestured an introduction: 'Archie Winterstone – Maurice Coverdale – my sister you know of course. You were out at the well just now – all right, is it? Water in it? Things working and so on? The report seemed to think it's viable.'

'It's never run dry,' said Coverdale. 'Yes, everything works, I just had a drink. Chain's a bit rusty, but they say you need a bit of iron in your diet!' His sudden grin invited, and enjoined, laughter. His shirt was open-necked, the sleeves rolled to the elbow; the tie he wore supported corduroy trousers much the worse for wear, yet his was a debonair presence, almost dandy, despite the foremost impression of animal muscularity.

Spen said, 'I thought it was time we should meet – all right getting away from work this morning? Good. I gather from Gower that you've found the last few weeks somewhat unintelligible, but I take it you now understand the delay?'

'Yes. And thank you.'

Spen waved a dismissive hand. 'Seemed good sense on several grounds. So. Now – I'd like to get some idea of the place, what you're likely to need here – you know of course that we can't connect electricity, too far from the mains, but Honoria tells me that there are portable gas gadgets nowadays, she'll be happy to sort out the kitchen end of things with you. Three rooms here? No "upstairs", is there?'

'No. And here there are four rooms if you count the

workshop –' Coverdale gave a nod in the direction of a corner door.

'Workshop!' Spen found the concept entertaining.

'He kept tools and things in there.'

'Ah – yes. You knew him, of course.' Spen regarded the door with amusement. 'Made his traps and snares in there, did he?'

'That's right.' Coverdale was unabashed.

'Pick up any hints?'

'A few.'

The two men smiled, each to the other.

Honoria, watching, thought, 'Heavens! They're . . . flirting!' She flinched, for Archie.

Spen was saying, 'Well, you know the place – so show me over!'

Maurice crossed the room, threw wide a further door and with a sweep of arm ushered his landlord on. 'The bedroom,' he said, and the two disappeared within.

Honoria found her tongue. 'I've seen this cottage before, in a sense!' she said cheerily. 'The boys' model-making, you know, so I've seen it all in miniature! And very good it turns out to be,' she gently propelled Archie into motion, 'but I'd like to see this kitchen I'm supposed to be advising about!'

She did her best; she kept going a stream of comments, hypotheses and observations as she toured the narrow lean-to, peering into the old brick boiler, opening and inspecting a decrepit meat-safe, guessing and assessing measurements here and there, examining the stone sink; involving Archie as she went, though not, she knew, engaging his attention. Her own was no less divided. She was indignant with her brother. Was this why he had made the morning's arrangement? To discomfit Archie – to indulge a little spiteful tit-for-tat over that Greek or whatever he was? A matter over and done with weeks ago? That would be disgraceful, and quite bad enough – but the alternative! Surely not! Spen could surely not be taking a fancy to young Coverdale – smitten with him? And as for *him*! What was *he* playing at, young Maurice? Playing – yes, that was exactly the word! Whatever that young man might or might not be, he had not 'been sent into this world in deviant form', as Spen expressed it. Far from it indeed, if gossip had any substance. She hardly knew with whom she was more indignant, her brother or young Coverdale; and she was confronted with the unpalatable fact that she now wished she had left well alone, not concerned herself with principles. What was it Archie had said? 'It sounds as though in the long run Hollisfont might be happier without him.'

At this moment of an April morning in the cottage kitchen, Archie glumly propped against the stone sink, captive to her constructed chat, the sound of voices and shared, quiet laughter floating to them from the 'bedroom', she was quite of that opinion. That young man had a talent for upsetting applecarts – intentionally or not!

The voices approached, and then receded. They had evidently gone out through the front door. Enough of this! thought Honoria. I can at least impose *some* restraint on their games by interposing my presence! 'Come on, Archie!' she said briskly. 'They must be looking at the roof, let's join them – I've finished here for now!'

Archie glanced at her. 'You go ahead,' he said. 'I'll take a look round inside.' He was, she saw, tight-faced; unhappy, angry.

Heading for the front door, she observed to herself with exasperation that sex in human affairs did not seem worth the candle! Forever bringing trouble!

It was a view she was at once disposed to revise as up to the porch bounced Nicholaus and Max, two products of the system that entirely justified it, and whom she hugged with delight. 'What a lovely surprise!' she cried. 'What are you young scallywags doing down here this morning?'

Nicholaus waved a tape-measure. 'We're going to make the well! We've finished the house and we're making the garden and we're putting the well in because the man *has* to have water!'

'And we're making the bucket out of a bottle-top,' said Max, 'but we haven't got a little chain so we'll use string, only it will have to be thin to wind round the roller.'

'I've got a little chain!' said Honoria. 'It's pinchbeck – I think it came out of a cracker, a long time ago!'

Max said, 'What's pinchbeck?'

'Oh, it's cheap metal, I'm not sure what kind – it's used for making pretend jewellery! I'll look it out today – it could be just the thing! Oh – Grace! Hello! And Tom! Good morning!'

'Aunt Honoria's got a chain!' Nicholaus informed them. 'She's giving it us today! Come on! Let's go to the well!' And he was off round the cottage.

'Wait – wait, Nicholaus!' called Grace. 'We don't want you falling in! Wait!'

'Oh, it's got a lid,' Max said.

The party hurried after Nicholaus. 'How nice to see you!' Honoria told Grace and Tom, a statement particularly resonant with feeling in her present circumstances.

Tom said, 'I'm playing hookey! There's a bell-ringing rehearsal this morning.'

'Oh, the . . .?'

Tom nodded. 'And Mrs Coverdale's there with Lilian, so they don't need anyone else supervising . . .'

'Ah!' said Honoria diplomatically. They rounded the rear of the cottage. By the well stood Spencer Seton and Maurice Coverdale. Nicholaus was dipping his fingers in the bucket and sucking them. Honoria said, '*We're* all here because . . .' She paused. Tom and Grace had clearly been surprised to see her and were equally surprised to see the others. 'Well, perhaps Spen should . . . well, it makes no difference now, *I* can tell you – it's all been kept dark, but Spen has bought the cottage and he's having it restored!'

'Oh, well *done*!' cried Tom. 'Splendid! Capital!' He beamed. 'Er – and is it to be let? Or preserved for posterity, or –?'

'Coverdale's to have it,' said Honoria. 'Instead of the bothy.'

Max clapped his hands together. 'Mo?' he cried and ran calling to Nicholaus, 'Mo's going to live here – in our cottage! He's going to live in it!'

Honoria laughed. 'Well! It's certainly a popular move in *one* quarter!' she said.

'Coverdale?' Tom was evidently putting two and two together. 'So he won't be leaving us, then?'

'Mr Sutton's very keen to keep him,' said Honoria, firmly opting for the simplest explanation.

She and Tom were looking at Grace who now spoke. 'Oh, it's splendid, as Tom says!' She smiled. 'Wonderful that it's going to be saved!'

'I knew you'd be pleased, my dear!' said Honoria. 'So's Lewis – he's going to be in charge of the restorations – very pleased to see it saved, such a rare period piece! Shall we join them? Look at this well?'

'. . . the way they'd heard?' Spen was intrigued, in conversation with Coverdale.

'No idea! He'd died in the night; he was all right the previous evening – just a bit tired.'

'Extraordinary!' Spen nodded good morning to the latest arrivals and told them, 'Extraordinary thing! Old Tully's tribe turned up here to collect the remains within hours of his dying – literally a few hours! But how did they know? No one in the village knew. Unless,' he said to Coverdale, 'one of them came after you'd left and was here when he died!'

Coverdale shrugged. 'He wasn't expecting anyone. It's possible, I s'pose, but the camp's the other side of Seddington – about twenty-five miles and they don't use cars, just horses.' He shrugged again.

'They were surely coming this way anyhow,' said Tom. 'A coincidence, I understood?'

'No!' said Spen. 'That's the point – they'd brought a coffin, in a wagon – they knew he'd died! Extraordinary!'

Nicholaus, round-eyed, said, 'A dead body!' Both boys were agog.

Their aunt said soothingly, 'He was a very old man, my dears – old, old people die, you know – it's natural!' She smiled brightly. 'Now let's get on with taking our measurements, shall we? You've brought a pencil – oh, good, and a pad.' She steered them into action, directing a discouraging frown at her brother in the process. But Spen either failed to read her message or chose to disregard it, being intensely interested in the mystery. 'Where did they bury him?' He turned to Tom. 'Do they qualify for Christian burial, travellers, gipsies?'

Tom said, 'Not strictly speaking – strictly speaking, Christian baptism is the qualification.'

'What do they do, then?'

'I'm afraid I don't know!' said Tom.

Coverdale said, 'They say the girl's buried on Chilley Hill.'

'Girl?' said Spen.

Honoria's voice rose. 'So that's four-and-a-half feet *that* way – what about this other side, it's not quite straight, is it? Come over this side and see!'

'The one they tarred and feathered,' said Coverdale.

'Tarred and feathered? Who? When?' Spen was fascinated.

'Gipsy girl. Sixty, seventy years ago – in Tully's lifetime, anyway. The villagers. They tarred and feathered her and chucked her in the river.'

'Good God!' cried Spen. 'For what?'

Coverdale said, 'Oh, a bit of . . . hanky-panky.' He grinned. 'With a married man from the village.'

Honoria, abandoning tactics, turned on the two men. 'I hardly think we need to hear *that* horrid story!' She glared.

Her brother, perhaps obtuse, but anyway unrepentant, regarded her with interest. 'You know the story! You never told me! Well, well! The dear good folk of Hollisfont!' He laughed.

Coldly, Honoria said, 'Weren't you particularly keen to inspect the roof this morning? Time's getting on.'

How Spencer Seton would respond to this rare demonstration of hostility from his sister was never put to the test. Guinness, at full stretch, hurtled among them and joyfully greeted Grace; down the garden in his wake came Lewis Gower and Archie.

Lewis stepped ahead. 'Good morning!' he called to the assembly. He brought with him all the good humour of his natural disposition, enhanced by the unexpected sight of Grace. To her, aside, he said, 'Darling! Lovely surprise!' and covertly pressed her hand. 'Tom!' He nodded greeting. 'And we're going to have the well, too, are we?' He smiled benignly at the boys. Turning to Mr Seton, he said, 'I was in the area – just been over to Brunley, the road business – thought I'd take another look at the end-beam here while I was about it!'

Archie strolled on and stationed himself to give close attention to the boys and their measuring. Grace, with a final hug to Guinness, did likewise. Tom took up with Guinness and made a tour of the boundary hedge while business was discussed. Scraps of that were audible to him on the warm, still air: '. . . move in now,' Seton was saying, '. . . get in anyone's way, would it?' Lewis: '. . . the end of the week perhaps . . . notified the office yet, so . . .' And Seton, laughing: 'Ah! . . . cat among the pigeons . . . friend Blow!' Lewis: '. . . the Board of Trustees . . .' And Seton again, laughing: '. . . yes, I know! Well, he's a by-the-book man!' enjoying irony. Guinness, bustling along the hedge, suddenly doubled back and energetically investigated a rustle. 'Watchagot, boy?' murmured Tom. 'Fetchit – seek!' But whatever it was had very sensibly made an escape, and Guinness resumed his bustling. Hands in pockets, Tom turned at the foot of the garden and began to pick his way back over the mess of rotting vegetation that had been Tully's kitchen patch. What, he mused, was going on? More than met the eye. He did not know Seton well; but he knew when a man was more excited than occasion demanded – the child in him governing the man. There were currents running that had little to do with simple property transactions, as had been made especially apparent in Miss Honoria's demeanour this morning. They had more to do with personal emotions; and unless he was very much mistaken, involved those least governable of emotions, our old incalculable concomitant, sex. He was mildly surprised, but not very. In his experience age did not necessarily modify its drive, particularly in men; and particularly, perhaps, in homosexual men whom society condemned to subterfuge? Subterfuge was a powerful aphrodisiac, if one were needed. As to Coverdale – well, he, alas, showed no sign of growing up as the years went by, captive as ever to the impulse of the moment and an easy target for flattering attention; he'd have no qualms about playing games with Spencer Seton this morning. What a pity, though. Sad, really, and a sorry adjunct to the worthy cause, the rescue of this building . . . He leaned and patted Guinness who had joined him. 'Find anything?' he inquired. As he resumed his progress, side-stepping the cabbage stumps, he glanced up. He saw Grace look at Coverdale, and Coverdale look at her. He blinked. Something very like a qualm shot through him and was gone. He blinked again, plodded on.

' . . . pepper-corn rent,' Seton was saying, and turning from Lewis addressed Coverdale, 'to cover legalities . . .'

'Teeny-weeny!' said Nicholaus, pronouncing on the bucket's dimensions.

'Will the bottle-top be too big?' Max was anxious.

'Oh, I don't think so,' Grace assured him. 'If it is, we'll make one out of plasticine!'

Archie and Honoria watched over Max's shoulder as he did a different sum. 'Can we have the chain *today*?' asked Nicholaus, and 'Please *may* we!' corrected Grace, slipping her arm round him and smiling. 'I shall bring it with me this very evening!' Aunt Honoria promised. 'That's right!' Archie told Max. 'Sixteen square feet – well done!' Busy good humour prevailed, earlier tensions so thoroughly dispelled that Tom fractionally wondered if they had existed. The benevolent effect of contented children! Grace said happily, 'Come and look, Tom – a proper scale drawing!' And he willingly hurried over.

Seton approached. He stood by Archie, obligingly admired the drawing. With the merest touch to Archie's arm, he then said, 'We're all finished. A drink before lunch, don't you think? Honoria?'

Everyone appeared to be 'finished'; and according to Honoria's watch it was quarter to twelve. The party drifted away from the well. Lewis joined Grace and the boys, bringing up the rear as the Setons and Archie led off round the cottage, Tom and Coverdale a pace behind. They stood for a moment in their groups in front of the cottage, making valedictions. Coverdale walked on and collected his bicycle. He mounted it and set in motion. 'G'bye!' he said and cycled off. Tom thought, *Lèse-majesté* if ever I saw it! My word, that's a cocky young man! Lewis said to Grace, 'Darling, look, I'll run you home! No – no trouble at all, jump in – Tom, can you cram into the back with kids and dogs?' But Tom opted to walk, escorting Miss Seton part-way.

As Lewis held the door for Grace, from St Aldhelm's tower in a sudden cascade of glorious tumult came the peal of wedding bells, flooding the sunlit air. He grinned. 'Our turn soon!' he said.

1930

May

CHAPTER SIXTEEN

Lewis hugged Grace in glee and relief. 'Oh, I'm so glad!' he cried. 'Of course I'm sorry about the measles but everyone has to have measles – and God bless Max!' The German trip was off. 'You're all right, aren't you?' He peered anxiously into her face. 'Not going to get measles?'

She smiled, shook her head. 'I've had them.'

She seemed a bit low. 'He'll be all right, Gracie – there are no complications, are there?'

'No.'

'I suppose Nicholaus will get them now – they're everywhere, half the school-children in Hestonborough down.' He somehow couldn't help sounding rather unsuitably cheerful – there would be no visit to Germany now, not in Grace's time. Herr Mayendorff was leaving for a six-month business tour in the United States shortly. He adjusted his tone. 'How's he feeling, poor little chap? I seem to remember it's jolly uncomfortable.'

'His temperature's high – 103 degrees. He feels rotten,' she said wanly, 'and the rash isn't through yet.' She sighed. 'Do you want to bring Guinness in?' They were still standing on the threshhold, neither out nor in, the Rover parked on the gravel sweep. Lewis carried the flowers he had brought her, a parting gift pro tem, this being his leave-taking before going to Cornwall.

'I gave him a run just now. He's all right where he is. These are for you!' He kissed her.

'They're lovely!' she said, and bent her face into the fragrance of narcissi. 'Lovely!' she said. 'Thank you!' She said, 'Come along in,' and she closed the door, led him into the drawing-room, explaining, 'Mrs Mayendorff and Nicholaus are out in the stables with the vet.'

'Don't tell me the horses have got measles!' But merriment was not the appropriate mode – she merely smiled briefly and said, 'They seem to think there may be problems with the foaling – something to do with Shenshi's pelvis.' She went on, 'I'll get a vase for these – would you like some coffee? Or . . .' she looked about vaguely, 'sherry, before lunch?'

'Sherry sounds nice – if you will too?'

'Yes,' she said, leaving to find a vase, 'it's over there – go ahead, will you?'

He set two glasses, poured their sherries and carrying his own wandered across to the fireplace, filled this warm spring day with an embroidered screen. Above the mantel hung in portrait the late Mrs Grantham Seton, décolleté silks and impressive jewels, the youthful mistress of Hollisfont. Quite a beauty, and it was to Spencer she had passed those attributes. He sipped the sherry. His sister, though, was far the nicer person. Not that Seton was difficult to get along with – practical, straightforward in the Poundell dealings. As to whatever was going on in personal terms in that quarter – and there was something or other – well, that was his business. He drank some more of his sherry. He wondered what they were going to have for lunch; he was quite hungry, had a scratch breakfast this morning, several things to cram into today, work to check, instructions to spell out before he left. Hang this trip! When he heard the glad tidings about the measles he had immediately thought to call it off – didn't really want to go anyway, duty stuff, and now that Grace wasn't going away . . . But he'd put it off last year, pressure of work, and he really couldn't bring himself to do that again, all those half-reproaches! The last straw was that he'd succumbed to requests to stay longer than the week – why not, with Grace away and they so insistent that he ought to visit assorted aunts and uncles long neglected! So now he was committed to ten days, dammit. Still, Cornwall was wonderful, that coast-line . . . he often missed the sea, so that would be a solace, beach-combing on his own, between relatives. And he'd find a remote place for the honeymoon while he was there – do a recce. Introduction tea-party with the clan – poor Gracie! – and then off to a secret destination, by the sea! Two whole weeks, and it could rain and blow all it wanted to, if it wanted to!

He sat down at last, nursing his diminishing sherry. She was being a long time . . .? Probably attending to the boy. She was looking pretty tired. Pretty, and tired. There was more to being in charge of children than met the eye, very demanding in fact. Different when it would be their own, those would be demands they would share, not be divided by! A door somewhere thumped and footsteps approached, and voices – Mrs Mayendorff speaking, Grace responding. So they weren't even going to get a few moments alone before this ruddy lunch! Oh, Lord! Very nice of Mrs Mayendorff to invite him no doubt, seeing that Grace was tied to the measles, but not a compromise he'd have chosen! He put aside his sherry and stood up.

Mrs Mayendorff, in jodhpurs and stockinged feet and wearing an abstracted expression, nodded: 'Oh, hello, Lewis! How are you?' and headed for the side-board where she poured herself a whisky. Grace, bearing vased flowers, followed her into the room and set them on a low table. Mrs Mayendorff swallowed some whisky. 'Got a drink, have you?' she asked Lewis. 'This yours? Oh, Grace's – well, let's take them in, shall we? Mrs Dunkerley says lunch is ready.' And without more ado they all trooped off to the dining-room. Grace collected Nicholaus from the cloakroom en route.

The food was good and abundant, but it was not a festive event. Even Nicholaus was subdued. Conversation of a sort was somehow maintained, Mrs Mayendorff making courtesy inquiries as to Lewis's work and gamely attempting to attend to his replies. Lewis asked politely about the horse and tried to look intelligent as to veterinary details. Grace said little, and that mostly to Nicholaus who dawdled over his food and rubbed at his eyes. It was a meal during which the click and clack of cutlery was noticeably audible. Mrs Dunkerley, collecting or delivering dishes, moved and spoke with deportment more appropriate to night-duty on a hospital ward than to a luncheon party.

'I don't want any more,' mumbled Nicholaus, pushing away his untouched pudding.

'Shall I put the coffee in the drawing-room, madam?' murmured Mrs Dunkerley. 'Or shall you have it here?'

'Oh, leave it here, thanks, Mrs Dunkerley – I won't stay myself – if you'll excuse me,' she said to Lewis, 'I'll get back to the yard,' she stood up, 'still got to exercise Villanelle, routine upside down today.' She said to Grace, 'What time's the doctor coming, did you say? I ought to be back for that.' She glanced at Nicholaus. 'Another patient for him by the look of things . . . Well, do excuse me – and have a good . . . holiday, you're going on holiday, aren't you? Oh, well, I hope it's enjoyable anyway . . .' She departed.

Grace said, 'Oh, leave it on the tray, thank you, Mrs Dunkerley – we'll take it to the drawing-room, Nicholaus looks as though a nap on the sofa's the best thing for him!'

Lewis carried the tray. Grace settled Nicholaus on the sofa, his head in her lap. 'No milk for me,' she whispered as Lewis poured. He placed it within her reach and with a sense of being entirely dispensable, sat to drink his own in an armchair. Grace, gently stroking the boy's forehead, whispered, 'The flowers are beautiful – I can smell them from here!' and smiled into his eyes from her entrenchment. 'I'm so sorry about all this, Lewis!'

'It's not your fault!' he swiftly assured her. 'I wish I could do something to help – you're tired – look, why don't I carry him up to bed for you?'

She shook her head. 'He's almost asleep.' She smiled again. 'Let sleeping dogs lie!' she explained. 'What time are you off tomorrow?'

'Straight after breakfast – unless there are any hitches this afternoon, I've still got to see the foreman on the Brunley job. Anyway, an early a start as possible.'

Desultory conversation, conducted *sotto voce*, touched on mileage, weather, the fact that as Honoria had never had measles she could not visit the boys, that the cancellation of the German trip had been made by Grace, not Mrs Mayendorff, on the telephone, that Lilian had by telephone expressed her satisfaction that the trip was off because Grace herself could now attend the remaining rehearsals and not put the Coverdales to the bother of finding a stand-in, and had dismissed the notion that Grace might not be able to be spared from the sick-room as 'plain silly, with all those village women she employs about the place!' And that she was jolly thankful that she hadn't got the boys as page attendants, as she had once considered! The shared quiet laughter drew them together in spirit if not in flesh. It was the best that could be managed in the circumstances, and soon Lewis needs must go. He had more business to attend to and also Guinness to be delivered to the Vicarage. Above the snuffling, somnolent head of Nicholaus he kissed Grace goodbye. 'I'll telephone, darling. I'll even send you a post-card!' Another kiss. 'Oh, Gracie, take care of yourself, won't you? Well. I'll see you a week on Wednesday. Goodbye, darling!'

Grace heard the Rover depart. She laid her head back, closed her eyes. She remained there awhile, hearing the tick of the clock, the breathing of the ailing child, and her own. Then she gently detached herself, slid a cushion beneath his head, and poured herself another cup of coffee. She carried it to the window, and stood gazing, wistful, tired and bemused, into the empty drive.

CHAPTER SEVENTEEN

The visiting organist from Peterborough, having more or less satisfied himself as to the quality of the organ in a two-hour practice session and partaken of a cup of restorative tea in Tom's study, climbed aboard his Ford motor-car and set off for home. 'See you in a fortnight!' Tom waved him goodbye and went to let Guinness out of the kitchen.

'Yes, you are – you're a good, patient dog!' Tom told him. 'And now you can come with me to shut up shop. We won't bother with your lead – you know how to behave in church don't you, old fella!'

Humming snatches of Bach still running in his brain from the afternoon's music, he made his leisurely tour, checked the necessaries for tomorrow's Communion, noted that the organist had tidily replaced things as he'd found them, the hymn-scores, Sam Wheatcroft's private cushion, on the organ bench. Making his way back down the nave, he lifted his head and voice and delivered eight bars of *Jesu, Joy of Man's Desiring*, complete with words. Guinness, trotting before him, wagged his tail encouragingly. 'Thank you!' said Tom. He could not manage *Toccata and Fugue*, nor attempted it. Neither could Sam Wheatcroft, bless him, whose arthritic fingers just managed to cope with the old familiar hymns; which was why, for the loftier demands of a Coverdale wedding, a crack performer had been delivered. He closed the huge studded door behind him and stepped after Guinness through the porch and into the gold and violet of the soft May evening. Beautiful, beautiful! A perfect day for Lewis's long drive today too. Should be there by now. The magical scent of mown grass greeted him; how well it looked, the churchyard, velvety gilded greens, ordered and tranquil. Another cut, a week on Friday, ready for the next day's wedding; unless, of course, it rained. Even Outwick House, he wrily observed, had no last say on the weather!

Passing Emily Bates's grave, he paused for a moment. She had at last gone peacefully and in readiness for death. Fresh violets, Emily's favourite flowers, put there by Biddy. The death had been a relief and release for them both, mother and daughter; it had been a long last winter for them, a very heavy strain on the devoted Biddy; herself in her mid-sixties and widowed. She would pick up now, summer coming – already looked fitter. He glanced again at the clean-cut new lettering on the headstone, simple statement of Emily Bates's mortal existence: Born January 12 1843 – Died March 30 1930. He moved on. Riding in his mind was the echo of Spencer Seton's laughter: 'Well, well! The dear good folk of Hollisfont!' Emily Bates would have been one of them; the last of that generation, here interred, who sixty, seventy years ago had lent themselves one way or another, in violent action or blind-eyed silence, to that fearful barbarity, the lynching. If it was true. Was it true? There remained no record. No legal proceedings. Conspiracy of silence? Or was it a lurid distortion of a familiar human aberration – sexual content always and ever a rich field for elaborators? Miss Seton had exhibited distress, a strong reaction. But then that might well have been nothing to do with the story's veracity, rather indignation at its being retailed at all in the presence of children; and quite right too – but then Coverdale was not thinking, he was, alas, courting attention and applause, regardless. He opened the wicket-gate for Guinness, followed him through: 'Come on, young fella-me-lad, time for your din-

dins!' Closing the gate, he glanced up and caught a movement in the lane beyond the spread of flowering white lilacs, someone hurrying along; it was Grace, he briefly saw, dark, bobbed hair, slender shoulders in her blue cardigan. 'Hello! Grace!' he called, but she hadn't heard, out of earshot; never mind. 'Yes! Din-dins!' he assured Guinness. She was out having a breather from the measles. On her way to the Hall. Honoria would be pleased, very frustrated to be debarred from visiting those particular sick. Humming – Vivaldi, this time – he set down Guinness's dinner on the kitchen floor. One of the many charms of that dog was his moderate behaviour with food; not a greedy, golloping dog; a neat and thoughtful eater. He went to get his own supper, courtesy of Mrs Cox, from the larder: ham and salad, very nice. The salads were from Honoria Seton, of course. Honoria's generosity was of a rare order – not only in the distribution of creature comforts. Attention, time and true concern, and universally applied, not just given where spontaneous affection moved her. Instance the effort and goodwill she had mustered in kitting out the cottage for young Coverdale, an enterprise, Tom guessed, that was not one hundred per cent approved by her; but she did it wholeheartedly, with all her good nature intact, and indeed, Coverdale was very comfortably set up down there. As to whether he was comfortable in the wider sense – well! Lewis had been right. The villagers had not liked it, special treatment for the fellow who had lost favour with them over his Union talk . . . And as for Mr Blow! Oh, dear, dear . . .

'Tom – cooee! Tom?'

'Honoria! Splendid! Come in! I was just this moment thinking about you! Come away in!'

'Hello, Tom! You look well! Hello, Guinness! Having your dinner! No, I won't stop, Tom, I just dropped by to let you know I've been with Bessie Goodson and she's *much* better and you've really no need to pop up there tonight because her sister's come over from Wakely – yes, she's staying a few days to help out. No, thank you!' Honoria smiled. 'I'm awash with tea!' They laughed together, victims both of ordeal by tea-cups on their pastoral rounds.

Tom said, 'You'll find a visitor when you get back – I just saw young Grace on her way down to you! Having a break from nursing – how is he, have you heard?'

'Oh, he's quite poorly, I'm afraid – I telephoned and spoke to Margaret at lunch-time. He's not at all well – and Nicholaus has got it now, poor chick, but then I suppose that was inevitable. And Margaret's got problems with the mare, as if there weren't problems enough. I checked with the doctor, though, I telephoned him last night and I'll be allowed back in the Dower House in about a week, so that's something – though it's right now that they could do with the help, really. Oh, well! I'll see you tomorrow, Tom. I'll away now – don't want to keep Grace waiting!'

But when she got home, Grace was not there.

'Are you sure?'

'Quite sure, madam,' said Parker. 'There have been no callers.'

CHAPTER EIGHTEEN

'I've brought this,' said Grace and thrust forward a small brown-paper bag.

Maurice, looking into her face, took the bag. 'What is it?'

'Just some lint and plaster and some antiseptic.' The tone was businesslike.

He said, 'I'd heard about the measles. Your trip's off, then?'

'Yes.'

'Well, erm . . .' He gave the bag a little shake. 'Thanks for this.' He took a step back. 'Um – d'you want to come in?'

'Well, I can't stay,' she said, briefly glancing at her watch, 'but – just for a moment.' She went down the two stone steps. She took in the room, now furnished, 'It looks very nice,' she said. 'How is it, the finger?' and without waiting for reply, 'You ought to have got something for it from Mrs Sutton, silly not to ask. Anyway. It needs attending to so I brought that.' She shoved her hands into the pockets of her blue cardigan. 'Well, how is it?' she inquired briskly.

He lifted his left hand, squinnied at the swollen middle finger. 'Throbbing a bit,' he said.

'Let me see.' She inclined her head, inspecting. 'Mm. It's septic. I should have brought a poultice. It's got worse. Needs a kaolin poultice. Is the thorn still in?'

'Don't know. Poked about with a bit of wire –'

'A bit of wire! Great heavens, that's the worst thing you could do! Blood poisoning!'

'Well, I got some out. But I think there's a bit left in.'

They still stood where they had halted, she at the foot of the steps, honeyed evening light framed in the doorway behind her, he a pace within. She frowned, admonished: 'You ought to have that covered. Don't you keep it covered? When you're milking?'

'Arnie gave me a rubber glove from the dairy. On the milk's account, not mine.'

'Quite right, though. Hygiene.'

He moved; he went to the table and emptied the contents of the bag: bandage, lint, a roll of plaster, a bottle of iodine. 'I haven't got scissors,' he said.

'Tst!' She was annoyed by her omission. 'Of course, scissors! Well, you've got a sharp knife, have you? That will do, I suppose.'

'D'you want to sit down?' he thought to suggest.

'I must go in a moment,' she said, perching on a chair-edge. 'You'll need to wash it thoroughly first. With boiled water. Then soak the finger. Hot as you can stand it, of course, to draw the pus out. Then put iodine on a strip of lint for the dressing.'

'All right,' he said. 'How is he, Max?'

'Quite poorly. Nicholaus has gone down now.' An impersonal medical report.

'I suppose he would,' said Maurice.

'Have you had measles?' The unrelenting brusqueness of her manner matched her posture, stiff, erect on her chair-edge.

'Yes, thank you.'

She laughed, as had been intended, she could not help herself, but immediately retracted, briskly pointing out, 'Well, if you were not immune you could have picked up the infection. It's obvious now that he must have been infectious, on Tuesday.'

Maurice fiddled inconsequentially with the things on the table, picked up the iodine bottle, put it down again. 'I thought you'd left for Germany. Then I heard.'

'Who told you?'

'Dan.'

'Oh yes, of course, Mrs Burtle.'

'Bush-telegraph. Hollisfont's favourite pastime.'

She ignored this further invitation to laughter.

Maurice said, 'Shall you go later, then, to Germany?'

'No. Herr Mayendorff is going abroad on business for six months.'

'Oh.'

'So we won't be going.'

'No.'

She looked at her watch, made an assessment. 'If you put the kettle on, I'll give you a hand with that dressing,' she announced.

'Oh.' He seemed uncertain of this demand on her time. 'I 'spect I can manage if –'

'Does it take long, the kettle?'

'Erm – no, not really. Well, it takes its own time –'

'Well, put it on, then.' She stood up and busied herself aligning the dressings. To his departing back she said, 'And find a sharp knife.' Arriving at another decision, she scooped up the dressings and followed him into the kitchen. 'We'll need a bowl too,' she said, standing there.

'This do?'

'Yes.'

'I'd just had some tea so it's quite hot already.' They both looked at the kettle, watched it, she with her hands holding the dressings, he holding the bowl.

'It's quite chilly in here,' she observed.

'Faces north,' he agreed.

'I expect it warms up when you have the oven on.'

'Yes.'

The kettle produced small promising sounds and a suggestion of steam.

'The knife?' she said.

'Oh – here.'

From her distance she gave it a cursory glance. 'Mmm, looks fairly sharp.'

'Oh yes, it's sharp.'

'Actually,' she bethought herself, 'have you some salt? If you've got some salt then we needn't be hanging about for boiled water, a strong saline solution will do just as well. Hot saline solution for the initial cleaning. Oh, good.' Impersonal, quick, efficient, she set out her medicaments, measured salt into the bowl, made the saline solution, while he hung back, shifted out of her way as she busied about, peered at his festering finger, shuffled his feet.

She placed the bowl. 'Try that.'

'Phoof – hell, it's hot!'

'It's meant to be. We want to draw the pus.'

He winced, whistled, a sharp intake of breath through his teeth.

'Well, if you can't stand it I'll cool it,' she said critically.

''S all right,' he mumbled.

'The hotter the better,' she told him.

'If it hurts it's good for you?' he sardonically inquired.

'In this case yes,' she said. '*Is* it hurting?'

''S all right.'

She said, 'You were very silly not to get it seen to. You should have asked Mrs Sutton,' and bent to frown disapprovingly at the submerged finger.

'Not likely!' he muttered. 'She wouldn't want to know about it.'

'What d'you mean? Of course she would, she seems a nice, sensible woman.'

'So she might, but she's gone right off *me*.'

'Gone right off you? What d'you mean?' she said again.

'Well, they all have.'

'They all have?' She flicked a glance at him. 'Keep it submerged!' she instructed. 'What d'you mean, "They've all gone off you"?'

'Since I came *here*.' He nodded indication of the cottage. 'That's Hollisfont all over. Cliquey lot.'

'I thought you liked it here – Hollisfont.'

'Farm's all right. Or was.'

She looked at him. 'What's happened?'

'What's happened?' he snorted. 'Well, what do you think? Squire's saved my bacon, set me up here, and they don't like it, do they? Petty-minded lot.'

'Surely not!' she protested. 'You're imagining things! Who could grudge you this place, for goodness' sake, when you'd nowhere else to go!'

He shot her an ironic look. 'Where've you been living?'

'What d'you mean?'

'Well, don't tell me you don't know!'

She faintly flushed; said nothing.

'The family freak?' he mocked. 'Bad apple, black sheep? You go about with that lot, don't you? Going to be one of my esteemed sister's bridesmaids? Don't tell me you don't know!' He gave a short, derisive laugh, then frowned. 'Hey, how long do I have to keep this in?'

She said quietly, 'You can take it out now.' She picked up the lint, took up the knife and expertly shaved off a fold. 'Give me your hand,' she said.

He raised his hand dripping from the bowl. Gently she took it, cradling it as she carefully dabbed, drying it. She said, 'I've heard the story. But not from Lilian. Lilian,' she said, head bent above her task, 'has never mentioned your existence.' She raised her head and met his eyes. The incredulity there dissolved away, the derision faded, leaving perplexity, a child's bewilderment. She bent again to the hand she held. 'You have never been mentioned between us. It is,' she said, 'a story that does your family no credit, in my opinion,' her tone now gently firm as her ministrations.

He said, and his voice was almost husky, 'I didn't – I couldn't make out – you know – when you kept coming with the boys – I didn't know – I didn't know what you made of me – and then coming with this tonight . . .'

She finished her drying, released his hand. 'Well,' she said, hesitant, 'we've never . . . talked.'

'No.'

She said, 'I'm only being a bridesmaid because Moira's had to drop out. They didn't really want me.' She smiled. 'I'm not,' she gave a soft laugh, 'the right type, I'm afraid!'

'Mother,' he said.

She smiled again, nodded. 'Lilian – well, she's – excitable, impulsive. It was a gaffe, Lilian made.'

He was nodding, absorbed, recognition in the dawning wry smile. 'Yes,' he murmured, 'yes, that's Lilian . . .' And then: 'My God! How insulting!' He was indignant.

She laughed. 'Oh, I'm not insulted! It's' – she shrugged – 'too absurd!'

'You're too nice!' In the meeting of their eyes, she flushed under his earnest gaze. 'No,' she demurred, 'not too nice –'

'You are,' he said.

She ducked her head away, rinsed the lint in the bowl. 'Give me your hand again,' she said. 'This might hurt a bit – I'm going to try to squeeze out the pus – hold still . . .'

'Sorry!' he said as his hand involuntarily jerked.

'It's all right,' she murmured, engrossed, plying deeper. 'Oop – sorry! Hang on – nearly done! Golly! Look at that! There *is* still something in there – look – but I – can't –

shift it!' She let out a pent breath and straightened up. 'Well, we've cleaned it out a bit,' she said dubiously, 'but I can't shift that bit of thorn, it's hooked right in!'

Heads together, they both peered. 'Well, you've got a lot of muck out,' he assured her. 'You've done a first-rate job!'

'Not good enough, I'm afraid.' She sighed briefly. 'I'm going to cover it now, put iodine on and cover it, and then you must take it to a doctor.'

'Doctor?'

'Yes!' she insisted. 'It's quite badly infected, it needs proper attention . . .'

'I don't know any doctors!'

'There's Dr Hazeldean in Hestonborough –'

'I can't get in to Hestonborough – anyway,' he headed off her protest, 'it'll be all right now, I don't need any doctor.'

Sawing a fresh piece of lint, she said, 'As long as that remnant of thorn is in there, it won't heal!' She made a pad of the lint and soaked it with iodine.

'You said something about a poultice.' He surrendered his hand for the dressing. 'Couldn't we try a poultice?'

Bandaging the pad into place, she made no reply. From the coppice birdsong carried, valedictory challenges and claims across the end of day. She secured the bandage, took up the roll of plaster. 'I might not be able to come,' she said, cutting a strip.

'Why not?'

'It depends on who's there. To keep an eye on the boys. Whether there's anyone there.'

She began to fix the plaster, encasing the bandage.

'There'll be someone, won't there?'

'I don't know – Sunday.'

A question occurred to him. 'Who's there now?'

'Mrs Dunkerley.' She turned his hand, frowning at the

difficulty of winding the plaster into position. 'Too tight? We don't want it too tight.'

'No,' he said. 'Does she know where you are now?'

'There,' she said, 'how does that feel? All right? Close your hand – see how it feels!'

'It's just right!' he said.

'Comfortable, then?'

'Yes,' he said. 'Does she know where you are now, Mrs Dunkerley?'

She was busily collecting up the bits and pieces. 'Where's the bag – or shall I just leave them here . . . No, I didn't mention where I was going,' she said lightly, 'why should I? I don't as a rule! Now then,' she was brisk again, 'try not to get that wet – in fact *don't* get it wet! Well,' she said with the air of one satisfied with proceedings and about to delegate lesser matters: 'You can clear up, can you? I must go now!'

He stepped aside to let her pass: 'Will you come, tomorrow?'

She said, 'If I don't come, you must get to a doctor on Monday – I mean that! Or you'll have serious trouble with that hand – understand?' She walked on out of the kitchen.

Beside her at the front door he said, 'You're coming, then, tomorrow?'

'I've told you!' she said coolly. 'I don't know whether that will be possible.'

He leaned against the door-jamb, scrutinized his repaired finger. 'When'll I see you, if you don't?'

'I shan't need to see that finger if you will do the sensible thing and go to a doctor, not later than Monday!' It was her governessy voice. She went up the two steps, adding, 'I'd like your assurance on that. If I don't come, the dressing will need changing by Monday at the latest, and there's still that fragment to get out.'

'I will if it still feels wrong.'

'Will what?'

'Go to a doctor on Monday if you don't come tomorrow.'

'Not "if it still feels wrong"! *However* you think it feels!' She stepped ahead into the garden.

'All right,' he grudgingly conceded. He mounted the steps, stood in the porch. He said, 'I'd rather you did it.'

'We'll see!' she said. And hurried away.

Grace gently slid the flannel back into the bowl of cold water and stood in dim, curtained half-light, looking down at the swollen, feverish face on the pillow. His breath laboured through parted lips; but the eyelids began at last to close. Across the room in the other bed Nicholaus stirred and coughed in his sleep. Making no sound, she stole to the window and eased the curtains apart, admitting cool evening air now that dusk had drained the daylight. With soft, adept movements she folded the towel, smoothed the sheets, restored the thermometer to its jar of antiseptic, picked up the pyjamas and set them outside the open door with the discarded pillow-cases ready for their journey down to the wash-house, and noiselessly set the chair beside Max's bed, there to sit and watch with him until sleep should come to his relief. The eyelids closed; inflamed, and swollen, even his eyelids. As Mrs Dunkerley had said, 'Spots! I've never seen measles like it – hardly a pin to put between them, poor little boy!'

Ah, Max! Dear Max! That you should be ill just now! It was true, what they said, the clever men in Vienna, patiently teasing out the truths of mind and body. He had not wanted to go, to go home to Vati in Berlin; and so his body had been allowed to have the measles . . . Nicholaus? That perhaps was not so easy to see; though once Max was ill and they could not go, perhaps he had lost interest for the moment, and succumbed in sympathy. Fanciful? Perhaps. But Max. Max had not wanted to go, to leave Mother, to go away without her. People disappeared when you went away. Vati had disappeared when they had gone to Reissen that last time. He was not there when they went back to Berlin. If you weren't watching, people disappeared . . . Fanciful? The body and the secret mind? She thought not, not at all. Ah, Max! What conflicts raged in that fever! The shako lay on the shelf below the bedside lamp flanked by medicine and pills and potions. Calamine lotion . . . but water was better, to relieve the heat, calamine quickly dried and crusted, added irritation to the itching skin. Better to swab with water.

She drowsed in her chair. Last night, again, she had dreamed she was in Germany. The same dream, she was there, alone, in a bright, pleasant room which was 'home'. It was nowhere she had ever been, except that it was Germany; and peaceful, very peaceful . . . Oh, Lewis . . . It *will* be all right! All right, in October!

She would not go down to Poundell tomorrow. She would not go again.

She was glad she'd been. Yes. That was all right. Sensible, and useful. Just as well she had – that could have turned really bad – possibly, well, gangrenous! It had looked pretty bad when they last saw him, the last time at the farm, Tuesday's milking – and she knew he wasn't taking it seriously, silly boy! She had told him to get it attended to, ask Mrs Sutton, but she could see he was not going to take the advice. Then, though, she had not realized that there was more to it than masculine stubbornness . . . She had not known about the hostility. If that were true. He believed it. It was true, for him; not just imagination. He'd looked – like a child, when he'd said it. An unhappy child. Yes, she was glad she had been. She was glad to have had the opportunity to tell him. To tell him that she at any rate did not subscribe to the Outwick family opinion of him. Telling him that, she had felt discharged of some irksome burden. She had put a record straight, with herself. A useful visit.

But she would not go again . . . She should not go again . . .

A board creaked on the landing: 'Oh – Miss Grace!' whispered Mrs Dunkerley, stealing heavily into the room. 'I've just brought this . . .' A fresh jug of barley-water.

'Oh – Mrs Dunkerley!' whispered Grace. 'How kind!' She stood up and took the jug. 'I could have done that – you're very kind – you've made yourself very late!'

'Not worried about that, Miss Grace! Only too pleased to help out – aah! look at him, poor little soul!' She took in the sleeping form in the other bed also and smiled fondly. 'Who-could-ever-hurt-a-child?' She murmured the comforting incantation.

Grace whispered, 'Thank you so much for watching while I went out – I'm very grateful!'

'Not at all, Miss Grace – no trouble at all – you go out whenever you've a mind – we're all helping each other just now, aren't we!' She nodded reassuringly and tiptoed away, scooping up the laundry as she went.

CHAPTER NINETEEN

'What's the trouble, Mrs D?' said Mrs Cox, arriving for her morning tea.

'Well, it's these shoes,' said Mrs Dunkerley, rummaging deep in the wall-cupboard, 'they're giving me gyp!' She withdrew, defeated. 'Tst!' she complained, 'it *was* there but it's not now!'

'What?'

'That roll of plaster.' She clumped the cupboard door shut and stumped to the stove.

'Well, what's the trouble?'

'It's these shoes.' She hauled a bubbling pan off the heat and dumped it on the draining-board. 'Cutting across my instep!'

'Tst!' Mrs Cox judiciously eyed the plump extremities: 'Mmm,' she said, 'that's the trouble with new shoes. Till you've broken them in.' She put down her dusters and polish. 'They're nice, though – nice shoes. I fancy a pair myself with the straps. Light, for summer.'

'Rubbing across here.' Mrs Dunkerley showed her.

'Tst!'

'I was going to put plaster across to ease it but it's not there!'

'Take them off!' said Mrs Cox.

'Take them off? Good gracious me, I can't hardly do that, can I?' Mrs Dunkerley said crossly.

'Why not?' returned Mrs Cox. '*She* does! Always walking about without shoes!'

'Well, so she might but *I* can't hardly, can I!'

'*I* would if it was me,' said Mrs Cox airily but with her main attention scanning for her tea, which was not in evidence. Indeed, the kettle was not even on the hob.

Mrs Dunkerley caught the glance. 'I haven't had a minute!' she declared. 'Running up and down with trays for this and trays for that and then a cup for the doctor!'

'Mad-house just now!' Mrs Cox agreed, and stepped into the breach. 'You just sit yourself down for five minutes, Mrs D,' she said soothingly, 'and I'll get the tea!' She bustled to the kettle.

'I've these potatoes to strain!' Mrs Dunkerley aggrievedly slung the colander into the sink.

'Well, you do that and then have a sit down, my dear – and slip your shoes off – you can do that while I get the tea!'

'Well, I won't say no,' said Mrs Dunkerley through a cloud of steam.

'You can use cotton wool – there's cotton wool, isn't there?' said Mrs Cox, reaching for the caddy.

'I can't go round with lumps of cotton wool sticking up! Unsightly!' Mrs Dunkerley was not available for solutions; stress and grievance were too heavily upon her. For days now, since Master Max was taken bad, there'd not been a moment's peace, no routine, didn't know where you were and what was coming next; never knew who'd eat what, or when; food spoiling, going to waste; special this and special that and no regard to time, only one pair of hands! And as if that wasn't enough there was the extra washing, sheets and pillow-cases extra, and not just the boys – now it was Ollie Furber! On a camp-bed in the stables, extra bedding, extra mouth to feed. Mad-house! And then Miss Grace and her going-for-walks – well, of course it was right she gets some time out of the house, stretch her legs, can't be on duty nursing all day, all night, and her looking very peaky, and small wonder, but all the same that's twice she'd come back later than she'd said, later than they'd arranged and made her late for getting back to see to Albert's food – ho, yes! day's not finished when day's done *here* – there's another lot waiting at home!

'Here you are then!' comforted Mrs Cox. 'Nice cup of tea! Biscuit? Slip your shoes off – that's right! Ooo dear, yes, I see where it's bearing – nasty! Left a proper furrow across your stocking!'

'I'll put my old ones back on for tomorrow,' grumbled Mrs Dunkerley. 'Where's Winnie got to?' She frowned at the clock.

'She had to leave off when the doctor came, she was doing round the boys' room. Oh – here she is! Come on, Winnie – tea's nice and fresh!'

'Gone, has he?' said Mrs Dunkerley.

'Yes,' said Mrs Burtle, 'just gone!' She subsided gratefully on to a chair. 'Had to strip the bed again, Mrs Dunkerley – yes! more sheets – well, it's the sweat, poor little lad! Not Master Nicholaus, his'll go another day.'

'He's bad then, still, young Max?' Mrs Cox prompted.

'Well,' said Mrs Burtle cautiously, 'I couldn't help but hear, I was on the stairs there getting on with the banisters – and, well, it seems he's infection in his ears now!'

'Hmm!' said Mrs Cox. 'There you are! You can go deaf with measles!'

'Oh, don't even think of it, Dora! Poor little lad!' Mrs Dunkerley's sympathies switched readily from her sore feet to the suffering child. 'Don't even think of such a thing for him!' She shook her head sadly.

'He's not as strong as Master Nicholaus.' Mrs Burtle dolefully sipped her tea. 'Still, they're doing everything they can for him!'

'Well, at least they'll take that hat off him!' said Mrs

Cox, selecting another biscuit. 'That's something that'll come out of it and about time too! Pressing on his ears it would be, doesn't even fit!'

The back door opened and a moment later the kitchen door. 'Oh, Mrs Dunkerley – could we have a mug for the vet when you pour Furber's? Soon as you can – thanks!' Mrs Mayendorff's face made a brief appearance and was gone.

'If it isn't doctors and grooms it's vets!' said Mrs Dunkerley, grimly hoisting herself upright. 'Well, it'll be another pot then, won't get two out of this!' She clunked the lid back on the teapot and painfully fitted her feet back into their shoes.

'Gone?' Mr Sutton frowned. 'Gone where?'

'I don't know, Boss. He just got on his bike and went,' said Dan.

'Where the deuce –!' Mr Sutton swept an exasperated gaze over the landscape. 'How long's he been gone?'

'Church clock'd just struck the hour.' Dan shrugged.

'Since ten!' Sutton was very vexed. 'And he didn't say where?'

'No, Boss.'

'Tell him when he comes back I want him down at the yard – that trailer load's still not been shifted – tell him to get down there and quick about it!' He strode off. Second time this week Coverdale had not been where he ought to be; this time Sutton was jolted, apprehensive and angry. What the hell was going on? He ducked through the orchard, passed the place where the bothy used to be, heading for the yard. Change in attitude – since the bothy came down. Or since joining the Union? Rumblings from the men; but it hadn't seemed to affect his work; till . . . well, very recently. Bloody fine time to be falling down on the job, everyone full stretch and the muck-spreading not completed! But as he rounded the barn, placatory sounds of the tractor spluttering at work met his ears, and his nerve-ends eased: well! that was all right, then – he'd not been swinging the lead! He'd used his common and come down to shift the trailer load! Relieved, he emerged into the yard. But immediately it was apparent that nothing had been accomplished. What the deuce?

Coverdale raised a hand. 'Carburettor trouble!' he called. 'All right now!'

'Hm – right! Carry on!' Sutton's nerve-ends eased again. He went his way into the house to complete the week's milk-yield records and check the gross margins on forage per acre . . .

'He turned up, then,' said his wife, setting a cup of coffee by him at his desk.

'Mm? Oh – yes! There all the time in the shed – trouble with the tractor!'

'In the shed?' she cocked her head. 'But I just saw him come in – not five minutes ago. On his bike – he just came in!'

Mrs Cox stood at the top landing window nibbling the biscuit from her apron pocket, feather-duster dangling. Mrs D's nerves no better for all she'd got her comfy shoes on today! Don't blame her either! Woman of her age, all these stairs, up and down, up and down! Expect too much, them as never turn a hand, just do this, just do that and never a penny extra. Well, I've said my say, but she's too soft, is Mrs D – she'll not say. Told her – it's your right! Extra work, extra pay – fair's fair! But she'll not ask . . .

Her ruminations were arrested by a movement glimpsed down below, way off along the shrubbery. 'Now, what's she doing there this time of the morning? Where's *she* been – and in her indoor shoes . . .' The grandfather clock in the hall struck eleven as Mrs Cox keenly watched Grace hasten along the boundary wall towards the house.

'Well,' said Mrs Burtle, 'if this weather keeps up they'll be all right – but you can't tell, can you? Might be wet. Still, it's nice for their rehearsal, today.'

'They're having a tent again, like with Miss Moira,' said Mrs Dunkerley. 'Too many folk to fit in the house though it's a big house, none of the rooms is *that* big. Another cup, Winnie?' Saturday being Mrs Cox's morning at the Vicarage, there was tea in the pot to spare, and Mrs Dunkerley topped up both cups.

'Funny sort of frock for a bridesmaid, though,' said Mrs Burtle, who had taken a peep when she was clearing the ashes in Miss Grace's room – well, it was on a hanger on the door, she wasn't nosing. 'Funny sort of colour – more slatey, if you follow me – sort of greeny-slatey, pale greeny. Funny sort of shape, well, no shape to it, though you can't tell really till it's on.'

'Well, funny ideas, Miss Lilian,' Mrs Dunkerley nodded.

'Well, she'll look nice in it whatever,' said Mrs Burtle. 'Always looks nice, Miss Grace.'

'Looking better this morning, I thought,' mused Mrs Dunkerley. 'Been looking very peaky but she looks brighter this morning.'

'Well,' said Mrs Burtle coyly, 'she would, wouldn't she! Had a telephone call from Mr Gower. Cheered her up! Like a spring flower in water!'

The outer door admitted someone. 'Oh – drink up, Winnie!' Mrs Dunkerley got quickly to her feet, 'Here's madam coming!' She hastened to the range.

Unshod, Mrs Mayendorff came in.

'Your coffee's ready, madam! Here – let me take that!' She relieved her mistress of Ollie Furber's empty tea-mug. Mrs Burtle gathered her dustpan and brush and set her chair back in place. 'Shall you have it here, madam?' asked Mrs Dunkerley. 'Or –'

'Oh – in a mug, thank you, I'll take it with me to the telephone. Thank you – a touch more milk – thanks.' She padded across the kitchen, sipping as she went. At the door she said, 'Oh, by the bye – you haven't been in the kitchen garden, have you? No, well, I didn't suppose you had –' She gave a little shrug. 'Ollie said someone went in there, the door was unlatched this morning. Not that it matters . . .' She smiled vaguely. 'Ollie's quite fussed about "prowlers", though goodness knows what anyone would be prowling for here – anyway, he asked me to mention it.' She padded away.

'Prowlers!' said Mrs Burtle, round-eyed.

'Tst!' Mrs Dunkerley was disdainful. 'Weather, more like – happens with our side gate when the weather warms up. Old fuss-pot, Ollie. When she comes back I'll tell her – happens with old wood come the summer. Goes back tight again when it rains.'

Lilian said, 'Gone? What do you mean?'

'She went – she left five minutes ago!' said Thelma.

'She can't have done!' Lilian protested. 'We're all going back to Outwick for tea!'

'She's probably in the churchyard – just gone out into the sun,' said Jean.

Mrs Coverdale and Frank approached the group assembled in the aisle. Mrs Coverdale drew her daughter aside. 'You and Frank cover the formalities here. Everything seems in order, quite a useful rehearsal, you can pass that on. I shall expect you for tea in quarter of an hour, you will have to be firm.' She turned, surveying the dozen or so young people perched or propped about the nave, chatting. 'We are already twenty minutes late.' The bridesmaids stood aside to let her pass, making her exit.

Lilian said, 'I'm just popping along to thank old Opie – round everyone up, will you, and get cracking – Mother wants us up there pronto, she's dining out tonight, all right? Round Grace up, she'll fit in Bonzo's car if you squash hard enough! Come on, Frank!'

'What?'

'Come *on*! Ps and Qs to the Vicar!'

He followed in her wake towards the vestry.

'This yours?' Liz proffered a handbag to Thelma.

'Oh, thanks!'

'Come on, everyone – tea-time!'

The party straggled out through the porch.

'Gosh, I could do with a large pink gin, never mind dreary old tea!' said Liz.

'Ssssh!' giggled Jean. 'Bertie's just behind!' And all three bridesmaids stifled laughter.

They did not find the fourth. They looked all around, but there was no sign of Grace.

Archie drove. Spen had met him at Hestonborough station. They had, not without a surprising amount of pain considering their ripe years, mended matters, restored peace. 'It was unforgivable, Archie. Very cheap. Stupid. I'm truly sorry.' The closing lines in the horrid sequence of mutual hurts: 'It's all right, Spen – it's all right. God knows, you had provocation enough. I'm sorry too.' And shared wry laughter, ten days ago, in town: 'Both a bit long in the tooth, old enough to know better!' A turn at the wheel of Spen's spanking new Alfa Romeo twin-overhead-cam two-seater sports was a consciously whimsical joke, schoolyard reparation, enjoyed by them both: 'You can have a go in my car if you want!' 'Oh, I say, Seton! That's jolly decent!'

Late afternoon sun behind them, hood open, hair buffeted, they bowled along the road to Hollisfont. Archie changed down, swung into the last bend. 'Sweet as a nut!' he grinned.

'Beats riding behind Murston, eh?' Spen called back, and Archie laughed: 'Right!'

The needle dropped to 40, 30, 25, the approach to the bridge. Ahead on the left, two figures threaded through the bushes, into Poundell coppice. One was Coverdale, the other a female, glimpse of printed cotton dress. No words were exchanged in the Alfa Romeo, just a brief ironic glance each to each, acknowledgement of follies past and laid to rest.

Across the bridge and nearing the Hall's entrance, Archie said, 'Great Scott! Like Piccadilly Circus!' as a swarm of motor-cars emerging from Church Lane roared off up the village street.

'Coverdale circus!' Spen enlightened him: 'One of their weddings – rehearsal, actual thing next Saturday. Mm? Good God, no, not I! Nonni will, she'll have to, poor girl!' As the car purred softly up the drive, Spen breathed deep the sweet green fragrance of the enfolding limes, and found himself to be quietly content; three months ago their snowbound tracery had touched in him a minor chord of melancholy, torment and despair. The wild card had been on the loose. Maybe now, at last, they'd learned enough to leave it in the discard pile.

Tom shook the tea-leaves round the roots of the climber rose as Honoria had suggested and carried the teapot back to rinse it at the sink. Curious, he ruminated, how everything related to Coverdalian enterprises smacked of combat.

Yesterday's rehearsal had gone perfectly tickety-boo once those two young ushers turned up, and yet a certain unease pervaded throughout, reminiscent of those periods known as lulls which were not lull-ish at all, between assaults, in France. Been the same with Moira's. Some mysterious disturbance, emanating from the mother, which was quite odd since she was without a doubt the very embodiment of Order!

He dried up the crocks from his tea-time snack and returned them to the side-board. Beautiful afternoon again. 'How about it, old lad?' he consulted Guinness. 'Little stroll before Evensong? Walk? Yes? Yes!'

Unlatching the gate he said, 'I'm going to miss you, you know! Yes. Another couple of days and you'll be back where you belong and I'll miss you!' Perhaps I should get myself a dog. Trouble is, it won't be Guinness; Guinness belongs to someone else, but it's Guinness that I – love! He almost flushed at this unwonted surge of sentiment, amused, slightly embarrassed. 'Now then, which way, eh? Not enough time for the Hill. Let's take a look at the river, eh?'

At its best, this high spring time. He leaned contentedly against the parapet watching the even progress of serene waters, the graceful swaying tendrils deep green in the limpid flow. A fish? No. Yes! Several. And birdsong. Lewis would know which birds, not an art I've ever mastered, but ignorance is no bar to this particular enjoyment! He bestirred himself, moved on.

Where had Guinness got to?

'Guinness!' He looked about. And caught sight of his disappearing back-end, beyond the bridge. He whistled, but jog-trotted on; he recognized in that quivering intense form, nose well down, that he was following a scent and was presently indifferent to summons.

He accelerated in pursuit. Not as much puff as he used to

have! 'Gui-nness!' he called, a last vocal effort, and chugged on, following the glimpses of movement through the scrub, into the coppice, and into the clearing before the cottage; in time to see Guinness vanish through the open door. He hurried on, surprised, puzzled, and preparing an apology for Coverdale. But he never used it. His plimsolled feet made no sound as he hesitantly stepped into the room, about to call out. Low, staccato voices drew him on. 'Hello?' he called. 'Hello?' and ducked through the open doorway of the farthest room. Across its floor a cotton dress; before him, standing stark naked, Maurice Coverdale; and on the bed, Guinness, joyfully licking the face of Grace Moon.

CHAPTER TWENTY

'She's taken him in the schoolroom – they're in there!' Mrs Burtle reported.

'Not the drawing-room?' said Mrs Dunkerley, eyebrows raised. 'P'raps it's that model they're looking at.' She answered her own query.

Mrs Cox arrived for her tea. 'Vicar's come!' she announced, snapping the door shut behind her. 'Grace let him in and they've gone in the schoolroom!'

'That's right, Dora,' said Mrs Dunkerley, introducing a note of anti-climax.

'Long face on him!' Mrs Cox challenged. 'What's he doing coming here?' She settled to her tea.

'It'll be about that model since they're in the schoolroom,' said Mrs Dunkerley, and then had a more satisfactory suggestion: 'Or about Miss Seton's book, more like.'

'She always goes down there for that!' said Mrs Cox.

'She's not the time just now,' Mrs Dunkerley pointed out, 'not for her drawings and such,' she added, repressing the observation that she seemed to have plenty of time for her walks, all the same!

'P'raps it's about the little lad,' Mrs Burtle wondered.

'About Max?' cried Mrs Cox. 'Not very likely, is it? What would he be wanting with a Reverend?'

'Well, I don't know!' Mrs Dunkerley was tiring of the subject. 'He's here for some good reason is all I can say.' And disproved that by adding, 'She's looking very peaky again this morning, so whatever it is I 'spect he's come here to save her going there.'

Mrs Burtle chimed in, 'And she was looking so bonny again last week! Still, Mr Gower's home on Wednesday – that'll cheer her up!'

Mrs Cox allowed a silence to accrue, before saying, 'I don't know so much.' She turned her biscuit over, examined the chocolate side. 'I'm not so sure,' she casually continued. 'There's something not right, to my mind.'

'Not right?' frowned Mrs Dunkerley, and dismissed the notion with asperity. 'Of course there's not something not right!' Sometimes Dora Cox went too far!

'Oh?' Mrs Cox was duly stung. 'Well, I'd like to know what she was doing of a Friday morning creeping about in the shrubbery in her indoor shoes!'

'Creeping about in the shrubbery?' Mrs Dunkerley snorted. 'And why shouldn't she go out for a breath of air? What's wrong with that!'

'Breath of air?' derided Mrs Cox serenely. 'Dodging behind the bushes? She didn't look to me like someone taking a breath of air! She'd *been* somewhere!'

Mrs Dunkerley found herself unaccountably disturbed and duly cross with Dora. 'You didn't say nothing on Friday!' she pointed out briskly, and stood up, having finished her tea, leaving the implications to mature as best they could.

'Didn't see you since,' drawled Mrs Cox, unrepentant.

Mrs Dunkerley stirred vigorously at the contents of a pan on the range and held her tongue.

'Well, we shall see what we shall see!' said Mrs Cox coolly. She rose, equipped her pocket with her extra biscuit and gathered up her dusters. 'Come Wednesday!' she said, and added conversationally: 'I'm over to Fold Cop again tomorrow, usual Tuesday now Mr Lewis's coming back. Get the place aired and ready for him.'

Mrs Dunkerley did not respond, stirring on.

Mrs Burtle said, 'Oh, I'm sure there's nothing amiss!' and glanced nervously at her colleagues; but Mrs Dunkerley was silent and Dora Cox just left the room.

'Grace – dear Grace – *think*!' Tom implored.

'We're in love!' she said again. 'I love him. And he loves me.'

She was . . . transfigured, quite, quite beautiful; his misery could not dim that perception. The upright figure before him almost emanated light, the wide eyes over spent and unrepentant tears shone with power, a kind of wild, exultant triumph. He knew himself defeated, he'd known last night; but on he went. 'You don't *know* each other, Grace! You don't know him!'

'*Everyone's* against him!' It was a personal rebuke, relegating Tom to the common ruck who did not understand Mo Coverdale.

'I am not "against him", Grace,' he told her patiently, 'but my dear – you have no *relationship* –'

'I've always loved him. I know that now. We've always loved each other.'

Tom did not attempt to dispute the term 'always'. But – love? He said, 'Love? Love, Grace?' He frowned in concentration, finding the words. 'Isn't what you have found merely sexual attraction? Sexual attraction? Oh,' he pre-empted any reply, 'I don't underestimate its force – nor yet its validity – but sexual attraction is itself not *love*. Sex in human affairs has importance, not least in the generation of children, though not only in that – but overall, in the greater span of things, Grace, sex is a side-show. A side-show to loving.'

'I want to have his child,' she stated. 'We shall have children.'

Wearily, he ran his hand over his eyes. He was tired,

very tired. He had not slept last night, sad, sick to the heart, sadder than he had ever known; knowing then that which was being confirmed this morning, that there was no point in appealing; that, he had known in one glance at her face last night: a dear, familiar face transfigured, defiant, radiant, refined to extraordinary beauty by a commonplace physiological urge of trivial importance; in itself, trivial . . . There was really nothing more to say. It had all been said. Lewis? She knew now that she had never loved Lewis. It would be wrong, for Lewis, for them to be married, and of course she was sorry, very – and indeed painful though unrepentant tears flowed upon this declaration – but she had never, never, intended to hurt him; she just had not understood herself, till now. Tom needed no persuasion that injury had never been intended; he knew that to be true. But, 'understood herself'? He had argued *that*, indeed he had, not hesitating to attack her intransigence with the sharpest weapon available. 'And the boys? The boys? *Leave* the *boys? Max?*' And the one moment in this lamentable morning when he had felt himself alienated, almost repelled, was when she replied, 'They'll be away at school soon.' It was perhaps at that moment that his swimming head began seriously to ache. He sighed. There was really no point, but he must go through with it, say it all, cover everything he had reviewed in the long wakeful night. He sat down, needing to, though Grace did not.

'If he is to quit his job, and you yours, you will have nothing to live on. Where would you go – how would you – manage? Practicalities, Grace.'

'I have money.'

He could not find the energy to press: enough? How far will it take you? Two people – have you any idea how much it costs to house and feed two people for a week – a month – how difficult it can be to find employment now?

How different from Hollisfont you would find the world outside? He could find no further energy to remind her of the difference in age, the ten years between them that could one day signify, begin to matter, though it mattered 'not at all!' today; nor of the disparity in tastes and aspirations. . . No point, really, after all. Not while sex held sway, the madness lasted. One final appeal, then, for time – time, to reconsider, to *think*; not about poor Lewis – that, doubtless, was past repair, done for. But marriage, marriage to Coverdale *need* not be the alternative – so! He was about to make his final appeal when his eye fell upon the ring; there, beside the model on the table.

She stepped forward, the first movement she had made; she briefly touched the ring. 'Would you give it back to him?' She spoke rapidly. 'Would you do that, please, and give him this?' She pushed forward an envelope beside the ring. And then stepped back.

'*I?*' He gazed at her, incredulous, yet unsurprised.

'I don't want to see him,' she said, low. 'It will be better, for him.'

He stared at the ring, and the envelope. At last, he said heavily, 'If you wish.' He made no move. Still looking at them though no longer seeing them, he said sadly, 'Perhaps it would be better, for him.' He slowly stood up. The visit was at an end. But he did not take the ring or the envelope; he made his final appeal: 'Grace, I ask one thing of you.'

She looked at him, waiting.

'I want you to do nothing, say nothing, I want you to pause, allow time for reflection – no, let me finish! If,' he said wearily, 'by tomorrow night you are are still of the same . . . persuasion, then – so be it! And I will do as you ask. But grant me, and yourself, that time for reflection. Please.'

She looked at the ring. Her face was expressionless. She met his gaze again. 'Yes.' She nodded briefly.

He turned away. 'I'll let myself out,' he said, and left.

Mrs Burtle said again, 'No – Dan says no one seems to know! Except Boss.'

'Well, I never!' Mrs Dunkerley gave the matter thought. 'It'll be his Union talk,' she decided. 'He's been asking for it, asking for the sack!'

'Oh, it's not the sack!'

'What, then?'

'He's just – going!' said Mrs Burtle. 'It's not the sack – Dan says as Boss looks like thunder – something about contract, Arnie heard them going on, something about contract . . .' She tailed off.

'Hmph!' Mrs Dunkerley took up another carrot and sliced off its top. 'Well – good riddance, I say!' and thought to add, 'And there's plenty others'll say the same, not to mention her up Outwick!'

'Dan says she was properly riled when Squire put him in Poundell – Dick Marsh said!'

'Well, quite right too – that's *one* thing we think the same, us and her! And Miss Seton didn't think much of it is my belief, good soul as she is!'

'Aye, well!' sighed Mrs Burtle, hanging her coat on the hook and going to fetch her dusters. 'That's that, then!' She set off for her Tuesday jobs, drawing-room, hall, library and lobby. 'Dora'll be interested tomorrow!'

Mrs Dunkerley beheaded another carrot. 'Dora Cox'll know already!' she declared caustically.

Mrs Sutton whispered, 'It's her – look! That woman from the Dower House –'

Her husband joined her at the kitchen window to watch

the governess hurrying across the yard towards the cowhouse. He glowered. 'Yeh! That's what it is – what did I tell you? That's where the trouble is!'

Mrs Cox, cycling home to tea from her day at Fold Cop, called, 'Afternoon, Grace!' and waved a cheery hand, cycling on. 'Hello-ello!' She tucked the information into place. 'Yesterday he's up at the Dower House and today she's down on a visit to the Vicarage, face like a yard of pumpwater . . .!'

Tom did not know what to do. He had seen men weep before; he knew about pain, and the delicate art of comforting, but he did not now know . . . what to do.

He gently pulled Guinness to him: 'Come on, lad,' he murmured, patting him in reassurance, soothing the dog's whimpering dismay at his master's rough shove, pushing the anxious, thrusting nose from him as he wept, 'Get away!'

'Come back with me, Lewis, come down to the Vicarage tonight –'

The bowed head shook, hands covering the face. 'No!'

The letter lay on the floor at his feet, the ring on the table.

Lewis should not be on his own tonight. Incredulity, total disbelief, a long blankness, gradual submission, shifting into rising rage, a storm of raging abuse, then despair, deep, retching sobs as tears spilled their tide of desolate grief.

'Come on, boy, c'm on,' Tom whispered to Guinness, and drew him away. 'It's all right, boy!' he told him, closing the kitchen door. 'Good dog! We'll make a cup of tea, eh? You sit there, and I'll . . .' He cast about in the unfamiliar kitchen, finding the caddy and the pot and the milk left yesterday by Mrs Cox, assembling the requisites for a cup of tea, needing to do something, when there was so little he could do. As the kettle heated he sat stroking Guinness's head, and watching the last of the sunset beyond the window. It was just now very difficult to keep sympathy with her; very hard to like Grace . . . I'll stay here, tonight. Lewis should not be on his own tonight.

With a face of stone Mrs Mayendorff said, 'In that case, the sooner the better, clearly.' She did not again look at Grace, left the drawing-room, shutting the door behind her.

'Friday,' she told Honoria.

Honoria said nothing. Her eyes were reddened, the powder with which she had attempted camouflage lay in patches on her stricken cheeks.

'What is it? What is it?' said Nicholaus from the schoolroom door.

'Now, Nicholaus – what did I say?' Aunt Honoria's quavering voice failed to sound jovial. She bustled him: 'Come back by the fire now, and get on with your plasticine! Doctor will have you back upstairs in bed if we don't do as he says!'

'What *is* it?' Nicholaus persisted.

'What, dear? Oh – nothing, dear – nothing – I mean, just a bit of difficulty . . . with a blocked drain!' she extemporized, closing the schoolroom door with a fleeting, miserable glance at Margaret's departing back. 'Now then,' she cajoled, 'let's get this finished!'

'I've done his head,' Nicholaus showed her. 'I'm doing his buttons now, and then we can put him in!'

'That's right!' said Honoria brightly. She found that she could hardly bear to look at the model of Poundell Cottage, awaiting its plasticine inhabitant. Her head throbbed. She felt slightly dizzy, rather ill. She tried again to pull herself together. There was nothing, nothing anyone could do to alter this appalling business; but at least she could lend Margaret a hand until the agency found a replacement, and she really must pull herself together. Tears again threatened; she gulped them back, those manifestations of a broken heart. Grace – oh, Grace . . .

'Here he is!' Nicholaus brandished the finished manikin. With satisfaction he climbed on to the chair and lowered it into the house. 'There he is!' he beamed. 'It's Mo! In his house!'

'It may well be, I'm afraid,' said the specialist. 'He's on the right treatment,' he endowed the doctor with a professional smile, 'but alas, that cannot guarantee total recovery – we shall have to wait and see.'

'How long?' asked Mrs Mayendorff.

'Ooo,' the specialist pursed his lips, 'another week, two – depends how soon the infection clears. Then we shall see.'

'Just the one ear, though?'

'Oh, yes, yes – his right ear seems perfectly all right, he'll have normal hearing in his right ear!'

'But there's nothing else you can do?' Mrs Mayendorff asked again.

The specialist shook his head. 'Damage done, I'm afraid – nobody's fault, just one of the hazards of the disease.' He transferred his gladstone bag to his left hand and proffered his right to shake. 'I'd like to see him again in seven days' time, and meanwhile, keep him quiet –'

'Yes, we've moved Nicholaus into another room now.'

'That's the ticket. Rest and quiet, no excitement.' He turned back as the doctor held the door for their departure. 'He's a nice child! Very nice boy, Mrs Mayendorff!'

'Tst tst tst!' Mrs Dunkerley mournfully shook her head.

The three women peered through the kitchen window at the figure of the departing vet laden with his sorry cargo wrapped in sacking. 'Well, at least they've saved the mare!' she said.

'One thing after another!' said Mrs Cox.

'Troubles never come singly,' said Mrs Burtle reverently. 'Poor madam!'

'She looks poorly,' said Mrs Cox, detaching herself and returning to the table. 'Doesn't look a bit well!'

'Who among us does?' sighed Mrs Dunkerley, joining her.

Mrs Cox settled back in her chair and folded her arms. 'Well – I said, didn't I? Didn't I say?'

'You did, Dora, you did. 'Mrs Dunkerley sighed again. She absently picked up her cup, found it empty and set it down again. She looked at the clock. 'P'raps I could make another pot?' she mused, but made no move to do so. They were killing time, staying put in the kitchen, by general agreement keeping out of the way until the taxi had been. 'I couldn't trust myself if I saw her face to face!' Mrs Cox had declared. 'Mucky hussy!'

'Miss Seton looks bad too,' Mrs Burtle volunteered.

'I feel for her, I do!' said Mrs Dunkerley. 'Thought the world of Miss Grace.'

'Thinks a bit different now!' Mrs Cox promptly returned. 'This's knocked her off her pedestal, little trollop! Well – she is! Mucky little trollop – two-faced, an' all!'

'That poor Mr Gower!' Mrs Burtle grieved.

'Well shot of her!'

The review rolled on, recapitulating all that had been said yesterday, losing none of its savour in the process, and collating fresh opinion culled overnight. How the Vicar had had the thankless task of telling Mr Gower, poor soul, how he'd stayed Wednesday night at Fold Cop – well, a man in that state, you wouldn't leave him on his own, would you? No knowing what he wouldn't do to himself. How Mrs Cox had got a message not to do her Thursday at Fold Cop – well, he couldn't face anyone, couldn't bear to see anyone except the Vicar, could he? How this business had been going on for months – months! The pair of them, carrying on – oh! many a time down in that bothy, back when he was in that bothy, there you are! Arnie'd seen plenty, many a time! Coverdale – well, no one's surprised about Coverdale – after anything in skirts, but *her*! Many surprised about her – but then turns out it's not the first time, not by any means! Carrying on with men for years before she ever came here, Ellie Furber had it from Joan Murston at the Hall. Well, it fits, doesn't it? Her with her airs – never seemed right, butter-wouldn't-melt! Common little schemer when it came down to it – reckoned she could have Mr Gower and keep her slutty ways! No – better he found out now than when she'd got him where she wanted, step-up-the-ladder, meal-ticket, house, and car! Better off without her, sly little madam! And those walks of hers – while Mrs Dunkerley did her job for her – ho, fine walks! How far do you walk on your back, eh?

'Her stuff's in the hall, I see,' said Mrs Cox.

'Ollie brought the trunk down this morning, madam had him bring it down,' Mrs Dunkerley told them.

'Been better employed taking his horse-whip to her, never mind fetching and carrying for her!' was Mrs Cox's opinion.

'Dear, dear,' murmured Mrs Burtle. She was finding the mixture somewhat high for her taste; but could somehow not forbear to add that Dan said as Coverdale ought to be flogged for his sins.

'Oh, he'll get his come-uppance!' Mrs Cox asserted.

'They both will! The pair of them,' she added with satisfaction.

'Hist!' Mrs Dunkerley cocked an ear. 'That's her!' she whispered.

Sounds from the direction of the hall suggested movement. They strained their ears and caught a trace of voices. 'Taxi-man!' hissed Mrs Dunkerley.

'Where's Miss Seton to?' Mrs Burtle murmured.

Mrs Dunkerley rolled her eyes aloft. 'Upstairs with the boys! Yes,' she confided, 'madam said to keep Master Nicholaus up there with Master Max, while she goes. I heard her say, to Miss Seton.'

'Poor little lads!' Mrs Burtle keened.

The boys had 'not been told'. 'Doctor's orders to keep her right away – Master Max too poorly for shocks!' 'She's ill, far as they're concerned – infectious, has to keep away!' A formulation that Mrs Cox had found to be rich in appropriate irony.

They sat in silence, ears acutely tuned for revealing noises.

Silence.

'Gone?'

Silence.

'I didn't hear no door!'

They listened again.

Silence.

'I'll just take a peek . . .!' Mrs Cox stole across the kitchen and softly eased the door ajar. Silence. And then, the faint thrum of a departing motor.

'Gone!' Mrs Cox announced triumphantly and smartly shut the door. 'Come on, Mrs D! Let's be having that pot of tea! I reckon that calls for a bit of a celebration!'

Across the fields and hedges the light breeze carried the

joyous clamour of bells celebrating Lilian's marriage, from St Aldhelm's tower to Fold Cop.

Lewis, at the table, raised his head from his arms. He blinked. A sob thickened in his throat. He jerked to his feet. Wildly, blindly, he swayed round. 'You bitch!' he cried. 'You rotten, treacherous BITCH!' The bells pealed on. He sank to his knees, racked by sobs: 'Gracie – Gracie – Gracie . . .' and enfolded the distraught Guinness in his arms.

Henry Coverdale folded his Sunday newspaper and set it aside. He consulted his pocket watch. Twelve-fifteen. Time for a sherry before lunch. He poured himself one and strolled to the window. The marquee drooped in the drizzle. Jolly lucky with the weather, got the do over just in time. All over and done with, no hitches. Last one, praise be. When Bertie came to take the plunge it would be some other unfortunate father-of-the-bride to soldier through it all and foot the bill. All went off pretty well. Vera good at that sort of thing, credit where it was due. Which reminded him, irritatingly enough, that he had a message for her from that catering Johnnie; forgot it last night – place crawling with people till Lord knows when, what with that and rather a plentiful intake of brandy . . . Not seen her about this morning. Didn't particularly want to see her now, but better find her. Hope to God it's not too late – something about the hampers and our staff and their staff . . . He wished he could remember. He hovered apprehensively, took another swig of sherry, and set off to find her. She'll know what it's all about, always does. Find her and get it over with.

He tapped tentatively on the study door, and as tentatively poked his head round it.

His wife, her back to him, was seated at her desk. Good Lord! He gazed, embarrassed. She was – crying!

He stood there for a moment, embarrassed and uncertain. And then he heard it. Laughter. Her shoulders were shaking; but not with tears! She was – laughing!

He withdrew his head and softly shut the door between them.

She was in there, on her own, laughing! There was no mirth. But it was laughter.